CW00701199

COPYRIGHT

Tempted BY A KING

B. LYBAEK & SARAH JD

FOLLOW

B. LYBAEK

B. Cybaek

FOLLOW
SARAH JD

DARK ROMANCE AUTHOR

ACKNOWLEDGMENTS

Bibi

I really need to thank Sarah first. Not only was she quick to jump on this venture with me, but she's also been a champ. Putting up with my random ideas and changes, all while doing her best to keep me in line. Seeing Zoe and Gray come to life has been a long journey. Sometimes it felt uphill, but thanks to my amazing co-writer and friend, I never faltered.

Sarah

Being an author is a very solitary career, which is why sharing it with Bibi has been a blessing. She has learned very quickly that I have a terrible memory. It's laughable how bad it is, yet she doesn't hold it against me, but offers me great support.

It's certainly a fun ride going on this journey with Bibi, and Zoe and Grayson's story has been such an amazing venture.

Aime & Jennifer—our amazing alpha readers. You ladies lovingly tore our manuscript apart, and helped us put it together to make it the best possible version. Also, thanks for starting #WakeGate 2023 ;-)

Anoesjka, Dorothy, Lisa, Melissa F, and Melissa M — our kick-ass beta ladies. You guys are the absolute best.

Cady — Thank you so much for putting up with our many, many, manyyyyy cover ideas/concepts. Your work is absolutely incredible, and we hope we haven't scared you away.
Emma — Thank you so much for taking the stunning picture. We love the embodiment of Grayson Black.
You... yes, you!!
If you're reading, we want to thank you for picking up our book.
We hope you've enjoyed the beginning of Zoe & Gray's story. And ummm... we should probably apologise for the cliffhanger.
We won't though. *Muahahaha.*

DEDICATION

Life is either a daring adventure or nothing at all.

-Helen Keller

Grayson

She stumbles through the dark cursing to herself like she hasn't known the garden bed she nearly tripped over has been there for years, the sight causing my lips to spread wide in a grin.

"Fuck. Ten bucks says she face plants before she even makes it to the door." Gunner chuckles from beside me, but I shake my head.

"Fuck that. It's a given with how drunk she is."

Gunner nods in agreement, drawing back on his blunt as we watch the show play out before us.

Zoe fucking Miller.

She's our MC's newest accountant's spoiled brat of a daughter. He has two daughters, and a trophy wife who's in a completely different league to Brian Miller in the looks department. The daughters obviously get their beauty from their mom Astrid, but little Leslie isn't on our radar. Zoe is.

Why?

She's sex on legs and then some. Fucking stunning, and knows it, and has a fucking sassy mouth on her that I'd love to fill with cum just to take her down a fucking notch. She loves to turn her self entitled nose up at the likes of us everytime she sees us lurking around her house or father.

Her designer clothes are fit for the classiest of celebrities, and tonight is no different. The curve hugging sequin dress that picks up every small bit of light around her helps to give away her location as she mutters to herself, trying to walk across the lawn in fucking stiletto heels. The pointy fuckers keep sinking back into the grassed soil, and I elbow Gunner as he chuckles again at the sight, a little too loudly.

The Miller princess doesn't hear him though, too fucking drunk to approach her family home quietly as one of her heels refuses to pull free of the grass, and she tugs her foot out of the shoe, stumbling around to try to grab hold of it.

It takes her three fucking tries before she crashes to her knees.

Gunner and I both lose it then, not able to hold in our laughter at the sight of the stuck up princess on her hands and knees.

She hears us now though. Her drunken eyes peering around and squinting to try to see into the shadows of the darkened yard.

"Who's there?"

We don't say anything, since annoying her is way more fun.

"I have a gun!" she whisper-yells, and we fucking lose it when she pulls a hairbrush from her purse.

Hot tears pool in my eyes as I let this light moment consume me. Something we rarely get in the MC of late, what with the Cali Reapers always trying to pick one of us off.

It's been that way ever since my club, the Cruz Kings, took over this territory. There had been a play for it, and surrounding clubs were happy for us to take control of it just so the Cali Reapers couldn't, so with the extra support, even though we were a new club, we won the rights to it.

Naturally the Reapers' aim is to make our lives a living hell because of it, and lately, they are attacking more frequently.

Since Brian Miller is a new consultant for our club, we keep extra eyes on him to make sure he's not playing two sides.

You can never be too fucking careful.

As the VP of the Cruz Kings, and with Gunner just a step below me in the hierarchy, we shouldn't really be doing mundane jobs like babysitting our consultants. But, we volunteer often just to get a glimpse of the blonde princess and see what things we can do to infuriate her each time.

"Ten bucks says she tries to shoot us with her brush." Gunner snickers next to me as we calm our laughter, still watching Zoe on her hands and knees with her hairbrush raised.

"Your bets are crap man." I grin at him, taking in his blond shaggy beard, and the way his blue eyes almost seem black in this light. "How about you bet on something that isn't a sure fucking bet."

The only reason I know Gunner is grinning is because of the way his eyes crease at the sides and the shaggy facial hair shifts like his lips have lifted at the corners.

"I will shoot!" Zoe whisper-yells again, and I smirk, glancing back at her.

Stepping from the shadows so she can finally see us, we loom in the corner of her yard, and her eyes widen.

"You!" She curls her lip before staggering to her feet and swaying, and all I can do is smirk, my arms crossed over my chest as I watch her point her hairbrush in our direction. "You sssshouldn't be here."

Her slur sends Gunner into another fit of laughter, and I manage to keep mine trapped in, even as my chest quakes.

"You seem a bit drunk there, Princess. I guess the two drinks you had were triple shots."

Her eyes widen at my dig that she's a lightweight drinker, and she staggers closer still pointing that fucking brush.

"I will have you know I had three very ssstrong drinksss."

Gunner clutches his middle this time, and I can't help but release a chuckle.

"Shut the fuck up!" she hisses, glaring at us before a click sounds, and a second later, the sprinklers pop up and start spraying the yard with water.

A gasp flies from her lips as she sucks in a shocked breath, right before she starts cursing way too fucking loudly.

Gunner and I take a step back, narrowly avoiding the spray of water, but not once do we take our eyes from the scene before us as Zoe throws her hands around like she has the power to block the spray.

"You fucking pricks. You did this, didn't you? Do you think if you soak my clothes that I'll take them off in front of you?" she hisses, her blonde waves drenched through as they start to cling to the bare skin on her shoulders.

"Now there's an idea." I chuckle, and she gasps again.

"As if I would ever take my clothes off for the likes of you-you-you... thugs!"

"Someone should fucking gag her on a cock to shut her up." Gunner chuckles, dropping the rest of his blunt and toeing it out.

My head darts to Gunner. "Now that's a bet I'll take. One hundred bucks says I can get her on her knees and choking on my cock in the next ten minutes."

Gunner's blond brows shoot up. "You that fucking sure of yourself?" he asks, his gaze shifting back to the bratty princess who has now resumed trying to pry her heel from the ground.

"Fuck yeah. She acts like she doesn't want a piece of MC cock, but she's been frothing for it."

Gunner angles towards me this time, tilting his head. "Fine, if you think it's a sure bet that you'll get her on her knees for you, I bet two hundred bucks that she won't let you make her come after you choke her on your dick."

Anticipation of the challenge tips my lips up. "Fucking deal, man."

Grinning back at me, Gunner offers his hand, and I take it, shaking on the bet before he gestures to Zoe, who is now sitting in the mud trying to put her shoe back on.

Shaking my head at the spoiled brat, I storm forward, ignoring the chill of the water spraying from the sprinklers, and before Zoe even knows what's happening, I bend and sweep her up, throwing her over my shoulder with ease since I'm over six and a half feet tall and she's a small framed five seven.

A squeal escapes her, and I give her ass a slap and march the rest of the way through the yard with her, to behind the pool house where the yard lighting is a little dimmer, casting the area in shadows.

Even as I tug her off my shoulder, I hear Gunner behind me. The fucker isn't likely to take my word for it of course. No. He's determined to fucking watch to make sure I can't lie about winning the bet.

Not that it's anything new. We share women all the time at the club. The Cruz Cunts, as we like to call them, are always ready to play.

Zoe is so far from a Cruz Cunt though, and even as she stumbles to her knees on the cushioned grass, half because she's so drunk, and half because I urge her down with my hand on her shoulder, she looks up at me with a venomous glare that a Cruz Cunt wouldn't dare direct to any of my club brothers. Especially towards someone like me.

My ranking in the club means nothing to this uppity princess, and fuck if that doesn't make me harder knowing I'm about to tarnish her pedigree mouth and pussy.

"Stop manhandling me!" she hisses, swiping her hand out to hit me, but meeting nothing but thin fucking air.

I chuckle. "I'm about to do more than manhandle you, Princess." I rasp, gripping her chin and directing her gaze up to me. "Do you like being on your knees for me?"

As if she's only just realizing what position she's in, she frowns, and before she can speak, I pop the button open on my jeans and ease down the fly.

"W-what are you doing?" she stutters, her big blue gaze dropping to my crotch.

Then she licks her fucking lips.

Fuuuck. She wants my dick bad, even if she *is* going to try to deny it.

Freeing my stiff cock right in front of her stunned face, I wrap my hand around its girth and give it a pump, squeezing all the way up to milk some pre-cum from the eye.

"What does it look like I'm doing?" I ask, not really wanting her to answer. "I'm getting ready to make you choke."

She sucks in a small gasp, shaking her head, her eyes darting up to mine briefly before they land back on my cock as I wipe up the bead of pre-cum with my middle finger before hovering it near her lips.

"N-no. I haven't-"

"Open!" I cut her off, and fuck. She does!

As her full pink lips part for my finger, her bright blue gaze meets mine, and for the first time, I don't see the distaste she normally glares at me.

This time, she's fucking hungry, and she lets me ease my finger into the hot heat of her mouth before she closes her eyes and moans around it, licking off my salty gift.

I chuckle, directing my words over my shoulder to Gunner. "Told you. Easy."

As if she's only just noticed my club brother standing off to the side, Zoe's eyes fly open and widen, her lips parting as she pulls back from my finger. I take that moment to stop any further words from leaving her lips, as I shove my angry hard cock into her hot little mouth.

The invasion makes her gag around my girth, and a grin tugs at my lips knowing she isn't used to a dick my size, so I weave my fingers into her still damp hair and firmly hold her in place.

"Suck!" I demand, and a whimper escapes her as her eyes water. "Suck!" I demand again, this time gaining her attention, and she does, relaxing her jaw and tongue, and sucking me.

"Now that's more like it." I chuckle, turning my gaze to Gunner's. "Listen to that silence."

Gunner chuckles. "I'd rather hear those choking sounds."

I nod. "Good point."

Even as Zoe sucks, her dainty hands grip my thighs in an attempt to hold herself back if needed, so I tangle her hair around my fist and take more control of her head.

Her eyes widen with fear, and I lower my head and grit my teeth. "Gag for me, Princess."

I shove her head hard onto me, her throat swallowing my dick, my balls resting right under her chin as she starts to gag.

The sound is like music to my ears.

"Fuck yeah." Gunner grunts low, and I just know he has his dick in his hand now.

I don't look because that shit doesn't interest me. The blonde beauty with trails of mascara running from her eyes as I let up on her head interests me a thousand times more.

Zoe gags again as I release my grip, allowing her to pull back as she nearly loses those three drinks she had earlier tonight.

I'm not really into chicks hurling on my cock, but there are some guys in the club that live for that shit, so really, this blonde princess should be glad that she's taking my dick and not theirs tonight.

Zoe does another gagging cough, and I give her a moment to compose herself, because I'm a nice guy like that, and when she gazes up at me again with the same anger from earlier, I smirk.

"What's the matter, Princess? You haven't had a dick as big as mine before?"

"I have vibrators bigger than your cock." She snarls, and fuck, her feistiness makes my dick jerk with more anticipation.

Fisting my hand in the top of her hair, I tug her head back as I grip my cock. "Is that so?"

"Yes." She hisses and I grin, jerking my dick faster.

"You know what your battery-operated toy can't do, Princess?"

"What?" She mutters like the brat she is, and I press the tip of my dick to her lips as my nuts start to tighten.

"Your toys can't fucking cream all over you."

Her blue eyes flare with what can only be excitement, and just knowing that she's practically salivating for my cum, sends me over the edge.

"Open!" I roar as the first wave hits, and she fucking does. Parting her full pink lips, her silky tongue making an appearance to catch the first rope of my cum.

I over fill her mouth, my nuts emptying completely, and when she goes to spit it out, I clamp a hand over her mouth and pinch her nose, blocking off her airways.

"Fucking swallow it!" I demand, and I feel her lips close properly as she does.

"Fuck that was hot." Gunner rasps from behind me as he looks down at Zoe from over my shoulder, and when she starts choking, I release her mouth and nose.

She gags and splutters, nearly fucking wasting the gift I gave her, but she manages to right herself before her expression turns venomous.

"You could have killed me!" She screeches, and I gotta hope that our distance from the main house will muffle the sound from reaching her parents' ears.

Not that they will do anything, but fuck, if Brian Miller goes whining to Rocco, our Prez, Gunner and I might find ourselves at the mercy of Mama C and one of her cock cages.

"I can think of worse ways to go." I mutter in response to Zoe, and if she were a cartoon character, I bet I'd see steam puffing from her ears right now.

"You are an animal!"

"Thank you." I grin, tucking my dick away and securing my pants.

"It wasn't a fucking complement!" Zoe grits through clenched teeth, and I lower to my haunches, coming face to face with her.

"Since you took my dick so well, it's only fair that you be rewarded." I smirk, remembering the second part of the bet. I need to make her come.

Her brows shoot up, and just like that, she's interested again.

"I bet your pussy is soaking after taking my dick." I reach forward and run my thumb along her full bottom lip. "I bet you'd love to feel my fingers slide deep inside you."

She whimpers.

"Would you like that, Zoe? Would you like me to stretch your tight pussy and flick your greedy clit until you come?"

She whimpers again, this time her lips parting even as her tongue darts out to taste my thumb.

"Take your dress off Princess," I demand quietly, and as if she's in a trance, forgetting all about her tirade on the lawn earlier, she starts to take it off.

Gunner is quiet, and I'm not even sure if he's still there. But I don't want to break the connection I have with Zoe right now since it may snap her to her senses, so I watch as she rises up on her knees and unzips the sparkly fabric before shrugging the thin straps off her shoulders and letting the dress pool around her knees.

"Lay back," I demand, and she does, her chest rising and falling with her building excitement.

Slowly tugging the dress the rest of the way down her legs, I toss it to the side and stare at the nearly naked Zoe Miller splayed out on the cool grass behind her pool house, just for me.

Silly girl should know better than to fraternize with someone like me, but she's not thinking clearly right now. Her only desire is to come on my fingers, and in the spirit of winning the bet with Gunner, I fully intend on delivering.

Leaning forward, I tug her panties off before balling them up and putting them in my pocket, and then I grip her ankles and spread her legs further apart.

Zoe bites her lip almost as if she's about to get all shy about exposing her cunt to me, but as soon as my hand is gliding up her inner thigh, she closes her eyes and loses herself to my touch.

When I called her pussy tight earlier, I had no idea how true the words would be. Not only is she well groomed down there, but it has to be the most perfect looking cunt I've ever seen.

Maybe that's because it hasn't been pounded for hours upon hours by six burly bikers like some of the Cruz Cunts endure, but really, I think the reason it's so pristine is that it's a classy cunt just to match its owner.

As I sink two fingers into her heat, my thumb finds her clit, and she parts her legs wider as she tilts her head back and palms her perky tits.

There's something fucking exotic about the daughter of our club accountant. Something so different from any-thing I've had before, and fuck, I just know this little bet between me and Gunner is only just the beginning.

How far will you let us push you, Zoe?

As I curl my fingers inside her, massaging the upper swollen wall, her slickness oozes around my digits tempt-ing me to have a taste.

But not yet. That's another bet I want to have with Gunner, because it's one I know I'll win.

Zoe shatters around my fingers only moments later, her mewling cries a turn on of their own, and as she slowly comes down from her high, her cunt's pulsing easing up, her lids lift lazily and her blue gaze meets mine.

I fucking grin.

Right before I lick my fingers clean.

Propping herself up on her elbows, she blinks rapidly as I stand and turn back to find Gunner with a shit-eating grin.

He doesn't even care that he just lost two hundred bucks.

"Are you leaving?" Zoe asks quietly, gaining my attention again, and I let her see how my eyes devour her before I answer.

"Clean yourself up, Princess. You're a fucking mess."

Her gasp is the last thing I hear as I turn my back and walk away, Gunner rushing to my side to keep pace.

"If looks could kill." Gunner chuckles, and I grin, pulling a smoke from my pack and lighting up.

"Pay up motherfucker." I smirk at Gunner as I hold my hand out. "Two hundred bucks."

Rolling his eyes, he tugs out his wallet and retrieves what he owes me before slapping it into my hand and muttering, "I'll make sure the next bet is fucking harder."

Throwing my head back, I laugh. "Bring it on, brother. Bring it on."

Zoe

The first thing hitting me as I wake up is how disgusting my mouth tastes, like, seriously gross. The second is that I'm naked and alone. The third thing is the fucking birds chirping and the sun that feels like it's baking me from the inside out.

I groan as I sit up to look around. Ugh, am I... why the hell am I outside on the lawn? This makes no sense whatsoever. I know I was drunk as a freaking skunk when I left Cassie's party, but that doesn't explain why I would end up back here.

As I look around, I notice I'm next to the pool house, which is at the back of our property, meaning I'd have to have walked all the way around the house, and by the pool to get here. Not a logical walk by any stretch of the imagination.

And why does my mouth taste so foul? This isn't merely a 'hey, I forgot to brush my teeth after drinking' taste. No, it's salty and... ugh. I need to get my ass out of here and back in the house. Preferably without being seen.

Since the bright light is hurting my eyes, I mentally make a priority list of what I need. My dress, which I find next to me on the ground and quickly put on. Then I look around for my handbag, and shoes, which aren't anywhere to be found. Oh, there is footwear, alright. But those ghastly, worn, black flip-flops aren't mine. And I sure as fuck didn't wear them last night with my newest designer dress.

"What the hell?" I murmur to myself.

Fuck it.

Fuck. It. All.

After correcting the spaghetti straps on my silver sequin dress, I stand up on wobbly legs. Jesus, I'm resembling a baby deer as I stumble around in search of my bag. When I feel nauseous from bending, I give up and, with a sigh, I pick up the horrendous footwear.

No way am I putting those on my feet, but I also don't want to leave them here in case mom notices. Sure, I could blame it on the pool cleaner or gardener, but somehow I don't think she'll believe these belong to either, since they're both middle-aged men.

With the flip-flops in hand, because I'd rather step barefoot on dirt than wear those atrocities, I make my way across the lawn back to the main house, walking as close to the surrounding bushes as possible so I can't be seen from the kitchen since it's facing our garden. I have no idea what time it is, so I don't want to risk mom or dad being awake yet. Ugh, or Leslie, my annoying little sister.

Luckily, I manage to make it all the way to the front door without being seen, and that's where the next issue arises. Without my bag, I don't have my keys. One glance at my reflection in the window next to the door confirms my suspicion. I look like someone doing the dreaded walk of shame after a night of debauchery.

My makeup is smeared, and... ew! There's even some dried drool at the corner of my mouth. I don't recall ever being this much of a mess after a party at Cassie's. Did someone slip me something?

While I did indeed indulge in alcohol, I've never touched drugs, and I don't remember having sex with anyone. I may have kissed one of the guys who kept grinding against me on the dancefloor, but I'm pretty sure that's all.

"Admiring yourself, Princess?"

My breath hitches, and my heart beats rapidly as I whirl around to see who spoke. "Oh, it's you," I sneer as I look at the jerk.

Grayson Black, or as I like to call him, the thorn in my fucking side. God, I hate the trademark smirk he's wearing, like nothing gives him greater pleasure than riling me up. Actually, I can't think of a single thing from his dark, tight curls to his black boots that doesn't irk me. And don't even get me started on the cancer-stick hanging between his lips.

The big bad biker, VP of the Cruz Kings MC. Also, dad's newest business venture. For the past few months or so, dad has worked as an accountant to the MC. I still remember how shocked I was when he announced the news during dinner, acting like it was nothing. Maybe it wasn't, because mom never said anything, only smiled as she refilled their wine glasses, making it a non-issue. It just was.

As their accountant, he's... an asset. My nose scrunches at the word. It sounds so cold, like he isn't worthy of being a valued person. But that's what I've heard Grayson and Gunner call him plenty of times, when they're bitching about being on 'babysitting duty' as they call it.

"What's it to you?" I sneer.

I *really* don't like Grayson. Unlike Gunner, he seems to go out of his way to antagonize me. Never happy to just watch from afar like I'm sure he's supposed to. Well, in the beginning, he did. But after I found him having cookies and lemonade with Leslie one afternoon, I threw the biggest fit, screaming at him until he left.

Honestly, I might give my sister a hard time, but that doesn't mean I want these thugs taking advantage of her naïvety. I know men like him, and there's no way he's only interested in sitting across from her while talking about her favorite music.

Disgusting prick.

I'm just about to turn my back to him when I notice my bag dangling from his hand. Narrowing my eyes, I point at the silver Mulberry, and say, "Resorting to petty theft now, are we?"

I loathe the smirk he sends my way. "Oh, this?" He lifts the bag further up so it's dangling in front of his face. "Didn't steal it, Princess. I found it."

Shaking my head, I scoff. "And where, pray tell, did you find it? Because I can see from here, it's an original Mulberry bag. No knockoff can make the stitching that perfect. So you might as well give it back before I tell my dad you're touching my things."

Grayson's eyes darken with... it's not anger. I don't know him well enough to read his expressions, but I'm pretty sure he's amused. "Ahh, the things of yours I've touched, Princess." He chuckles darkly, making sure I know it's an innuendo.

As if I'd ever willingly let him touch anything of mine.

"But since this isn't really my color, you might as well have it back."

I barely catch the bag with one hand as he tosses it to me with an infuriating smile. A smile that hints of dirty secrets.

"Fuck you," I mumble.

Then I turn my back on him, and without saying another word, I find my keys and let myself into the house. Once inside, I don't waste time on trying to decipher what Grayson was hinting at. Instead, I bolt up the stairs to my bedroom as quickly and quietly as possible.

I breathe a sigh of relief as I find my phone in my bag along with my keys—even the credit card and emergency cash are still there. Hmm, so maybe Grayson didn't steal my bag. All that wouldn't be here if he did, right?

Since I don't want to take him at his word, I scrutinize the lining and stitching of the inside of my beloved handbag, making sure he hasn't tricked me with a cheap knockoff. But no, sure enough, this is an original—almost one of a kind. Okay, five thousand of a kind, but still. That's pretty damn rare.

Leaving the bag on my bed, I head to my walk-in wardrobe. "What the hell?" I murmur, confused as to why the stilettos I wore last night are placed neatly in front of the double-doors.

Seriously, how much did I drink last night? I don't understand why I would walk in here, leave my shoes only to walk back outside, and then pass out behind the pool house.

With an angry shake of my head, one I regret as soon as it feels like someone is holding my temples in a vice-like grip, I let out a frustrated huff and head towards the shelves with my PJs.

I manage to ignore any mirrors or shiny surfaces for as long as it takes to find my clothes and shower. With my hair wrapped in a turban and another towel covering my body, I finally study myself in the mirror. With the caked makeup gone, I look like myself. My blue eyes aren't as shiny as usual, but I guess that's to be expected since I still have no idea what time it is. All I know is it feels like it's too early to function.

Brushing my teeth has never felt so good. Ever. I swear, with each brush stroke, I could feel the disgusting coat disappear, leaving behind the minty freshness of my toothpaste.

After dressing in my light blue sleeping shorts and top, I gather the evidence of last night, i.e. the dress I wore and... wait a fucking second. Now, I know I didn't wear a bra because it's not that kind of dress. But how the hell didn't I notice my panties have gone missing? I'm pretty sure I didn't take them off before I showered.

I just about tear the bathroom apart, looking every-where for the small scrap of fabric. I even go as far as to look in the drawers and on the shelves with my beauty products, needing to make sure I haven't accidentally placed them there while making myself more human after washing the filth of a night sleeping outside from my body.

A knock on the door interrupts my frantic searching.

"Are you done soon? I need the bathroom."

Ugh, Leslie's whining is not helping the building headache.

"Go use one of the other ones," I snip, not in the mood to deal with my sister.

"Come on, Zoe. You've been in there for over an hour."

I have? It doesn't feel like it.

Not wanting to gain the attention of our parents, I roll my eyes and gather the soiled dress before unlocking and opening the door.

"Here you go, brat."

Leslie eyes me warily. "Why are you always so mean?"

Her weakness makes me bristle. I'm not being mean to her, I just don't have time for her or the rose-colored glasses she sees the world through. I swear, I'm just waiting for her to bring a homeless guy or a three-legged dog to our house.

"I'm not being mean," I sing-song while ruffling her hair that's already resembling a bird's nest. "I'm simply preparing you for real life."

"Fudge you," she retorts, like her faux swear holds any fire. "I'm only three years younger than you, so it's not like I need a life lesson from you."

Rather than wasting my breath arguing, I head into my room and slam the door behind me. After throwing the dress on the floor in my walk-in wardrobe, I retrieve my phone and throw myself onto the bed.

I send Cassie a quick text, asking if I left the party with anyone, before I switch to Instagram. Surely there'll be evidence of whatever happened to me there. Neither me nor my friends have accounts under our real names, because no one wants parental snooping. But there are usually a lot of pictures after a party like last night.

It only takes a bit of scrolling before I come across what I'm looking for. Sadly, none of which answers the pool house mystery. Yawning, I decide to let it go when a notification of a new text pops up, and I immediately tap it.

A video plays of me, on my knees... and I'm... I'm... well, there's no delicate way to describe the scene playing out in front of me. I'm sucking someone off. Something I've never done before.

There is no sound, but before the image zooms in on the dick and my face, making it impossible to discern who it is, I can see the grass I'm kneeling on. It doesn't take a genius to put two and two together. I'm behind the pool house... where I woke up not too long ago.

Just before the video ends, there's a distorted voice. *"I'd rather hear those choking sounds."*

It's embarrassing how many times I replay the disgusting video, looking for clues as to who's behind this. But apart from a pair of black boots in the background, directly behind the man I'm blowing, there's nothing. Fucking Unknown Number.

I pull the pillow from under my head and hold it firmly over my mouth as I scream into it. What in the ever loving fuck is happening? All thoughts about sleep are forgotten, and I stomp into the wardrobe and pull a random summer dress from the hanger.

It takes me less than an hour before I'm fully dressed, my long, wavy hair is gathered in a high ponytail, and I'm wearing enough makeup to hide how rattled I am.

Downstairs, I bump into dad in the kitchen, and it takes all my strength to feign a cheery greeting.

"Good morning, Zoe. Are you joining us for breakfast?" he asks jovially.

I give him half a wave before darting past him, yelling over my shoulder. "Can't. I have something to do."

"Don't forget it's family day today, Zoe."

I almost run into mom as she comes into view.

"Yeah, but—"

She shakes her head. "No buts, Zoe. We all agreed to make more of an effort. So go take care of whatever it is you need to do, and then we can all have lunch together by the pool." The need to argue hovers at the back of my mind, but before I can think of what to say, mom carries on. "If you really can't spare some time to be with us, you should be studying. You're eighteen now, and high school is almost over. Harvard isn't a place for slackers."

I hate that she's throwing my early acceptance into the Ivy League college in my face like that. But just because I dislike it, doesn't mean she's wrong. The imminent move from Santa Cruz, California to Cambridge, Massachusetts, is the reason mom decided we need to have family time every Sunday.

While simmering over mom's words, I look out the glass next to the front door. Of course, Grayson is there, right where I saw him earlier. Only, this time, he isn't smirking. If anything, he looks downright furious. Maybe I shouldn't care, but it's giving me the much needed strength to embrace family day.

I may not be able to prove it, but my instinct tells me that Grayson has something to do with the vile video on my phone. All I can do now is pray he isn't the owner of the nice-looking cock.

"Let's do it," I say, smiling warmly at mom.

In true Miller fashion, we have a big breakfast while we each talk about how our week has been. As per usual, mom's highs involve me and Leslie, and her low is that I'm leaving home at the end of summer.

"This is why we need to make the best of the time we have left living under the same roof. Don't get me wrong, honey. I can't wait to see you soar. But this..." Trailing off, she points at each of us. "This time is special, and none of us should take it for granted. One day you'll look back and wish time didn't move so fast."

A few tears fall from her eyes, making their way halfway down her cheeks before she wipes them away. Seeing her this happy and emotional has me feeling bad for almost blowing my family off to go demand answers from Grayson. And for my earlier behavior towards Leslie. I should probably apologize to her, but I don't. I can always do that tomorrow.

"My high is right now," I hear myself say, surprised that I mean it. "My low is studying for my finals."

There's no way I can tell them my low is that I'm apparently starring in some kind of distasteful amateur porn.

Dad's high is today, and his low is that he has to leave us for a few days due to his business with the Cruz Kings. Although we all know he works for them, he's very secretive about what it all entails. To me, that can only mean one thing, the work he's doing isn't above board. Not that I care, at least not as long as he's discreet.

"My high was my horseback riding lesson the other day," Leslie says proudly. "I jumped higher on Kaya than I have before."

I smile as she avidly explains about her lesson, and how the other students and even the teacher clapped.

"They even mentioned she might get an award," mom says, proudly.

Dad smiles warmly. "If you get one, we'll frame it and put it on your trophy shelf."

For hours, we do nothing but sit there and talk about everything under the sun. Mom and I share our thoughts on how I should decorate my dorm room at Harvard, and Leslie keeps talking about wanting my room when I move out.

"Should we move out to the pool?" mom suggests when it's a little after noon.

We all agree, and after getting changed into the blue bikini that perfectly matches my eyes, I plop down next to dad and Leslie on the sunlounger that really should have my name on it.

I try to ignore the feeling of being watched, but it's impossible. Even though there's no trace of anyone else, I can feel Grayson nearby. Call it an asshole sense if you want, whatever it is, having him close to my vicinity makes me annoyed, whether I can see him or not.

With a huff, I turn onto my back and close my eyes. I'm determined to enjoy the time with my family. It doesn't take long before the soothing sound of mom flipping the pages of her magazine and the soft jazz Leslie is playing lulls me to sleep.

I startle awake as something wet hits my skin. "What the hell?" I shriek, scrambling to sit up. "Leslie!" I can't see my sister, but it has to be her.

"I've been called many things, Princess. But a girl's name isn't one of them," Grayson drawls before throwing more water from the pool onto my heated skin.

"What the fuck are you doing here?" I growl.

Looking around, I'm surprised my family isn't here anymore.

"Don't be an ass," Gunner says as he strolls towards us. "Your mom, dad, and Leslie went to buy ice cream. They wanted to wake you up, but we promised to look out for you."

The glare he sends in Grayson's direction is downright lethal, and I can't help grinning as he winks conspiratorially at me.

"So why are you here?" I ask, making sure to put as much attitude as possible into the words. "You don't have to be next to me."

"That's what I said," Gunner easily agrees.

Grayson shakes his head and flips his club brother off. "But where's the fun in hiding? After all, I've seen what you're hiding beneath those scraps of fabric you call a bikini."

I immediately bristle. "I knew it was you," I hiss. "You're a fucking psycho."

Standing up, I plant my hands on my hips, doing my best to stare him down. Something that becomes much harder as he straightens to his full height, towering over me. I hate that Grayson is actually good looking. Someone like him should be covered in warts, and not walk around in an enticing exterior.

"You sent me that video, didn't you? Do you enjoy recording yourself? Does it make you feel like a man?" I spit.

Grayson doesn't answer me. Instead, he just slowly looks up and down my body while licking his lips.

"Come on, let's go back," Gunner says, sounding like he feels sorry for me.

I can't say I welcome his pity, but if it gets Grayson far, far away from me, I'll take it. I'm way too tired and hungover to deal with that prick. Besides, knowing he's taken advantage of me while I wasn't aware, that shit stings.

"Yes," I seethe. "Best run along before someone finds out what you did to me."

Grayson merely raises an eyebrow. "What I did to you? Oh, no, Princess. You fucking enjoyed what I did to you. Don't come crying now just because I didn't stick around to spoon afterwards."

I rear back at his open dismissal. Fuck, I didn't expect him to admit to anything, let alone turn it around.

Looking at Gunner, I'm surprised that he looks torn—between what I have no idea. That's just what he looks like to me.

"Fuck this," I huff.

Not wanting to deal with either of them, I pick up the few things I brought outside with me, and disappear into the house. I refuse to admit to myself that I'm hiding. No, this is just a strategic retreat until I have the brainpower to deal with Grayson.

3

Grayson

Something isn't right. When I received a message earlier with a video attached, I was sure Zoe must have sent it. I didn't really think she'd have the balls to do that but who else could have sent it given it came from the security camera behind the pool house.

But then, she accused *me* of sending it to *her*.

It threw me for a moment, confused as fuck, but I went along with it anyway, tormenting her. Which honestly is more fun than sitting around the clubhouse and watching the Cruz Cunts stick their tits in my club brothers' faces looking for their next fuck.

Still, it doesn't change the fact that both Zoe and I received a video message from a blocked number, with video footage that came from the Millers' surveillance. As far as I know, aside from the Millers, my MC are the only others that have access. Unbeknownst to Brian, of course.

I glance at Gunner, watching him eye Zoe through the window as she makes herself something to eat in the kitchen. Like me, he finds tormenting the Miller princess one of his favorite things to do, however, when the real interactions happen, it always seems to be me and Zoe while he watches.

I think the prick likes seeing Zoe tear into me with her sassy mouth, trying to rip shreds off me, because then he sweeps in and says something to make me seem like the only asshole, when he was silently there for the torment as well.

Fucker.

"You get any messages this morning?" My voice snags his attention, and he drags his blue gaze from the window to frown at me.

"Nah. All quiet. Why?"

Frowning I shake my head confused. "Nothing. Doesn't matter," I mumble, turning my back on him to step further into the shade of the trees that line the Millers' perimeter.

Maybe Prez sent the video message. A way of making it clear that he knows I'm fucking with our asset's kid. But fuck. Rocco wouldn't send it to Zoe as well. What would he gain from that?

Raking my hand through my hair, I turn back to see Gunner still fucking hovering by the window, watching the show Zoe doesn't know she's putting on.

Actually, knowing that bratty princess, she probably knows Gunner is watching. She's probably putting extra fucking sway in her hips as she moves about. Fucking little dick tease, she is.

Slipping a smoke from the pack hidden in my cut, I light up, drawing back until my lungs fill, and hold it there for a long moment as I think over the video, and also Brian's behavior today.

It seems odd to me that he was so adamant to have us stay and watch Zoe while they went and got ice cream. He knows we're here to watch *him*, yet I agreed to his request, following Gunner's lead who was a little too obvious about how much he'd like to watch Brian's daughter.

Opening my phone I click into the app I use to track Brian. We have a GPS locator in his car, phone, and that stupid watch he only takes off to shower or swim. He doesn't know of course which helps when he's acting sketchy. We also have trackers in the phones of his wife and two daughters, just to be thorough.

A live map appears on my screen showing both Astrid's and Leslie's phones together, hovering near the ice cream shop along the main beach. The problem is, Brian's phone, watch and car are not with them.

Zooming out on the map, I quickly locate Brian's phone and watch tracker moving on a path that runs along the San Lorenzo River, with his car parked in a nearby parking lot. It's far enough away from his wife and daughter to look really fucking suspicious, so I pull out my phone and call Slayer as I release the smoke from my lungs.

Slayer and his brother Slasher are two mean brothers that you don't want to fuck with. Not only are they built like a brick shit house, but they have scars they aren't worried about showing the world. Slayer even has an eye patch to cover his empty socket that makes him look like a berserker pirate.

"VP?" Slayer's mumbled voice comes through the speaker.

"I need you to go for a ride down past Old George's Hardware. Miller's car is parked in the lot across the road, and he's gone for a walk along the river. I'm not sure what he's up to, but I'd like you to be at his car when he returns."

"Sure thing. Am I roughing him up?" Slayer asks, and from the mischief in his tone, I can tell the fucker is grinning.

"Nah. Just having you standing there for when he returns will make him piss his pants." I chuckle, and Slayer grunts. "Send Slasher to Maggie's Ice Cream Van. I want him to babysit the wife and daughter until Miller returns to them."

"You want him to hang back?" Slayer asks and I shake my head, even though he can't fucking see me.

"Nah. Tell the grumpy fuck to get an ice cream and join them."

Slayer chuckles. "Roger that."

The call ends and I take another drag of my smoke as my eyes lift back to Gunner who just fucking waved through the window at Zoe.

Jesus fucking Christ. The last thing we need is for the brat to think we are her fucking friends.

"Hey dickhead," I snap, and just like I knew he would, Gunner turns to look at me, flipping me off. "Stop fucking drooling over the stuck-up bitch and get over here."

Rolling his eyes, Gunner takes one last look through the window before walking across the grass towards me.

"What's up your ass?" He grunts coming to my side, and this time I roll my eyes.

"We aren't here to play with her. We are meant to be watching her."

Gunner chuckles. "So choking her on your cock last night wasn't playing with her?"

I glare at him. "Shut the fuck up."

Gunner throws his head back laughing, and I bite back my smirk.

Fucker.

"I bet you a hundred bucks that I can get her to let me in her bedroom." Gunner beams, not at all looking like a threatening biker with the way he's wagging his blond fucking brows.

I scoff. "I bet you two hundred that I can get her to let me in her bedroom, and spread her legs for me."

Gunner frowns. "She's not gonna let you fuck her. Besides, I'm the one making the bet, so it will be *me* getting her to spread her legs."

"You don't sound so sure. You really think *you* can get her to spread her legs?" I counter, smirking at how he looks worried about me being right. "I bet I'm the one who gets between her legs, and not you."

Gunner's eyes turn hard, glancing from me, to the house.

"Come on, asshole. You accepting the bet or not?" I push and he returns his glare to me.

He never can turn down a fucking bet.

"Deal." He holds out his hand, and I fucking smirk even more as I take it, knowing I'm going to be two hundred dollars richer very fucking soon.

Again!

I march towards the house while shooting off a group message to Slayer and Slasher to ring me when Brian and his wife are heading back home, before climbing the steps leading up to the back porch of the Miller house.

Trying the handle, I find it locked, so I key in the pin code to open it, smiling to myself that Zoe can try to keep me out, but if I want in, then I'll fucking get in.

I hear Gunner trailing behind me, and as soon as I step through the door he pushes past me, on a mission to find Zoe first.

She isn't in the kitchen anymore, and since I know she spends most of her time in her bedroom, I don't bother looking for her anywhere else while Gunner starts searching for her in the living room.

I haul ass up the stairs, hearing Gunner curse from somewhere behind me, before the thuds of his heavy feet dash quickly to catch up. I don't bother keeping my steps quiet, not caring if Zoe can hear me coming. I hope she gets fucking scared.

Gunner lunges for me halfway up the stairs, but I manage to escape his attempt, and when I reach the landing at the top, I grab the decorative pillows off the ornamental chair by the wall, and toss them at his head.

"Ahhh, fuck!" He hisses as I chuckle, enjoying the sound of them slapping against his head.

My attack only momentarily slows him, so I spin and bound to Princess' door.

As soon as I reach it, my hand gripping around the handle, I hear a faint moan, and freeze.

Is she?

No?

She can't be.

Gunner slams into my back, the momentum pushing us forward, my grip turning the door handle as we stumble into Zoe's room.

Zoe's eyes flare wide like a deer in headlights while my eyes travel over the way she's splayed out on her bed, legs spread wide with her fingers pressed between her bare thighs.

Fuuuck.

What a sight!

It takes a moment for her to react, and when she finally moves, it's to reach for her pillow, before holding it to her front, covering everything I want to see.

"Get out!" She hisses, baring her teeth, but I grin, crossing my arms over my chest.

"Ahhh. Sorry." Gunner offers, and I see him turn his fucking back in my peripheral.

This is why I am going to win this bet.

The thing about Gunner is, he's all bark with no bite when it comes to chicks. It's a contradiction to the beast that lurks beneath the surface. He is a brutal killer, and an even more merciless torturer, often taking pleasure in delivering pain and suffering to his victims. But sex and chicks? He's like a nervous fourteen-year-old boy that wants to be a man, but hasn't quite grown the balls to step up to the task yet. This is why I know *I'm* going to win the bet.

"Now. Now Princess. You know, and *I know* that there's no way I can leave you in this state." I gesture to her on the bed, her cheeks flushed and her blonde hair a little tousled. "Were you thinking about me when you pressed your fingers to your clit?"

Her cheeks turn redder and she balls her fists tightly against the pillow, hiding her pussy from my gaze.

"I said, get out!" She forces out, ignoring my question.

"Why would I do that?" I ask, and her nostrils flare.

"Because I said so!"

I shake my head as I start shrugging my cut off. "You don't mean it. I think what you really want is for me to join you on the bed and replace your fingers with mine. Don't you?"

Her lips part as if she's going to speak, but the words never come as she watches me hand my cut over to Gunner who still has his back to Zoe. He automatically takes it, and for a moment, I feel bad.

If I were a nicer guy, I'd help him get his dick wet, and perhaps if it were any other chick than Zoe Miller on the bed, I'd do that.

But fuck. There's just something about the idea of filling her cunt to the brink and tainting her high-class pussy that has me not willing to fucking share her.

"What are you doing?" She whispers, and I shrug before reaching behind my neck to grip the back of my shirt and pull it off, blindly reaching back and passing it to Gunner as well, as her bright blue eyes travel over my bare chest, taking in my inked skin.

"I'm taking my clothes off." I deadpan before I start on the button of my jeans.

"Why?" She mutters, looking really fucking confused, crossed with arousal, as she obviously fights herself on whether or not she likes what she sees.

"Why not?" I state, dragging my zipper down. "You're in here all hot and bothered, needing to come, and I'm here, offering to help." I shrug. "I mean, you were already thinking about me while you flicked your bean. May as well have the real thing."

"I was not." She rushes out, but her words mean nothing as her eyes follow my hand slipping into my jeans and jocks to readjust myself, letting the tip of my dick peek free.

Just like last night, Zoe seems to be in a trance, her heated gaze practically devouring the tip of my cock as she licks her lips.

"Can I join you?" I ask quietly, not wanting to drag her out of her lust drunk state.

"Yes."

Her eyes widen as if she just realized what she said, and she shakes her head.

"I mean no."

Pushing the fabric of my jeans and jocks down further, I release my rigid cock, giving it a pump.

"Are you sure, Princess?"

Her eyes flicker to my dick, her lips parting as she presses the cushion tighter to her, almost like she is trying to cause friction between it, and the pretty cunt she's hiding.

"Yes." She breathes, even as I step forward.

"Yes, I can join you?" I urge and she nods.

"Yes."

I try not to laugh at Gunner's curse from behind me, knowing that even though we were already in her bedroom, Zoe's acceptance of me joining her on the bed is basically the next best thing, meaning I've just successfully completed the first part of the bet.

Slowly closing the distance, I push my pants further down my thighs as I stand at the foot of her bed.

"Get rid of the pillow," I demand, and like my puppet, she fucking obeys.

She tosses the pillow aside, exposing herself to me again, and she shuffles back on the bed a little.

Shifting forward on the mattress, I'm well aware that if Gunner is lurking nearby watching, then he's getting an eyeful of my ass. I'm not sure where he is though, and Zoe is giving no indication of his presence, her eyes trained on me as I settle between her legs.

She looks like a goddess splayed out before me, and fuck I want to taint her so badly I'm almost shaking with the desire. The only scrap of fabric left on her body is her bikini top, so I finger the fabric before tugging one cup down and exposing her tit and the dark pink of her pebbled nipple.

"Look how hard they are for me, Princess." I rasp, flicking my thumb over the peak which causes her chest to drive forward, seeking more of my touch.

A moan escapes her lips and I take that as my invitation to continue, one hand stroking her nipple while I let go of my dick with my other hand and glide it up her inner thigh. The moment I glide my fingers over her bare mound, she gasps and grinds up searching for more friction.

"Do you want me to fill you, Princess? Make you feel so fucking full that nothing else will ever compare?"

A whimper escapes her, and as I glide my fingers through her swollen folds, her arousal coats my fingers. She's so turned on right now, I don't even think she realizes that as she cups her other tit.

Technically, the bet I had with Gunner was that I could get her to spread her legs for me, which she has already done, but Gunner mentioned that she won't let me fuck her, so even if this pedigree pussy doesn't deserve Grayson Black's cock, she's going to get it, because a bet is a fucking bet.

I take a moment to admire the beauty of the brat before me. She is fucking blessed with perfection, that's for sure. Any man's wet dream with her long blonde hair, big blue eyes, and full lips that I already know look good wrapped around my dick. But fuck, her cunt looks so tempting, glistening, and flushed with a deep pink as all the blood rushes to the area. Makes a man want to drop to his knees and have a taste.

But no. I'm not here to indulge. I'm here for a bet, and to torment the princess with it afterwards, because if there's one thing I know, even though she's in a lusty daze right now, when she snaps out of it, she's going to be fuming.

And fuck if that thought doesn't make me harder.

"You ready for me to fill you?" I ask her, not caring what her answer is going to be, because I don't give her a chance to answer as I grip her thigh, spreading her wider before pressing my hips into the valley between her legs.

"W-wait," Zoe gasps. "Condom."

"Oh come on Princess." I smirk knowingly at the way she can only form one word at a time. "I know you have a birth control implant. There's no need for a condom. Besides, I'm clean. You're clean. I promise it will feel so fucking good."

"But... how-"

I cut off her attempt to question how I know those personal things about her, not wanting her to know that her family doctor can easily be paid off for information, and brush my thumb over her needy clit. She gasps, her cheeks flushing as she forgets about questioning me, her blue eyes latching onto my cock jutting out like it's seeking a wet warm hole.

Without any more hesitation, I guide my cock, finding her entrance before sliding a little way in, thanks to her slickness.

The moment her molten heat engulfs the head of my cock, I surge forward and squeeze into her vise like grip. She cries out, throwing her head back, her spine arching and pressing her tits higher, her pebbled nipples straining.

Digging my fingers into both her hips for better leverage, I start pounding into her hard and fast, wanting to get this over with, because after all, it is just a bet, but also, maybe, I'm fucking horny as fuck, especially after gagging her on my cock last night.

"You like that Princess?" I rasp through gritted teeth, gaining her attention as her lids flutter open. She doesn't answer me, just grips the sheets under her and holds on as I piston into her. "You like Grayson Black's cock don't you." I urge, and this time she bites her lip like she's trying not to answer me.

I still, leaning down and roughly gripping her chin. "Fucking answer me."

"No." She spits, curling her top lip. "Your dick's so small I can't even feel it."

Gunner's laughter comes from behind me, but I ignore that fucker. He's the one who's two hundred bucks broker, not me.

Zoe's eyes widen a little at hearing Gunner, and it's like she's only just realizing he's in the room.

Didn't she see him there before?

"Is that so?" I ask, gaining her attention again. "You can't feel this?" I draw back and slam into her, causing her back to arch off the bed even as she holds back her moans.

When she composes herself, she nods, glaring at me. "It feels like a little tickler."

I ignore the laughter coming from my club brother again as I glare down at Zoe.

"Well, I guess it won't matter if I stop then."

A whimper escapes her as I tug my dick free, wrapping my hand around its slick girth, thanks to Princess, and start pumping it, watching as her eyes widen.

"You think this cock is small, Princess?" I hiss, and she ignores me looking partly aroused by what I'm doing, and partly worried. "You don't think it could have gotten you off? Filled you so full of cum that it would be running down your thighs for days?" I squeeze tighter, chasing my orgasm. "Just look at it." I hiss, watching how she does exactly that, her blue gaze filling with more lust. "Look how fucking perfect it is. How good it would have felt to feel me explode inside you."

The moment she whimpers, is the moment I erupt.

Hot jets of cum shoot from the eye of my cock as ecstasy rushes through me in waves, painting Zoe's ribs and tits with my creamy offering.

When the last rope of cum cuts off to a drizzle, I grip the end of my cock and flick the last remnants in her direction, the creamy droplets slapping onto her chin, cheek, and nose.

"Next time, you'll remember to watch that smart mouth of yours, and maybe you'll get to come too," I snap, shoving my dick back in my jeans as I re-dress.

Wiping at the mess on her face, Zoe's cheeks redden in anger.

"There won't be a next time!" she yells, her eyes glazing over as her emotions get the better of her. "You're a sick bastard!"

I shrug. "Maybe. But you're the one that willingly spread your legs for me." I smirk, ignoring the look of betrayal that crosses her expression, reminding me that Zoe Miller is nothing more than our asset's bratty daughter who could use a fucking lesson or two in toning down her stuck up mannerisms.

Turning my back on her, I snatch my t-shirt and cut from Gunner's hand as I push past him in the doorway, the action causing him to stumble out into the hall.

"I HATE YOU!" Zoe screams from inside her room, and I chuckle, once again holding my hand out to my club brother.

"Another two hundred bucks. Thank you very fucking much."

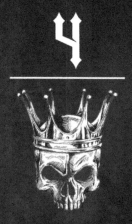

Grayson

Brian Miller is up to something. Since the day last week when he supposedly went for ice cream and ditched his wife and youngest daughter while out, we have increased our watch on him, which is a pain in the ass given the Reapers' hit Hugo's Butcher Shop a couple of days ago.

They fucking blew up the entire store, which took out the dress shop on one side, and the flower shop on the other. Hitting our citizens is a low fucking blow, and yeah, Hugo would give us all the access we wanted to his industrial fridge, but now there's nothing but charred remains which means we now don't have access to a cold room to keep our kills on ice until we can dispose of them.

The Reapers knew somehow that Hugo turned a blind eye to what we did on his premises, and since there have been no reports of suspicious behavior, it's safe to assume we have a mole in the club.

"What did Miller say when he got back to his car last week?" Rocco asks Slayer, who takes his time blowing out the smoke he just inhaled before answering Prez.

"Nothing. Just looked like he was going to piss himself."

"Did you ask him where he'd been?" Prez asks and Slayer sighs.

"Yeah. And he didn't fucking respond. Just got in his car and sped through the streets until he got back to Maggie's Ice Cream Van."

I glance at Prez and take in his frown. We have already been over this, but like me, he's concerned about a mole. I probably should have told him about the video that was sent to me and Zoe last week, but shit went down and it just never came up. I need to tell him though.

"What were Astrid's and Leslie's reactions to you joining them, Slasher?" Prez asks, and Slasher, being the creepy fucker he is, smirks.

"They weren't thrilled by my presence at first. I'm pretty sure Mrs. Miller has the hots for me though."

Chuckles rumble up into the smoke hazed room as we sit around the table for church. "The kid though. She's ok. Started talking to me about horses or something."

"Anything suspicious happen while you were with them?" Prez asks and Slasher shakes his head.

"I'm the only suspicious thing that happened."

Everyone nods, because let's be honest, Slasher is suspicious as fuck to the normal world, and Prez moves on to announce that we are starting more patrols of downtown to make locals feel safer, but also to catch anything suss before it escalates.

Because there's no way the Reapers should have been able to drive through town and break into Hugo's Butcher Shop without being seen. Not unless they had help.

Prez closes church, and I stay seated as everyone files out, Gunner the last to leave as he shoots me a curious glance. I don't react because I'm not inviting him to this discussion with Prez. There are parts of my role which warrant only Rocco's presence, and I know it annoys Gunner deep down. After all, he was an original like me, Rocco and Mama C, yet he doesn't hold a rank or have a leadership role.

Our men look at him as a higher up, naturally, but when it comes down to it, my best mate is ranked at the same level as the rest of the guys who joined up when we first started.

Since it was me, Rocco, Mama C and Gunner who left the Diamond Crew together to start a new club, we typically share most of the goings on between the four of us, but sometimes, it's just Prez who needs to hear what I have to say.

"There's something I should have told you last week," I state, and Rocco shoots me a raised brow.

"What the fuck now?"

Sighing, I lean forward to rest my forearms on the tables. "Last week, I was sent a video that came from the Millers' surveillance cameras. Zoe, the oldest daughter, was sent the same video."

Rocco frowns and shakes his head. "What was on the video?"

"Me. And Zoe."

Rocco's frown deepens before it morphs into anger. "You're fucking kidding me, right?"

"Nope." I shake my head and sit back in my chair. "The thing is, I don't know who sent it, and Zoe doesn't either because she accused me of sending it to her. The number was listed as unknown. I'm not sure if it's relevant, which is why I didn't tell you in the first place, but given everything that's happening..."

"Hmmm." Rocco grumbles, looking nothing but pissed at me. "You and the Miller girl a thing?"

"What?" I spit, jerking back. "Fuck no."

He glares. "Why the fuck were you messing with her then? I assume you were balls deep in her in the video?"

"Nope. Choked her on my cock and then made her come. All for a bet."

Slowly, Rocco smirks. "You're such a fucking prick. The bratty bitch is going to go crying to her daddy, and then I'm gonna have to listen to him bitch in my ear about his innocent daughter being stained."

I shrug. "I won two hundred bucks. I'll give you half for your trouble."

Rocco throws his head back laughing, and for a moment we aren't Prez and VP. He is the guy that took me under his wing when I was sixteen, and I am the guy, despite the age difference, that became his friend.

"If Daddy Miller comes hounding me about you spearing his daughter's throat, I'm gonna take the full two hundred."

"Come on. That's not fucking fair." I whine and Rocco stands.

"No, it isn't. Maybe next time you'll turn down the bet and keep your cock in Cruz Cunts instead."

He slaps me on my back as he passes, chuckling to himself, but when he reaches the door, his laugh fades and he turns back to me.

"I don't think we have a mole in our club, but just in case, we keep everything between us, Gunner and Mama C. Got it?"

I nod. "Yeah. Got it."

The main room in the clubhouse is loud when Rocco and I enter, everyone's attention on the row of Cruz Cunts lined up on the long table top as five of my club brothers work their hands over their exposed cunts, seeing who can make them squirt the furthest.

Meanwhile, a bunch of the younger members, prospects included, are on their knees getting drenched from the spray.

Fucking hell. Live porn at its best.

I automatically think of Zoe, even though I fucking shouldn't. But fuck I'd like to make her squirt like that. Milk every last drop from her quivering body until she passes out.

I sigh, breaking off from Rocco to head to the bar where Gunner is sitting, his back to the live show going on.

That's not like him. He fucking loves watching.

"What will it be, VP?" Tex asks as he wipes the bar top down.

"JD on the rocks." I nod in Tex's direction, and he gives me a nod back before retrieving my order.

Gunner turns to look at me as I take the seat next to him, a grin tugging his lips as he catches me rearranging my stiff cock.

"They're giving a good show tonight." Gunner chuckles as he slips his phone into his pocket, and I nod.

"Yep. So why the fuck aren't you over there on your knees too?"

He shrugs, sneaking a glance over his shoulder towards the cheers as Sasha cries out, spraying the guys on their knees, and the fellas standing behind them.

"I'd rather watch Princess squirt."

His comment stills me as Tex slides the glass of amber before me, and I glare at the back of Gunner's head.

It's not his comment that shocks me.

It's the fucking way I feel like swinging fists and telling him to keep his fucking hands off what's mine that has me freaking the fuck out since I don't typically mind sharing Cruz Cunts.

But she's not a Cruz Cunt.

"Another bet?" I grit through clenched teeth.

Gunner turns back at me and shrugs.

He seems flat. Quiet.

Even though he tried to brush off not getting involved in the porn sesh, it's not like him to not be in the thick of it. For all his timidness with chicks, Gunner seems to do ok in group scenarios. He's normally in the middle of a gangbang, slamming his cock into whichever Cruz Cunt put her hand up for the railing.

"Making Princess squirt is just another bet you'll win." He sighs, and fuck, now I feel bad.

"How about we ditch the bets and go over there and show her what Gunner cock tastes like?"

Gunner's eyes flare wide at the idea of that, and once again, I feel like throwing punches.

Jesus fucking Christ. I need Sasha, or Alana, or hell, maybe even Rose to let me fuck their ass so I can stop imagining what it'd be like to claim that part of the bratty princess.

"Actually, I have a different bet for you." Gunner smirks, his spine straightening as he finally snaps out of his somber mood.

"Yeah? What?" I grin before downing some of the JD and reveling in the burn as it goes down.

"We all know you put any chick that looks at your dick in a trance, which is why you keep stealing cash from me."

"I fucking won it. Don't whine like a little bitch just because you lost." I tease and Gunner's jaw tics.

"Well, I bet you that I can make her fall in love with me."

I nearly spit out the drink in my mouth at his words, only just managing to swallow it down before a laugh rips from me.

"Are you fucking crazy? She's already in love with me. I have the magic dick remember?"

"She doesn't fucking like you." Gunner sneers. "She fucking hates you."

I chuckle. "Yeah, that's why she keeps spreading her legs for me."

"Because you give her no fucking choice."

I stiffen at Gunner's dig, and slowly lower my glass back to the counter before tilting my head towards him.

"I'm not a fucking rapist." I hiss, and Gunner's eyes go wide.

"Nah. No. That's not what I meant."

"Then what the fuck did you mean?" I curl my lip as anger that I've never had towards my club brother rises to the surface.

"I don't know. Not that, man. You know I'd never think that."

I roll my tongue in my mouth as I suck in air through my nose. I'm coiled so fucking tight right now I could kill.

"I may coerce Zoe, but she fucking consents."

Ok. So I know there's a fine fucking line with what I did behind the pool house, but she never said no or stop. If anything, it was dubious.

"Yeah. I know man." Gunner shakes his head, a flash of worry crossing his features. "I made the wrong remark. I'm just trying to challenge you with a bet... That you're gonna lose."

Slowly, a smirk lifts his shaggy blond beard, and I can't help but smirk back.

"Is that so?" I ask, and he nods. "You're serious about this bet. You think you can make her fall head over heels for you?"

Gunner beams. "Yep. And I've already started."

I frown. "What do you mean?"

"Well, while she thinks you're a fucking prick, she thinks I'm the nice one. I've been messaging her for a couple of days. She even said I'm nice."

I chuckle. "And you think that nice will win the stuck up Princess' heart?"

He nods. "Yeah, I fucking do."

"Ok then. How much are you willing to lose?" I snicker and Gunner's smile drops.

"I won't lose. So I bet five Benjamin Franklins."

I throw my head back laughing. "You fucking idiot. What are you gonna do if she falls for you? Run off and marry her and pop out a bunch of bushy beard brats and live in a house with a white picket fence?"

"I don't know." He shrugs. "Might not be so bad."

My brows shoot up.

"The fuck?"

Gunner shrugs, and a strange feeling twists my gut. I don't know what the fuck it is exactly. I just know that I don't fucking like the sound of Gunner settling down with Zoe.

She doesn't want him, anyway. Right?

Not that it fucking matters. I don't want the brat. But I do want to win the bet.

"Fine." I huff. "So it's the first one to get her to confess her undying love gets five hundred bucks?"

Gunner nods. "Yep."

"You got yourself a fucking deal." I grin before we shake on it, and I down the last bit of my drink.

As if he thinks he's already fucking won, Gunner pulls his phone out, grinning as he slips off the barstool and walks away with his eyes plastered to the screen.

So he thinks he can win with text messages.

Sure, words are nice, but actions are better.

And on that note, I walk out of the clubhouse and swing my leg over my bike.

I have some Princess Pussy to devour.

5

Zoe

"I can't believe it. You're all grown up, baby. In a few months you're leaving home, and..." Mom's voice cracks, and her eyes become glassy as she smiles at me, "we're just so proud of you."

Dad clinks his glass to mine, his eyes are glassy as well. "We're so proud, baby girl."

"Does this mean I can have your room?" Leslie's predictable question has me laughing.

All year my sister has been badgering me relentlessly, reminding me my room is the biggest one and that it's not fair I hold on to it when I'm going to Harvard.

"We'll see," I say, trying hard not to roll my eyes.

"Les," mom scolds. "Tonight we're celebrating Zoe's amazing achievements, so let's cool it on the room talking."

All my life, I've been Ivy League bound. The funny thing is now that it's so close, I can't remember if it's my parents' dream or mine. But with all the money my parents have spent on private tutors and prep schools, it's just always been a given.

"Okay, okay, I'll admit it's rather cool that my sister didn't just get the highest GPA at Santa Cruz Prep, but is also going to Harvard." I'm just about to ask Leslie if she's been body snatched when she adds, "You're still a pain in the ass, though." And now I recognize my annoying little sister again.

As the waiters bring our food over, I look around the super fancy restaurant dad picked. I was so sure we were going to Parallel like we usually do, but dad totally stumped me when he surprised all of us with a last-minute change in plans. While looking smug in his suit, he declared that the only place good enough for an evening such as this, is Fuego—and now that we're here, I have to agree.

When we got to our table, the waiter asked us what our favorite animal was, and then folded the napkins into said animal. My sister's penguin doesn't look as good as my mom's swan, but that's hardly his fault. Who the hell asks for a penguin? My embarrassing sister, that's who.

"I'm sorry, mom, but I don't think I can ever be happy with your cooking again," my sister quips, rubbing her stomach for good measure.

Dad orders more wine, allowing my sister another half glass. She's only fifteen and I think this is the first time our parents let her have wine with the food. I guess it's fitting, since they keep talking about how special tonight is.

Even though they're right, I wish they would stop saying it. Yes, I graduated high school today and soon I'll be walking the hallowed halls of Harvard. But that's not until the end of summer. There's still almost three months, and I don't want to treat them like a countdown—I want to live, to have fun.

When we're done eating, I check my phone. As I skim a text from Gray, pleasure thrums through my veins, and I squeeze my thighs together to get rid of the tingle. Christ, with the way my body is acting, as though it's conditioned to tingle and throb as soon as I think about him, I need to get to the bathroom or I'll leave an embarrassing wet patch on the chair.

It's hard to believe that mere weeks ago, receiving this sort of attention from him would have repulsed me. Though, I wouldn't say I like it per se... maybe a little... no. It's intriguing... yeah, that's what it is. I'm not sure how or when it happened, but he's managed to worm his way under my skin, searing me from the inside out, even when he's infuriating me.

G: I miss the way your soaked cunt feels around my cock. Why don't you give me a preview to get going?

Me: Dream on!

G: It's cute you still think you have a choice. Give me what I want, or your family is about to find out what it feels like to see their princess choking on my cock.

As every time Gray lords that threat over me, my blood runs cold. He already knows I'll do anything to avoid him leaking that video, so I don't even know why I try to fight him.

Me: You think my dad is going to continue working for you if you leak that shit?

G: You think I care? Tick-tock, Princess.

An involuntary squeak leaves me, but it's not from fear, it's excitement. I hate that I can't stop imagining his dark, smoldering eyes as he groans my name before sinking all the way inside me, like he's done so many times lately I've lost count.

"What's up?" mom asks, leaning closer, and I immediately lock my phone's screen. "Are you wondering when you can ditch us?"

I laugh nervously, feeling caught out.

After tucking my phone away, I say, "No, it's just—"

"We understand, baby. Look, I know you're probably getting impatient. But this evening means so much to us. How about we have dessert together, and then we can drop you off at your friend's party?"

I look down at myself, frowning at the elegant dress I'm wearing. It's perfect for this restaurant, I'm just not sure it's what I want to wear on the back of Gray's bike. I contemplate changing before I go to meet him, but then again, it might be better to have him rip it off me.

Ugh, I shouldn't care. It's not like it's a date, or that I'm even choosing to meet up with Gray. He made it clear he's going to pick me up, and I... well, I go along with it because of the incriminating video he has of me. And that's the only reason.

"Okay," I agree as I stand, grasping my clutch. "I'll just head to the bathroom." With those words, I rush away, needing a few minutes to myself.

Luckily, there's no one else in the bathroom. I get into one of the stalls and swing my leg up on the closed toilet. After moving my thong to the side so my pussy is bared, I position my phone so it's perfectly capturing my glistening folds. Knowing that I'm doing something this depraved on a family night is enough to send another rush of wetness to my core.

It's wrong.

So deliciously wrong.

Rather than dwelling too much on just how much it turns me on, I quickly attach the photo to my reply and send it.

Me: Here. Are you happy? Have fun tugging your pin prick of a dick over this.

While I wait for Gray's reply, I scroll through our messages. Most of them are him commanding me to do something, like sending him a picture of my used underwear, of my vibrator, and even of me playing with myself on one of the kitchen chairs. Each one was more outrageous than the last, and it's mortifying to admit to myself how much I like him forcing me to do those things for his entertainment.

G: I'm pretty sure a pin prick wouldn't make you gag the way my cock does when I fuck your mouth. For even suggesting that, you'd better be ready for me to fuck your throat so brutally that you won't be able to fight it. Fuck I can't wait to see the tears in your eyes as you beg me to let you breathe.

Heat flushes across my skin as I read his message. Though I shouldn't be turned on, I can't resist moving my hand between my legs, rubbing my clit while imagining it's Gray's fingers touching me. Trying not to moan out loud as I rub my clit is hard. His words do something to me. As much as I hate Gray, which I do, I love the way he's skillfully playing my body and mind, like I'm his Fender Stratocaster.

At twenty-six, Gray's eight years my senior. Something I could probably overlook if we didn't also come from different walks of life. Where I know I'm meant for more, he's willing to settle for less. Am I judging his lifestyle as a criminal? Yes, I suppose I am.

Despite the fact he's a fucking criminal that's blackmailing me, Gray is a master at disarming me with his rugged but handsome looks. Where his deep, dark brown eyes always feel sharp, like they see more than I'm comfortable with, his face is slightly rounded. His jaw lightly dusted in dark facial hair that perfectly matches the tight curls on top of his head.

I don't know why, but I find that the springy locks make him less serious—less intense. Especially with how short he cuts the sides and back, giving off an almost military vibe.

Then there's his body... Lord have mercy. He's beyond ripped. Intricate lines of his countless tattoos cover his neck, stopping just under his jaw. The designs span across his shoulders and down his chest and back. His stomach is the only part of his torso that isn't covered in ink, making the hard ridges of his abs even more pronounced.

Even when he's threatening to leak the obscene video of me sucking him off, I can't stop wanting him to command me. A sick part of me is getting off on it. I think I actually like that he isn't giving me much of a choice.

G: I'll pick you up in two hours. Be fucking ready.

I'm tempted to tell him that I won't leave with him, but who am I kidding? Even if he didn't have that damning video, I can't deny the way he makes me feel when we're together. Wild, uninhibited, and seen. Yet, when we're apart, he's nothing but a dick. Mr. Hot & Cold indeed.

Me: And if I'm not ready to be picked up when the almighty Grayson Black arrives, I suppose you're going to threaten me with the video again?

G: It's good to see you're learning how this works. Be fucking ready. I'm not a patient man so don't test me. I will carry you screaming from your friend's party if I have to!

There's a party at Cassie's house, and even though I'm not much of a party girl, I really want to go. At least that's the public story, which is much better than telling anyone I'm going to meet up with Gray for a night of what I can only imagine will end in hot debauchery.

Feeling annoyed with his text, I hit the call button before thinking better of it.

"Princess," Gray rasps, and I can hear the smirk in his voice. "To what do I owe this pleasure?"

"Why are you being such a dick?" I seethe. "I've done everything you ask of me."

"That I have to ask for it doesn't convince me you want it. Maybe I should just send that video—"

Interrupting him, I stammer, "N-no, I'm sorry. You know I've been busy with exams, and..." I don't really have anything else to say, so instead of completing the sentence, I just trail off. The way he can strip me of any confidence with only a few choice words is loathsome.

Rather than answering, he scoffs and my breathing quickens as I mentally panic. I don't know if I should say something, or what to even say.

I need to stop kidding myself into thinking what Gray and I have is mutual, because it isn't. My body might like the way he manipulates me, but I need to stop forgetting that it isn't by choice. Just because it makes me wet doesn't mean I like it or agree with it. Does it?

Pinching the bridge of my nose, I slow down my breathing. "I'm sorry." The words taste wrong, but I forge ahead. "You don't have to convince me. I want you, Gray."

The low chuckle coming through the phone grates my nerves. "That's more like it, Princess. Do you want us to be exclusive? Is that it? Do you want Grayson Black to be yours, and only yours?"

Not trusting myself to not just blurt out 'hell no' I pinch my lips together.

"Answer me," he growls, and the sound causes my nipples to tighten into hard buds.

"No," I grind out.

What kind of game is he playing? That's not what I want, and more importantly, I don't for one second believe it's what he wants.

Now it's Gray's turn to keep quiet, and as I strain my ears, I swear I can hear the sound of skin against skin. At first I don't get it, but when it finally dawns on me that he's jerking off, I whimper into the phone.

"Oh fuck, Princess." Gray's lustful growl has my nipples pebbling further. "Moan for me."

My body obeys the command instantaneously, and I moan into the phone as images of our previous trysts play like a movie across my inner eye. With Gray, it's always intense. Softness isn't a word in his vocabulary, and I love the way he's always rough and demanding in his touch.

The few times he's snuck into my room while my family was asleep, we had to stay quiet. Which always proved to be harder for me than for him. But fuck me, so worth it.

The rush of knowing we could get caught made my body soar to new heights every single time.

"I can't fucking wait to be buried inside your hot cunt," Gray rasps, and the sound of his hand moving along his thick, long shaft becomes louder. "To feel you come on my tongue so I can lick your slick cunt clean. Would you like that, Princess?"

Shit, I'm so fucking wet I can barely stand it.

"Y-yes," I moan. My hand moves under my dress, and I slide two fingers into my heat. "I can't wait to have you inside me."

Gray groans my name, and his breathing picks up. As the sounds of his hand moving grow louder, I move my fingers to my clit, eagerly rubbing the nub until my legs shake and his name tumbles from my lips when he growls my name in the way he only does when he finds his release.

"Did you come, Princess?" Gray asks.

"Not yet," I pant. "I'm so close, Gray."

The low chuckle is the only warning I get that he's about to say or do something that doesn't bode well for me. "Well, that's a shame, isn't it?"

"W-what?"

The sound of the call ending is like cold water on my overheated body, and I curse his name as I tug my hand from between my legs. Stubborn fucking bastard.

My phone vibrates in my hand, and for a split second I fantasize about getting a text from Gray where he apologizes. As if.

G2: Congratulations on graduating today, Zoe. Your dad's been boasting about you getting the highest GPA. We should celebrate sometime.

G2: Are you spending all night with your family or are you going to your friend's party?

I smile at the easy text from Gunner. Last week I confided in him that I didn't really want to go to Cassie's party, it felt more like a rite of passage, something expected of me. Don't get me wrong, I love letting go and having fun, but since I know I'll never keep in touch with any of them once I go to Harvard, what's the point? Then again, I don't want to sit around at home and play monopoly or something equally boring either.

Me: Thank you!! I'm so glad it's finally over because I don't feel like there's any more room in my brain for anything. If I'm not careful, I'll forget how to spell my name.

The more I talk with him, the more I learn that my first impression of him was wrong. Gunner really is the light to Grayson's shadow. The calm to the chaos Gray brings. Darkness comes from the absence of light, which seems accurate—for some reason Gray is worse when Gunner isn't around.

As I watch my phone, the dots indicating Gunner's writing keeps popping up and disappearing again just as fast. I don't know how long I've been in the bathroom, but I have to get back or everyone will start suspecting I've either been kidnapped, or am suffering from a mean case of food poisoning. Ew.

Me: Yeah, I'm going to Cassie's after we're done with dinner and I've changed. Want to take me?

Gunner's told me numerous times to let him know if I need a ride anywhere. He seems genuinely worried about my safety, plus he has a car as well as a bike. And if I'm going to a party, there's no way I'm showing up with helmet hair. Just no.

G2: Glad you're going, especially if you're about to forget how to spell Z-O-E

After cleaning up and washing my hands, I return to the table, where my family has ordered dessert for me. I'm glad it arrives quicker than the rest of our food, and within the hour, we're ready to leave. While dad pays the bill, Leslie keeps going on about the crème brûlée that's apparently to die for.

"Maybe we can try to make it at home," she says, giving me a hopeful look.

I scrunch up my nose, but before I decline her offer, I'm reminded that this is our last summer of living together.

As I look at my sister, I wonder what kind of memory this moment will create. One laced with regret over not spending enough time together? Or one that makes me smile because I made an effort? I know regret is part of life, but that doesn't mean I won't try to avoid it where possible.

Hell, maybe I should even let her have my room. Why do I care when I'm leaving?

"That would be fun." I give her a quick hug, clearly surprising her. "Consider it a date," I grin.

With how nostalgic this evening is making me, I'm beginning to wonder if I can even survive moving across the country. I've always thought it would be a breeze, but now I'm no longer so sure.

Right now, I just can't imagine not seeing the faces of my family every day. I'm sure I'll even miss bickering with Leslie just because I hate agreeing with her.

Dad leads us outside, holding the door open for us. "I'm a lucky man," he says as he walks out behind us. "Getting to spend the evening with my three favorite women." Mom takes his hand and kisses his cheek while Leslie links her arm with mine.

Now that we're no longer protected by the restaurant's A/C, the Santa Cruz summer heat smacks me right in the face.

My breath hitches as I hear the faint rumbling sound of bikes in the distance. Whenever I hear that noise, it reminds me of him. Grayson Black. My heart skips a beat, and my lips part to say his name. To cover up my almost blunder of saying his name, I force out a laugh.

"What's so funny?" Leslie gives me a hopeful smile. "Are you laughing because you've decided to give me your room?

"As if," I say, shaking my head.

As we slowly walk towards our car, I get lost in ideas of what to wear to Cassie's party. Most of the girls will want to show off their newest designer outfits, and that used to be enough for me. Only, tonight I find myself wishing I owned something risque to wear. Like, a long dress or skirt with a slit so high not wearing underwear would be downright indecent, or a top so see through my nipples would make a guest appearance all night long.

"Watch where you're going, Zoe." My mom's words snap me out of my thoughts as I almost walk into the lamppost in front of me.

Oops.

"What's with the goofy smile?" dad asks, smiling knowingly like he thinks he knows exactly what I'm thinking about.

I try to smile back at him, but it's more of a grimace. My cheeks burn as I swallow, hoping he really, really doesn't know what's on my mind. Then again, I can't imagine a man as sophisticated and proper as my dad ever having an indecent thought, let alone as depraved as mine.

No. Ew.

Thoughts like that about either of my parents make my stomach churn. I prefer to think of them the old-fashioned way, the one where intimacy doesn't exist, and thanks to them not sharing a bedroom, it makes it easier.

"Maybe we should go away for a few days," dad suggests. "Go to the beach and rent a cabana or—" Before dad can finish his sentence, three men jump out of the shadows.

As I notice a gun pointed directly at my chest, I let out a blood-curdling scream of terror. My breath gets caught in my throat, and my world feels like it's closing in on me.

I barely notice I'm being thrown to the ground, or the gunshots and screams around us. It's like I'm in one of those silent movies, however, instead of music, the scene is being set by the thunderous roar of my blood rushing to my ears.

"Leslie!" As I scream my sister's name, a hand is clamped over my mouth.

Oh, God... this is it. I'm going to die.

"Don't move, Princess."

I know that voice, low as it is there's no way to mistake it. Despite knowing it's Gray, I keep trying to move. I need to find Leslie. We were... her arm was linked with mine, wasn't it? Where is she?

When I try to call for her again, the hand over my mouth slips between my lips and I bite down while fighting Gray's hold on me.

"I said don't fucking move," he hisses. "I can't fucking protect you and fight you at the same time. Do as you're told and lie fucking still."

Protect me? Is that what he's doing? But... but who's protecting Leslie, and mom and dad?

As something shatters close to my head, I'm roughly being pulled by my hair. The movement is followed by my head being pushed down against the rough asphalt. I think it hurts, but I can't be sure. I can't feel anything but all-consuming panic.

When the grip on me disappears, I immediately curl in on myself in a fetal position with my arms curled around my head protectively. My body is shaking with tears and silent screams that I don't dare let out.

"Zoe? Are you hurt?"

In response to the voice I don't immediately recognize, I try to make myself smaller.

"Leave her alone, Gunner. Go check on the others instead."

That voice I recognize.

Gray.

The two of them talk about something regarding a perimeter and backup, but I can't make sense of most of their words. My mind reels as I try to recall where I am and what I'm doing on the ground. I was... walking... I think. Did I fall? I try to move, but my body doesn't obey. It feels heavy, as though it's being held down by an unseen force.

"Leslie... oh God, Leslie. Astrid. Zoe... answer me." My dad's heartbroken shouts bring me back to reality.

I scramble up, looking around me at the carnage. Next to our car is... no... no, no, no.

"Leslie?" I scream, barely getting her name out before Gray grabs my shoulders and spins me around, holding me tightly against his chest.

"Don't look, Zoe," Gray whispers directly into my ear.

Anger takes over, and I do my best to fight him off me. "Let go," I screech. As I finally get my arms free, I dig my nails into his arms. When the bastard doesn't even flinch, only making shushing sounds, I quickly lift my knee, ramming it right into his junk.

Rationally, I know I only got the upper hand because he never expected me to even consider doing something like that, but I don't care. I need to get to Leslie.

I'm surprised when Gray doesn't let go, but instead takes me to the ground with him as he falls to his knees while groaning in pain.

"Let me go," I scream.

I swing my arms wildly while screaming at him, but it does no good. He only clutches me tighter, and there's not a goddamn thing I can do about it. He's easily overpowering me, even while being in pain.

"Gray let her go, man."

Ignoring Gunner, I move my hands to Gray's face, scratching him so viciously I feel my nails break his skin.

"Let go of my fucking daughter." Dad's booming voice slices through me, making me cry out in relief.

"Dad?" I cry out to him. "I'm here. Dad, I'm here."

There's a grunt followed by my body being jostled, then I'm free. I blink, confused by what happened, but when my eyes land on Gunner, who's holding Gray in a chokehold, it all makes sense. I quickly crawl towards my dad.

80

He's close, leaning over... I begin to shake as fear and grief tear at my insides. Although I know I shouldn't, I can't stop looking at the bullet hole in my sister's forehead. Tears stream down my cheeks as I look at Leslie and her wide, unseeing eyes as blood runs down her face. It's all around her, seeping into her new dress.

A part of me wants to leap up and move her. She loves that dress. It took her endless arguments and coercion before mom finally caved and let her have it. And now it's being ruined... that's not fair. Leslie loves that dress.

Pressing my fist against my mouth, I try to silence my sobs.

No!

This can't be real!

This has to be a dream. A nightmare.

Please, God, let this all be one big horrifying dream—one I can wake up from.

I bite into the soft skin on my hand, not stopping until I'm drawing blood. But it's no use. Despite the pain, I'm not waking up.

Leslie... I can't remember the last time I told her I love her. And... she wanted my room so badly. Why didn't I give it to her two years ago when she first mentioned it?

I don't know how much time passes before dad comes over. "Zoe, are you okay?" he cries, emotions thick in his voice. I can only nod as he pulls me into a bone-crushing embrace.

"Mom?" I croak, and when I feel his big body shake, bile creeps up my throat.

No!

In a rush, I push him away, crawling to the side on all fours, and empty my stomach into the bushes.

This can't be real. It has to be a nightmare because there's no way this is the end to my perfect day.

6

Zoe

The days are blurring together, much like the tears and snot on my face.

Is it Monday? Tuesday? I don't have a fucking clue.

Days are a way of measuring time, a way to divide our existence into neat packages. People are creatures of habit, so we love sticking to a schedule, a pattern. In the end, it doesn't matter. Or maybe it does, because all I can think about is that I need to find out what day it is.

Leslie has horseback riding lessons on Wednesday, and someone needs to call her Olympic gold medalist coach and tell him that Leslie is... Leslie is... she isn't coming.

On Thursday she has her ballet dance class, they also need to be notified.

My sister will never again show up at the stables with sugar cubes in her pockets for her mare, just as she'll never take center stage and dance her little heart out.

Mom is on the garden committee, but I'm not sure what all she does to fill her time aside from that.

A list... I need to make a list.

There are so many things to do, and since I don't know what fucking day it is, I don't know how much time I have.

I scramble to get out of Leslie's bed, but the pink throw blanket is tangled around my legs and I end up falling to the floor with a startled cry. My head bounces off the soft carpet lining the floor, and I scream in frustration, in pain, and because life is so fucking unfair.

How am I meant to go on living when I can't even manage a simple task like getting out of bed?

Shaking myself off, I slowly stand up and look around Leslie's room. It's the only place in the house where I can breathe without the walls closing in on me. So I stay here every night. When I close my eyes to go to sleep, I tell myself my sister is at camp and that she's coming home soon.

"She'll be so pissed if she comes home and finds her bed unmade," I murmur to the empty room, allowing myself to indulge in the lie for a bit longer.

Tonight... tonight I'll open my mind to reality, and I'll no longer lie to myself.

I make my sister's bed, even going through the motions of lining her stupid unicorns in the order she's received them in. An order I know well since I'm the one who's bought her most of them.

Leslie is beyond obsessed with unicorns, and for some reason I've never been able to come across a stuffed unicorn without buying it for her.

Even though we've fought countless times, and I've told her she's embarrassing, I hope she knew that she was always in my heart. But how could she? I didn't even know how much I loved her until she was ripped away from me.

A sob escapes me as I make my way to the bathroom. While I strip out of the clothes I slept in and step into the shower, I feel an overwhelming sense of despair threatening to drown me.

How hard would it have been for me to be nicer? I should never have let a single day pass without telling Les how much I loved her.

There's no excuse great enough, I know that now.

Tilting my head back, I let the warm water drench my long blonde hair. Droplets cascade down my face, mingling with the tears that are now free-falling anew.

After shampooing and conditioning my hair, I reach for the razor that's perched on the shelf in the shower. Like in a trance, I close my hands around the handle and move the item closer. I open my eyes and study the blade. Some hairs are stuck between the plastic and the metal, and I idly wonder if I should be missing this part of myself.

I don't recall ever looking this closely, and I never feel anything when shaving. But that's just another part that we humans close our eyes to, isn't it? We can rake the metal across parts of our bodies to rid ourselves of unwanted hair, but do we ever feel it?

Shaking my head, I close my eyes again, wanting to get rid of my thoughts that make no sense. I have more important things to do than turn wistful over some stray, unwanted hairs.

As soon as I'm done, I dry myself before wrapping my hair up in the towel. Then I go to my room and find the clothes I need to face the day. A light-blue summer dress and wedges. Not something I'd normally pick when moping around the house, but I need it. The expensive designer stuff makes me feel empowered, and right now, I need all the strength I can get—even if it comes from being shallow.

After I'm dressed, I reluctantly sit down in front of my vanity mirror. "Fake it until you make it," I whisper to myself, rolling my shoulders back as I stare down the sickly version of myself that's peering back from the mirror.

Doing my makeup and hair is second nature, something I can do without thinking. Which is good, because I don't like my thoughts. They're becoming more and more strained, and it's a battle to keep reality from knocking down my carefully erected walls.

As soon as I'm done, I reluctantly leave my room, surprised to see dad pouring himself a cup of coffee.

"Good morning," I say tentatively, trying to smile at him, but it's forced and hurts my cheeks, so I quickly let my face fall into the mask of sorrow that's forever etched into my flesh.

After placing the cup on the counter, dad turns around and his red-rimmed eyes meet mine.

"I'm glad to see you're up, baby girl," dad says. His voice is hoarse. "The detectives will be here soon with more questions. Do you think you can manage that today?"

Confusion causes me to frown, something I shouldn't do unless I want premature wrinkles. I heard mom once saying that to one of the women in the neighborhood.

"What day is it?" I ask, unable to focus on anything else until I know.

"It doesn't matter—"

Shaking my head, I interrupt dad. "It matters to me," I cry. "Someone needs to call Leslie's trainers to let them know... and what about her school? And her friends? I think she was planning something this weekend—"

The inhuman cry coming from my dad breaks through my tirade.

"Zoe, please take a breath."

Even though I feel ridiculous, I do as he says. I close my eyes and inhale deeply before slowly expelling the air from my lungs.

"Do you remember the last three days?"

My eyes fly open, and I glare at dad. "Of course," I snap. "Why are you talking to me like I'm stupid?"

Raising his arm towards me, dad tentatively takes one step and then another in my direction. It really fucking hurts my feelings that he's acting like I'm a wounded animal, like he doesn't know what to do with me.

Propping my hands on my hips, I demand, "What's going on?"

Dad comes to a stop in front of me and places his hands on my shoulders. "Baby girl, you... when the ambulance and police arrived, you fainted and hit your head pretty bad on the concrete."

My hand darts up to my scalp, and I prod it until I find a bump with a scab on it. How did I not feel that when I was brushing my hair?

"Why am I not in the hospital then?" I ask like that's the most important question.

"Because..." Dad looks around with a wild look in his eyes before continuing. "It wasn't safe, baby girl. I called Dr. Hemphill, and she's been here to see you multiple times a day."

"That's a lie," I blurt out. Taking a deep breath, I slowly sag against the wall. "I don't fucking believe you."

"Zoe... every time you woke up, you kept screaming for Leslie. You tried attacking Dr. Hemphill, myself, and even..."

When it becomes clear that dad isn't going to finish his sentence, I ask, "Even who, dad?"

He slowly shakes his head. "Grayson and Gunner were here a few times. They claimed to want to look after you, but I didn't believe it, so I spoke with the Cruz Kings president and had him make them both stay away."

None of this is making any fucking sense to me. Gray wouldn't be here to check on me, that much I know for certain. But that doesn't matter. Now, my lack of memory, I need that to make sense.

"Why don't I remember anything?" I ask accusingly.

"Dr. Hemphill says it's likely trauma paired with your head injury."

Though I'm not sure I believe dad, I nod. I feel tired, and my clothes are no longer making me feel anything but uncomfortable. I frown as I look down at the dress I'm wearing. There's a memory lodged in my brain, wiggling as it tries to break free.

"Leslie," I gasp. When dad looks at me with unshed tears in his eyes, I carry on. "What happened to her dress?"

"Baby girl, both your mom and—"

Not wanting to hear the words, I interrupt him with a cry. "They're at camp," I insist in a way that makes it clear my lie isn't up for debate. "Now tell me what happened to her dress? She really loved that dress, you know."

We're interrupted by a knock on the front door.

"That must be the detectives," dad says robotically. "Go sit down at the table and I'll let them in."

While dad disappears, I pour myself a cup of coffee before sitting down in my usual seat. I don't know what the detectives will ask, and I don't remember talking to them before. But I do suspect it'll be less awkward if I can keep my hands busy.

The two people trailing behind dad look frumpy. The suit the man is wearing is too short on the legs, making it look like the edge of his pants are enemies with his lime-green socks. And don't even get me started on the woman. Her pants are crinkled, and there's a coffee stain on her white shirt. It's like they're purposefully trying to drive me insane.

If mom was here, she'd pretend not to notice. She is—*was*—graceful like that. But I'd know she'd have noticed, because she would narrow her eyes and then quirk one of her eyebrows. Probably the right one.

"Good morning. How are you feeling today, Zoe?" the woman asks, holding out her hand to me.

I know I should take it, shake it, and return her greeting. But I'm not going to.

"Please call me Miss Miller," I say. When the woman rolls her eyes, I straighten. "We're not friends and we do not know each other. Please don't offend me by pretending otherwise." Smirking, I lean back and take a sip of my coffee.

"Of course, Miss Miller," the man says. "I'm Steven and this is—"

"I'm Detective Nelson," the woman says, interrupting him.

Does she think she's being clever or something? Oh, for fuck's sake, is she one of those petty women who thinks she has something to prove?

Clearing his throat, dad says, "Steven, Tania, please sit down."

Even though it's immature, I can't help smirking at Tania, who looks like she's bit into a sour lemon. Ugh, if only Leslie was here, she'd be giggling to herself. I miss her laugh.

After accepting the offer of coffee from dad, the detectives sit down. Steven pulls out a sleek, black tablet and takes notes after each question he asks.

"Do either of you remember noticing anything unusual before the attack?" Tania asks while looking at me.

After each question, I have to swallow the growing lump of emotions in my throat. I can no longer lie to myself about mom and Leslie's whereabouts. They're dead. Gone. Never to be seen or spoken to again. They're... fuck.

"No," I croak. As I feel tears fall from my eyes, I angrily swipe them away.

"Why were you at that particular restaurant, Zoe?" Tania asks almost unkindly. "It's not your usual place to go, is it?"

I look helplessly at dad who shakes his head at me before barking, "We won't answer any more questions without our lawyer present."

Try as I might, I find it hard not to show how surprised I feel. I don't understand why he invited them inside without a lawyer here if he isn't going to answer their questions. And I definitely don't get why he doesn't just answer when we have nothing to hide.

"Because I just graduated from Santa Cruz Prep," I say sternly. "I don't know if you've heard of the place? It's pretty fucking elite, and I won the spot as valedictorian with the highest GPA. So no, Tania, it wasn't a restaurant we frequented. Just like it wasn't an average night out."

I know I shouldn't speak to her like she's dirt when she's just doing her job. I should show her respect, and be grateful she's working to solve... well... no, I can't say the words, let alone think them. Either way, she's getting on my last nerve with her attitude.

"I'm glad to see you're feeling better," Steven suddenly says. "Do you remember the last time we were here?"

Rather than answering with words, I shake my head.

"When will we be able to bury my wife and daughter?" dad asks angrily. "I thought that's what today was about. We want to say goodbye."

The rest of the time with the detectives is as uneventful as the cold coffee I'm sloshing around in the cup. They won't tell us anything, and in return, we tell them nothing. At least I think that's why dad is being vague.

"Right, well, if that's all, we have another engagement," dad says brusquely when Steven asks if I've ever been to Fuego.

Honestly, either the man has the attention span of a fruit fly, or he's fishing for something.

"Of course," Tania says as she stands up. "Please make sure to come to our office tomorrow. We would advise you to bring your lawyer so we can talk freely."

"Why do you—"

Dad interrupts me. "I'll be there tomorrow afternoon."

I should be relieved it isn't me they're wanting to see, but I'm not. Something is wrong with the way my dad's acting, and the detectives keep asking the same stupid questions. It makes no sense. Though I want to ask more of my own questions, I hold them back. Dad always has his reasons for doing what he does.

As soon as the detectives leave, dad suggests we order breakfast before going to the lawyer's office to hear mom's will. I agree, even though all I want to do is go back to Leslie's bed. The pancakes and scrambled eggs that I end up wordlessly pushing around on my plates aren't doing a good job at convincing me to stay up.

Dad insists I have to be present, though, and that's the only reason I walk out in the garden instead of back to my sister's room.

My head is throbbing, and the bright sunlight isn't doing me any favors. I sit down on the edge of the pool. After kicking my shoes off, I dip my toes into the water. It feels amazing on my skin, and for a moment I contemplate pushing off the edge and hiding below the water's surface.

"Hey Zoe." I'm startled by Gunner as he walks closer. "How are you doing?" He cringes like he's just realizing it's a stupid thing to ask.

Rather than giving him a quick quip, I ponder the question. Truthfully, I don't know how I'm doing. I'm confused, angry, sad, overwhelmed, and tired—bone-deep exhaustion, to be exact.

Settling on a statement, I croak, "I'm alive."

Gunner nods as he sits down next to me, folding his long legs under him. "That you are," he says softly. "Do you—"

"Please don't ask me about that night," I whimper.

I remember seeing Gunner there, in the parking lot. Well, I think I remember seeing him, but I could be wrong.

Shaking his head, he says, "I wasn't going to. I wanted to know if you need anything."

I pull my legs up and rest my head on my knees. Then I peer at Gunner from beneath my lashes. He looks solemn, like he's afraid of doing or saying the wrong thing.

"Not really..." I trail off as a thought hits me. "I need my sister's dress. The one she was wearing..."

The look on Gunner's face is almost comical. "I think it's ruined."

"I know that," I snap. "But I need to fix it so she can wear it again." I'm surprised by my words. I didn't even know my thoughts were heading in that direction, but now that I've spoken the words out loud, it feels right.

Leslie needs to be buried in that dress, and with some of her belongings. I don't know what comes next for her and my mom, but I don't need to. My sister deserves the best send-off, and she deserves to look her best.

"I don't think that's possible," Gunner says thoughtful-ly. When I look away to hide the tears quietly falling from my eyes, he adds, "But I'll see what I can do."

"Thank you," I murmur. Then I reach out and stroke his inked arm in a placating gesture.

Gunner looks down to where I'm touching him, and opens his mouth like he wants to say something but he never gets the chance.

"Well, doesn't this look fucking cozy?" Gray's voice and angry footsteps slice through the peace and quiet. "What the fuck are you doing here?" He points an angry finger at Gunner.

"I was just asking Zoe if she needs anything," Gunner answers smoothly.

Gray's so angry he's practically vibrating. Hell, I'm not sure it would surprise me if he starts to spew fire through his flaring nostrils.

"Get the fuck back to your post," he thunders. "You know your fucking orders. Don't stray."

After mumbling something that sounds like an apology, Gunner gets up and slinks back around the house to where they usually stay when they're watching. Before disappearing completely from view, he turns around and says, "I promise I'll try to get the dress for you."

"What dress?" Gray barks the words like it's a declaration of war rather than a question.

Closing my eyes, I once again consider diving beneath the cool water to hide. The way the sun sparkles makes the bottom of the pool look inviting.

"What dress, Princess?" Gray asks again, his tone softer this time.

When I finally lift my head to look at him, he gasps like my face is shocking him. Which is ironic since he's the one with deep scratch marks on his face. Maybe one of the Cruz Cunts got him good.

The stunned surprise doesn't last long. Gray lifts one of his dark eyebrows, silently willing me to speak. But I don't. I have no words for him. A part of me feels like this is his fault. He's the VP, so it should have been him protecting us and not Gunner. Since I don't remember seeing Gray there, I'm confident he wasn't at the restaurant.

Like that's not enough, I also remember spending a good part of my family night in the bathroom, sexting and talking to him on the phone. Time I should have spent with my mom and Leslie. That time is now nothing more than a memory, one where I have severe regrets.

"Doesn't matter," I mumble, unable to look away from him.

"If I can help you, it matters."

Lowering my legs, I look back at my reflection in the water. Despite the water-proof claim on the tube, there are twin black streaks on both my cheeks. Fucking rip-off mascara.

"It's too late." I barely recognize my voice with how hollow it sounds. "You should have been there to protect us, and you weren't."

Gray's face morphs into confusion but I'm saved from having to say more when dad calls for me, so I quickly get to my feet and walk back inside without looking back. I can feel his dark eyes bore into my back, but I ignore it.

Throughout the drive to the lawyer's office, I try to pretend not to see the three bikes trailing behind us while dad white-knuckles the steering wheel. He's beyond tense, has been since the detectives said they want to see him alone.

"Why do the detectives want to ask you more questions?" I ask as I look at his profile. I can't help smiling as I notice he has some white powder-like substance stuck under his nose. Hmm maybe it's sugar or flour... but we didn't cook our breakfast, so that doesn't make sense.

After I point it out, dad wipes his nose and says, "I don't know, baby girl."

I frown. "Is it because of mom's parents?"

Although we never talk about mom's family, I know she comes from money—big money. Her dad was big in technology, allegedly he was working with Bill Gates on computer projects in the early days. So when she married dad, they were far from impressed, and basically disowned her. I had only met my maternal grandparents once, and even though they smiled, they seemed stuck up, even to me.

"It could be," dad says on a sigh. "I hate talking about money, but your mom had some of her own that she inherited from her parents. I'm assuming..." His voice cracks, but I don't need him to finish the sentence.

Now that mom is dead, it will all go to dad. Something mom's parents wouldn't want to happen, and they're not above fighting it even from beyond the grave.

After parking in one of the visitor spots, we enter the building where we're met by Graham, our family's lawyer. I don't recall meeting him before, but he acts like we're old friends, even goes as far as kissing both my cheeks. His gross cigar breath is almost as offensive as his crooked tie, and the small seed stuck between his front teeth.

Graham ushers us into his office, which is filled with knick-knacks. His credentials are all framed, lining the walls. There's a single sunflower in the window, and a few stray petals on the gray carpet underneath.

"Right, so we best get to it," Graham says, like it pains him to speak the words. "As I explained on the phone, there's no law declaring I have to read out Astrid's will. You're more than welcome to read it yourself."

I look at dad, not understanding why he brought us here if it isn't necessary.

"And as I explained," dad says, exasperated. "I think it's better if you read the will. We might as well do it the proper way."

Despite the severe situation, I want to roll my eyes at dad's need for things to be done in a way he deems proper.

"Of course," Graham says easily.

Then he opens his drawer and pulls out a box of tissues that he places on the table. He follows that by pulling out two envelopes that are sealed shut.

"Astrid left three letters, one of which has been destroyed per her will, and I'm forbidden from reading out loud."

"Why—"

Holding up his hand, Graham interrupts dad. "It's in her will that she wants them read privately. The instructions she's left is that once her will has been read or shared, I am to hand the corresponding letter to you, one at a time. Astrid wishes for you to read them separately."

Although dad looks like he wants to protest, I nod. I can't claim to know why my mom has chosen to do things this way, I just know that she wouldn't do it if she didn't feel it was necessary.

"O-okay," I say.

Graham begins to read out loud from his laptop. "I, Astrid Victoria Miller, hereby leave all my earthly belongings to my two daughters—Zoe Isla Miller and Leslie Hannah Miller. They are to inherit everything enclosed. If I die before they turn twenty-one, everything must be kept by my trustee, Graham Silver. In turn, Mr. Silver must make sure all expenses for my daughters are provided from the trust, for which he has received specific instructions. If one of my daughters is unable to receive their portion of the inheritance, the full sum will befall my other daughter. If both my daughters are unable to inherit, all items are to be sold and donated with my money to the Wilko Foundation for Young People—"

"That's preposterous," dad shouts. He stands up so quickly his chair falls to the carpeted floor. "There's no way my wife would—"

Graham, who's struck me as friendly so far, looks anything but at this moment. "Sit down, Mr. Miller," he says, coldly. "I will not tolerate any outbursts in my office. Are you accusing me of falsifying your wife's will?"

Dad looks chastised as he raises the chair back up. "No, of course not. But—"

With a sly smile, the lawyer steeples his fingers together. "Now, I would advise you to take a deep breath and compose yourself. If you do not, I'll have no choice but to disclose, ahh, certain things in front of your daughter."

My eyes are flicking between dad and Graham, but I can't make sense of what they're saying, or why dad looks so scared. A part of me also doesn't care. I want the letter my mom left me, I don't care about anything else.

"I want my letter," I say, looking straight at the lawyer. Then for good measure, I add, "Please."

When dad complains and tries to insist he wants to stay with me, Graham calls security and two big, burly men come to escort dad out. I feel bad as he calls for me, but I don't turn around. I need that letter. I need to see my mom's handwriting.

"I'm sorry, Mr. Miller," Graham calls. "But since Zoe is eighteen, she doesn't need supervision and this was your wife's wish."

As soon as the door closes behind dad and the security, Graham hands me the envelope with my name on it. The wax seal is an eagle, the logo of her dad's company.

My dearest Zoe,

I don't know under what circumstances you're reading this. But I hope it's after you've graduated Harvard, met a nice man, and settled down. Maybe you've even gotten married and have kids of your own.

God, I hope so.

Since we never know what life might bring, there's no telling when you get this letter. You might be reading this earlier than you should, and if that's the case, I hope you're sitting next to Leslie. Please look after your sister, Zoe. Her heart is big and kind, maybe too much. So she'll need you to help her.

I stop reading as the letters become blurry, and I hiccup into the tissue.

You might have questions about why I'm giving everything to you and your sister, and I want to be as honest with you as I feel I can be. Please know this part isn't in Leslie's letter, because I don't want her to worry. But you're stronger, baby, you're cut from the same cloth as I am.

There are many things you don't know about your dad. He has problems and demons of his own, which is why I've fought tirelessly to keep my estate from him, so he can't take it away from you or Leslie.

Your dad is a good man, please don't think he isn't. But he's too comfortable living above his means. That's the real reason he had to start working for the Cruz Kings, he needed to earn more money to support his habits and our lifestyle.

I know I'm to blame as well. I'm too comfortable with wealth and can't imagine living without it. I suppose that's my fatal flaw, and I hope you can forgive me.

Zoe, I know you might think you're reliant on material goods, too. But that couldn't be further from the truth. You're strong, baby. You're going to be a force to be reckoned with once you find your footing.

With all my love,

Mom.

I re-read the letter until my entire body shakes from the force of the sobs I can't hold back. I even look to the side as I re-read the part about Leslie sitting next to me, and for a second, it's as though I can feel her hand in mine.

Graham excused himself as I did my second read through, and he still hasn't returned.

"I'm so sorry," I whisper to the empty room, hoping my voice carries to heaven where my mom and sister are now. "I should have looked after you better, Leslie. I... I—" My cries turn to wails, stealing my ability to continue what I want to say.

Mom is wrong, though. I'm nothing more than a spoiled, rich girl. Without material goods, I don't know who I am, and I'm not sure I dare to find out.

According to the itemized list Graham left on the table, I'll be worth a lot on my twenty-first birthday. Yet, if I could bring mom and Leslie back, I'd burn it all right this second.

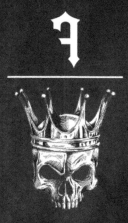

Grayson

Something I'm not privy to happened inside the lawyer's office. Brian and Zoe were in there for longer than I expected, and when they stepped out, Zoe was a tear soaked mess, and Brian was agitated as fuck, taking his anger out on his car door with a slam. I stepped forward, almost approaching the car to stop Zoe from getting into the passenger seat, but her red-rimmed eyes met mine across the small parking lot, and she halted my steps with a small shake of her head.

Now I watch from the dark backyard of her house as her dad paces the lower level of the house, tipping back beer after beer, as Zoe's bedroom window on the second floor remains dark, but her sister's window lets out a warm glow.

"Has she responded to your message?" Gunner asks as he approaches me from the side, leaving his fucking post once again. I shake my head, and glare at him.

"Has she responded to you?" I snap, and Gunner shakes his head, too.

Fuck.

I don't know why it matters. Zoe Miller is nothing more than something to entertain us but her words from earlier slam into my head.

"You should have been there to protect us, and you weren't."

I fucking protected her! Doesn't she know that? I couldn't get to her mom or sister, and I would have if it were safe to leave Zoe, but it wasn't.

Maybe when she said 'us', she meant her mom and sister?

She's hurting right now, and lashing out is expected. I know I'm a fucking prick most of the time, but I am also damn fucking good at my job, and I fucking protected her as best I could given the circumstances.

I push those thoughts aside, because right now, they don't matter.

I guess what does matter, more than anything, is how fucking on edge Brian is.

"Go back to your post. I'm going in to have a chat with Brian," I state to Gunner, and he hovers for a moment, his eyes boring a hole into the side of my head, before he finally turns and leaves.

As soon as Gunner disappears around the corner of the house, I make my way across the lawn, and climb the back steps, onto the porch where the back door is. It's locked, as usual, but like always, I know the code, and key it in, hearing the lock click open.

As soon as I step into the room, I hear Brian's voice, laced with anger as he mutters either to himself, or someone else, perhaps over the phone.

Stepping into the living area, Brian's gaze darts up to mine in panic, and he stumbles back a few steps.

He's definitely not on his phone, so the words he was muttering must have been to himself.

"What's wrong Brian?" I ask, sounding amused.

I'm not really amused, but it's a scare tactic that works well for people not accustomed to my world.

They expect angry and brooding. Or calm and happy. What they don't expect is someone so relaxed that they seem amused. It freaks them out.

"What do you think is wrong? My wife and daughter are dead!" Brian spits, his beer sloshing in the glass bottle as he waves his arm around.

"I'm obviously aware of that," I say lazily as I take a seat on his recliner and get comfortable. "What I'm referring to is how fucking angry you have been since stepping foot from your lawyer's office."

"That's none of your fucking business!" Brian snaps, taking a menacing step towards me, yet I don't move a muscle. I remain relaxed in his recliner.

"I think you will find it *is* my business, Brian. Everything you do is my business. You fucking know that working for CK means you give up your privacy when it comes to us. So how about you calm the fuck down and tell me what I need to know."

"And i-if I d-don't?" He stutters as he slowly steps back, trying to put distance between us.

I sigh, rather fucking dramatically before sitting forward a fraction to reach behind me. Slowly, I tug my Glock free before bringing it around and pretending to inspect it.

Even though I'm no longer looking at him, I can see Brian hovering nearby in my peripheral, shifting from foot to foot as his nervous energy almost explodes from him.

"Okay. Fine. If you must know, my darling dead wife didn't leave me a fucking thing in her will. Now I'll need to sell this house, and my car, and... and... and..."

In defeat, Brian flops down to sit on the sofa and starts to cry.

Fuck.

I have more fucking questions for him relating to his agitation, as well as other things like why he changed the location of Zoe's graduation dinner. I'm really fucking curious about that. But in this moment, I just don't feel that fucking heartless. He's grieving. And feeling jilted obviously, about not being left anything in his wife's will.

For the first time in a long fucking time, I decide to give Brian a break. This questioning can wait until after he buries his wife and kid.

I don't offer Brian any comfort. I just up and leave him to his grieving knowing I can't do a fucking thing for him, or his only daughter left alive who is most likely just as distraught upstairs in her dead sister's bedroom.

Returning to my post, I take out my phone to see a message from Rocco stating that he is sending someone to take over for me and Gunner because we are needed back at the clubhouse.

I feel anxious about leaving Zoe. Her dad is uncharacteristically unstable. I understand that he feels jilted, but something in my gut says it's more than that.

I shoot Rocco a message asking him to send extra men to cover us, and as soon as they show up, Gunner and I head back to the clubhouse.

When we pull up, I can see why we were called back.

A police cruiser sits outside our clubhouse, and most of my club brothers are loitering around outside instead of lounging around inside, enjoying some drinks.

"What's going on?" I ask Slayer as I set my helmet on my bike before climbing the steps to the closed doors.

"Fucking pigs are here to see you man." Slayer grunts, his only dark eye giving me a hard look that tells me if I were inclined to go in guns blazing, he'd be right there by my side.

"I've been expecting them. Can't hold the pricks off forever." I slap Slayer on the shoulder as I pass, before turning back to Gunner. "Stay here, man. They'll be gone in no time."

Gunner pulls up short, a look of disappointment flashing over his face.

I don't know why the fuck he'd be disappointed about not going inside to talk to the cops, and I don't have time to analyze it, turning my back and pushing through the door.

Normally stepping inside the club you are greeted with loud music, and some sort of moaning from a Cruz Cunt or one of my brothers, but now the music is turned down so low I can't even tell what's playing, and there's no sign of the Cruz Cunts.

Mama C and Rocco are sitting lazily at a table drinking and eating peanuts while two cops stand before them, looking annoyed. They all turn to see me as I walk through the space, my eyes not even bothering to meet the cops as I reach the table, bump fists with Rocco, lean down and give Mama C a kiss on her cheek, before flopping in the spare chair and grabbing a handful of peanuts.

"You must be Grayson Black." The female officer snaps, unimpressed, and I nod, tossing a peanut up in the air, and shifting quickly to catch it in my open mouth. "We've been trying to catch up to you for days. You're a hard man to catch."

I shrug, catching another peanut.

I've been hard to catch on purpose, just like the way I avoided them at the scene where Astrid and Leslie were killed. These two detectives aren't on our payroll, so they are nothing but trouble for someone like me.

"Yeah, it took threatening Mr. King with a potential warrant to search this establishment before he gave in and asked you to show your face." The male officer remarks, gesturing to Rocco, and I shrug, stuffing the rest of the peanuts in my mouth.

"Whatdoyouwant?" I ask, my voice muffled by the mouthful I'm munching on.

"I'm Detective Nelson," the female states, looking annoyed by my vile table manners, "and this is Detective Caruso."

I nod at them, swallowing the mouthful of peanuts before reaching for Rocco's beer and taking a swig.

"Are you done?" Detective Nelson snaps, and I flash her a toothy smile.

"Sure." Gesturing for her to continue, I relax back in the chair and cross my arms over my chest, waiting for her to hurry the fuck up and get on with it so I can get back to the Miller house.

"We saw you at the scene Mr. Black, yet you seemed to avoid being questioned. We also have video surveillance of the shooting, and it clearly shows you running into the scene with a raised weapon," Detective Nelson glances down at the file in her hand, opening it to flick through a few pages before looking back up at me, "a Glock if our imagery is correct. You fired some rounds towards the attackers and then you protected the eldest Miss Miller, dragging her away from the line of fire. Does that sound correct?"

I shrug. "You have the video footage, so I guess so."

"Do you have a permit for the Glock?" Detective Caruso asks, and I smirk.

"We both know you don't need a license for a handgun in this state."

"It's registered though, right?" Detective Caruso smirks back, and I roll my eyes.

"Are you here about me carrying a weapon or about finding those fuckers who killed two innocent people?"

"Why were you at the scene, Mr. Black?" Detective Nelson asks, taking over the questioning again.

"I was passing by. Heard the gunshots and saw an innocent family being attacked."

"That's a bit of a coincidence, don't you think?" she asks, raising a questioning brow.

"How so?" I ask back, igniting her annoyance.

"The Cruz Kings are clients of Mr. Miller's, isn't that correct?" She glances back inside the folder for a moment before lifting her hard glare back to mine. "He is your club accountant."

I nod. "And? What's your point?"

Detective Nelson huffs, flapping her file shut as her cheeks go red in anger. "The point is, Mr. Black, that it's a little too coincidental that you just happened to be across the road from the restaurant that your club accountant was dining at with his family, right at the time your arch enemies, the Cali Reapers, attacked."

My brows shoot up. "How do you know it was the Reapers?"

We already know it was the Reapers, but they weren't visibly wearing their club logo, so unless they have facial rec to pick up the Reapers members, then they have come upon this knowledge another way.

"We found a Reaper dead in a back alley a few blocks over." Detective Caruso interjects. "Died from a bullet wound. From a Glock 19."

"Was this a club hit?" Detective Nelson steps back in. "Is the war no one admits is happening between the Cruz Kings and the Cali Reapers escalating?"

It's at that moment that Detective Caruso's phone starts ringing loudly, causing Detective Nelson to shoot him a glare like it's his fault his phone is ringing.

Detective Caruso answers it, and we all fall silent waiting for him. His eyes widen, darting to Rocco, and then to his partner before he agrees to something and ends the call.

With a frown creasing his brow, he leans in and whispers something into his partner's ear, who then curses, her cheeks flaring redder than before, before she glares at Rocco, and then me.

"It must be nice having friends in high places." Detective Nelson spits, her remark aimed at Rocco as she pins him with a look that I'm sure scares most people. Just not us.

"I don't know what you mean." Rocco says smugly before taking a swig of his beer.

"So you have no idea why the police commissioner has just ordered us to end our questioning and leave your clubhouse?" she asks with venom in her tone.

"Nope. But thanks for stopping by." Rocco grins.

She glares at us for a few long moments before turning on her heel and storming away, her partner in tow.

"Well, that was fun." Mama C smiles and Rocco grins back, nodding.

"I always love the moment they realize their attempts are fruitless."

"You could have told me why I was summoned," I bark at my Prez, who rolls his eyes before responding.

"Where's the fun in that?"

I shoot him a '*really*' glare, and he chuckles.

"Look, it was only a matter of time before they were going to catch up with you." Rocco concedes. "Better to happen here where we can make them feel the most uncomfortable."

"It was the most entertained I've been in a while." Mama C snickers and I roll my eyes at both of them.

"Good to see my discomfort is fucking amusing to you."

"Oh, don't whine like a little bitch." Mama C points her claw-like nail towards me. "You weren't the least bit uneasy. Don't pretend like it was a difficult conversation to have."

"I've got a difficult conversation for you." Rocco inter-jects, and the grin that had tugged my lips momentarily, drops away. "Why do you keep fucking insisting on taking the watch shifts at the Millers' house?"

I shrug, standing from my seat. "The Reapers set out to take out that entire family. They didn't succeed, so it only makes sense that they will try again."

Rocco shakes his head. "I'm not so sure. They haven't even tried to get close to them again. We've been watching the area the Millers live in. It's been quiet. I think with the hit on Hugo's Butcher Shop, we should be looking at protecting our smaller partners."

He has a point. Word on the street is that our local businesses are scared. Their affiliation with us has made them a target, and the Reapers are determined to get people to turn on us, as much as to take us out one by one. Hitting our local businesses will scare away their loyalty to us, making it easier to move in and claim our territory.

"So what do you want me to do?" I ask, and Rocco's shoulders relax.

"Tomorrow, start visiting our small business owners, one by one. Reassure them that they are safe. Put extra patrols on the streets. Let's start making them feel safe, and hope if the Reapers sneak into the area, we either spot them, or they back away with our extra presence." Prez sits back in his chair. "As for the Millers, I've already organized some of our loyal cops to stand watch at the start of their street. That's about as much as we can do right now given we need the manpower elsewhere, but perhaps tell Brian to reach out if they need to leave their property. We will provide protection outside their home."

"Will do," I agree, knowing Prez is right. We have to protect our community. Not just the spoiled little rich girl living up near the DeLaveaga Golf Course.

Leaving the clubhouse as my brothers start to file back in, I find Gunner waiting for me, leaning against the post.

"All good?" he asks, and I nod.

"Yeah. Prez is calling off the watch on the Millers. He's stationing some pigs on their street, but we are still to provide them protection when they leave the house."

Gunner's brows shoot up at this information, but I ignore his weird response and brush past him, striding to my bike.

"I guess that puts a damper on our bet."

I still at my bike, replaying Gunner's words in my head. Did he really just say that?

Slowly I turn to take in my club brother. The guy who has been my best buddy ever since we met when I was sixteen. Twelve years of knowing this guy, and all of a sudden he is saying insensitive shit that makes me feel like he's been possessed by another being.

"Are you talking about the making her fall in love with us bet?"

Gunner nods, frowning. "Yeah. Why?"

Rolling my tongue in my mouth, I close the distance between us, jabbing my finger to his chest.

"The moment her family got filled with lead was the moment that fucking bet ceased. What the fuck is wrong with you?"

He balks at me, taking a step back. "I thought it was still on since you've been going inside most nights. Haven't you been fucking her?"

"No!" I snap. "I'm not that fucking heartless, Gunner. What the fuck, man!"

"Then what the fuck have you been doing?" he snaps, and my lips thin.

Fuck.

What have I been doing?

Watching her sleep. I can't tell him that. He will ask why, and I have no fucking answer to give because I don't fucking know. She's just so fucking broken. Her old man has been giving her less and less attention, leaving her to suffer alone with the pain I know all too fucking well is unbelievably excruciating.

It's taken me back to that day, when I was sixteen, in an alley, watching my dad die. I had no one to help me through until Rocco took me under his wing. My mom was too heartbroken to remember I even existed. Or maybe she wasn't heartbroken. She didn't seem so distraught when I sprang her getting railed by my dad's best friend at the fucking funeral.

Fuck!

I drag my hand over my face as the exhaustion from the last couple of days starts to seep in. I've barely slept. When I haven't been helping my club hunt down motherfuckers for answers about the Miller hit, I've been watching over Zoe.

I need a night alone to fucking sleep.

To forget.

"I've been trying to get closer to Brian to see if there's any dodgy shit happening. I still don't trust him after the day he slipped off while Astrid and Leslie were getting ice cream."

Gunner nods. "Okay, man. Sorry, I thought we must have been still working Zoe."

I shake my head. "Nope. You may as well stay here. Party with the Cruz Cunts tonight. I'm heading to the Millers, checking in with the cops patrolling."

Gunner nods, but doesn't say anything as I get on my bike and ride away.

When I arrive at the mouth of the Millers' street, I'm met with Hunter and Rodrigo, who have been assigned to watch the street for the night, thanks to Police Commissioner Johnson.

We have at least a dozen cops we can call on at any time for assistance. They get paid well in cash, and access to Cruz Cunts for their services, and we get extra protection, police paperwork going missing, as well as evidence at times. Also, a heads up if a raid is possible.

It works well for all involved.

They fill me in that all has been quiet, and I leave them to do their job as I cut the engine on my bike and walk it up the street, parking it in the bushes in the Millers' front yard.

The house is dark and quiet, the only sound is the rhythmic ticking of the clock on the kitchen wall. Making my way silently up the stairs, just like I've done each night since the shooting, I notice that as usual, Brian Miller's bedroom door is closed. There's a faint light glowing from under it, indicating that he's in there, so I move slowly, making sure to make no sound.

My eyes fall to the other two remaining bedroom doors, and I note them both ajar with only darkness beyond.

I don't bother going to Zoe's bedroom. Since the shooting two nights ago, she hasn't slept in there. Instead, I move to Leslie's bedroom door, and peek in, letting my eyes adjust to the dark to see a familiar, yet heartbreaking sight.

Zoe, curled in a ball as she hugs her little sister's pillow.

Sneaking inside I move to her bedside to look down at my princess in the faint glow of the moonlight beaming through the shutters on the window. Her cheeks are still damp with tears as she finally sleeps, and her fingers are still clutched tightly to the pillow making me think that she's not long dozed off.

As I've done each night since the attack, I take the pink throw blanket at the foot of the bed, and gently drape it over Zoe's sleeping form, hoping the warmth helps her stay asleep for longer than the night before.

Then I sit on her sister's small velvet desk chair and watch Zoe sleep.

She looks more innocent than she really is, sleep making her appear so sweet. She's not so sweet though. She has a sassy mouth and attitude to boot, and when she's awake, she seems to be wearing a constant resting bitch face.

Thoughts of her sassy mouth cause my dick to stir, and I know it's just the beginning because that fucker won't go down until it finds its release. So I have two options.

The first is to head back to the clubhouse and find one of the Cruz Cunts to get lost in. Sasha comes to mind, her ability to gag on dick without losing her lunch is popular amongst my club brothers. I'm feeling rather aggressive tonight, so fucking her mouth could be just what I need.

My eyes rake over Zoe again, and my dick jerks, telling me that what it wants is right fucking in front of me. I could wake her, spread her wide and fuck her until she screams. That would get her dad's attention, though, and so far, he has no fucking idea that I've been defiling his daughter.

It hasn't been long since she watched her mom and sister get killed in front of her, so I haven't even attempted to start anything with her, despite what Gunner fucking thought.

Who the fuck does he think I am?

Even as I think that, the urge to sink inside Zoe's tight cunt makes me ache to come.

But waking her isn't a good idea. She needs to sleep.

What if I didn't wake Zoe up? What if I just jerk off and feed my cum into her pretty little mouth.

The thought has me standing abruptly, my zipper down in a flash as I free my dick and give it a pump.

"You wanna taste, Princess?" I whisper, knowing Zoe can't hear me.

I grin.

I probably shouldn't do this. Not after everything she's been through, yet I find myself holding my dick out with one hand, and bracing myself on the bed to hover over Zoe's head with the other, before I run the tip of my cock along the parted lips of the sleeping princess.

Her lips open a little more as I paint her lower lips with the bead of pre-cum.

Fuck. That's hot.

Heat flushes over my body as intense need slams into me, and I know I'm actually going to do this as much as I know I'm going to fucking hell for it.

The mere thought of what I'm doing tightens my nuts, so I give in to the need, gripping my cock hard and start pumping.

With each pump, the bed moves, and I watch Zoe for any sign that she is going to wake, but her emotional exhaustion has her deep in sleep.

Pumping faster, the pleasure starts to consume me from the inside out, and I let my eyes travel over Zoe's sleeping form, and the innocence she exudes right now.

Thoughts of that first night behind the pool house when she took my cock and didn't even try to fight me off has me pistoning into my fist.

Fuck, she might deny her attraction to me, but her body doesn't fucking lie.

I want to dirty her up even more. Cover her in the filth that lurks in my head.

A picture of Zoe covered from head to toe in sweat and cum flashes in my mind. She'd look so fucking good with mascara running down her face, lipstick smudged, frothy drool dangling from her chin after I choke her on my cock.

A grunt escapes me as my pleasure builds to the point of no return, and as my balls tighten and my back coils, I press the head of my cock to Zoe's parted lips, and watch as my cum starts jetting into her mouth, on her lips, and down her chin.

Even as I fill her mouth, Zoe doesn't stir, still trapped in the land of slumber as I gift her my cum. Pulling back, I squeeze one last drop from the eye of my dick, and wipe it off with my thumb, before gently wiping it on her cheek.

Jesus fucking Christ. Why is this whole scenario so fucking hot?

I'm definitely going to hell for this and I'm not even mad about it.

As I stand back, I take in Zoe's sweet face, marred with blobs of my cum, while a trail oozes from her parted lips, onto the bedding below.

For a split second. I feel some guilt.

I feel guilty for not feeling guilty.

Shouldn't I care more that I did something so depraved to someone who is suffering and vulnerable? Shouldn't I be holding back until she snaps out of her grief before I use her body again?

I probably should, but you can't take the asshole out of someone like me.

As I stare down at the sleeping princess, the only regret I have about tonight is not waking her up so she could enjoy that too. For some reason, I think she would have been all for it.

I guess I'll find out when she wakes and tastes me on her tongue and lips.

Fuck yeah, I look forward to her wrath.

And yeah. That makes me a fucking prick in light of the situation.

8

Grayson

The suit and tie I'm wearing feels like it's strangling me, but Prez insisted that we leave our cuts at home today and wear suits out of respect for the funeral of Astrid and Leslie Miller.

As I lean against the stone wall of the old Anglican church, my eyes are trained on the two white caskets at the front containing an innocent mother and daughter who were the collateral damage of the lifestyle both the head of their family and I live in.

I try to ignore the sounds of young girls crying as they huddle together, their mothers close by with glassy eyes, probably wondering how they can console their daughters and help them through losing a school friend. There's no room for emotions in this business. Emotions get you killed.

Today though, I'm feeling some fucking emotions I'm not used to feeling. Emotions I've kept buried for a long fucking time.

I put it down to seeing so many innocent, naïve women and children mourning.

And perhaps, I feel fucking sad for Zoe.

This shit should never have touched her.

Deep down I know my past is coming back to haunt me. Dad's words. The gun shot. The frozen look on his face the moment his heart stopped beating. His funeral.

Shit.

The faint music playing in the background of the church seems to get louder as the crowd hushes each other, and all eyes move to the entrance.

I hate this part about funerals. As if the mourners want everyone gawking at them in their time of fucking grief. It's not a fucking wedding. People should look away, but they don't. And neither do I as the two remaining members of the Miller family come into view.

Brian is a noticeable mess. His suit is creased. His tie is crooked. And his hair is a shaggy mop which suits the unshaven shadow lining his jaw. What I notice the most about Brian isn't his frazzled appearance, though. It's the way he keeps space between him and his daughter, not even bothering to hold her hand and offer her support as they walk.

I know the police investigation delayed holding the funeral, and has likely taken its toll on Brian, but shit. What about his daughter, Zoe? I know that he's just lost his wife and youngest daughter, but he still has one walking right beside him, who is clearly in need of comfort, yet he doesn't even attempt it.

Zoe, unlike her father, is well put together. Her black dress is crisp, hugging her curves in a way I shouldn't be noticing at her mother and sister's funeral. Her stunningly blonde hair is long, worn down in a middle part, smooth soft curls falling down her back and over her shoulders acting like a blanket of support. It's the way she hugs herself that shows how fragile she is, though. Her eyes, rimmed red as tears fall while her gaze lands on the caskets at the front of the church.

It doesn't matter that I'm a number of feet away from her. I, like everyone else in the room watching Zoe, can see the pain in her eyes.

Fuck I hate funerals!

Before any more useless emotions come to the surface, I push them down and remind myself that this is a cruel fucking world we live in, and yeah, I'm part of the fucking cruelness, but it beats being vulnerable and feeling the sort of pain most are feeling here today.

Zoe and her father sit at the front of the church, and silent sobs spread through the space as the minister starts the service. My eyes remain on Zoe as she suffers in silence, alone, while her dad pays her no fucking attention.

As far as services go, it's fucking heartbreaking but a nice send off to the mother and daughter duo. The only time I glance away from Zoe is when they play a video on the big screen above the caskets. Memories of two lives cut short, and two lives that have to somehow figure out how to continue on.

From where I'm standing, I can see the side of Zoe's face. She bats the tears away as she looks up at the screen, not missing a moment of the memories she created with her family here in Santa Cruz. At times a small smile tugs at her lips, and fuck, I feel fucking bad that I couldn't save her mom and sister so she could continue making memories with them.

Some people get up and speak about Astrid and Leslie, each person struggling to handle their own loss and remain composed.

One of the hardest parts of a casket service is about to take place, and as everyone watches Brian Miller walk to the side of his wife's casket to stand as a pallbearer, my eyes remain on Zoe, as she stands and watches her dad pass by with a handful of men as they carry her mother out of the church.

The hushed cries throughout the church suddenly increase as Zoe, trembling with grief, moves to the side of her sister's casket to be joined by a handful of others as she clasps the handle and lifts her sister.

The moment a gut wrenching sob flies from her lips, and her knees nearly buckle from under her, I find myself darting forward, pushing through the crowd until I'm right there with her.

"It's okay. I've got you," I rasp quietly so only she can hear, and her blue tear filled gaze locks on mine before I shift behind her and clasp the same handle she's holding, taking the weight of the casket.

When she looks over the top of her sister's casket to the woman holding the front on the other side, she gives her a nod and they start walking.

Given that I'm holding the same handle as Zoe, it means I'm pressed close to her back as we walk. I thought it would be more difficult than it is, but when her right foot steps forward, so does mine, and when her left foot moves, mine follows.

Zoe's sweet scent engulfs me, and I have to fight the urge to reach out with my free hand and wrap it around her middle to pull her back against me.

Yeah, even a fucking funeral can't hold my depravity at bay.

The walk out of the church doesn't take long, and the funeral attendants take over to load the caskets into the two hearses parked right out front. I take a step back from Zoe, giving her room as people swarm her, their arms wrapping around her as she stiffens. Those blue eyes find mine through the chaos, not looking away until I'm pushed back so far from the other mourners that I can no longer see that beautiful white blonde hair, or those broken blue eyes.

Not that I fucking care.

The next part of the funeral is the committal service, and not everyone attends. I probably shouldn't be attending this part, but Rocco insists we do, so Rocco, Gunner, and I follow the funeral procession on our bikes—wearing fucking suits—making the slow ride out to the cemetery. I guess we should be thankful the Millers decided against having a viewing prior to today's funeral. Whether it be that Brian just wanted today over with since the police investigation held things up, or perhaps because little Leslie was shot in between her eyes and wanted to avoid traumatizing themselves and others any further, I'm glad it won't get dragged out any longer.

We stand behind the small crowd of mourners opposite where Zoe and her dad stand as a prayer is said and the caskets get lowered into the earth. As more words are spoken and people start to approach the grave side to throw roses into the open earth, Zoe's eyes find mine.

She keeps her gaze locked on mine, tears still pouring from her blue pools like an endless stream. The mourners begin to dissipate, and Mr. Miller walks away, his head bowed as he turns his back on his daughter, not bothering to see if she's following, or needs any support.

My lip twitches in anger then, and I have to suppress the urge to reach for my gun, hidden away under my jacket.

I guess murdering Brian at his wife and daughter's funeral is a fucking bad idea.

Gunner slaps me on the shoulder as he passes by, and he joins Rocco, as they move to Brian's side, offering their condolences as they all walk away.

Zoe's bloodshot puffy eyes remain on mine, and we stare at each other silently as the last of the mourners disappear through the cemetery gates leaving the two of us alone.

She doesn't speak, her thin body looking frailer than it was a couple of weeks ago, the stress of watching her mom and sister get killed in front of her, and the vigorous police investigation taking a toll on her health.

I wait a few moments, waiting for her to react. She normally has a snide remark to throw my way, and I wonder if today is different.

"What the fuck do you think you're doing here?" she whisper-yells. "You're not welcome. You never are, but especially not today."

Okay, so today isn't so different. She's pissy, but not the typical too good for everyone pissy attitude, pretending to be better than the likes of me.

No. Today's level of pissy is downright rage.

As I stare at Zoe, her face turns redder with fury, and as much as I enjoy riling her up, I can tell that whatever is happening here isn't the type of situation where I should do that.

"What's your issue with me attending the funeral?" I ask, slowly walking closer to the open graves.

"Are you kidding me right now? You don't deserve to be here! They died because of you!"

I can't help it, her words sting, and I flinch back before I can hide it. She doesn't seem to notice though, her hands balled in fists at her sides as her blue gaze turns glassy.

"I didn't kill them," I state, edging to the side of the grave so I can get closer to her. She doesn't take her eyes off me, their deadly glare following me as I move.

"You didn't save them either!" she screams, bursts of tears springing from her eyes to tumble quickly down her heated cheeks.

"I could only be in one place at a time. I don't have superpowers," I tell her calmly, stepping over to her side of the gravesite.

She shakes her head vigorously, her eyes falling to the ground before she bends and picks up a rock.

"You didn't save them!" she screams, and then she throws the fucking rock at my head.

"Shit." I duck out of the way just in time, but then more rocks and clumps of dirt come my way, and I raise my arm to shield the attack as I dash forward.

"You didn't even try to save me!" she screams, just as I reach her and grip her wrists.

"Stop!" I yell, but she struggles against my hold, baring her teeth.

"Why didn't you save me?! Where were you?!" she screams and I realize then that she really doesn't remember that it was me that shielded her with my body.

I tug her to my chest, releasing her wrists and wrapping my arms around her middle to hold her to me, but she thrashes in my hold, her fists pummeling my chest as she screams.

"Why did it have to be him and not you?!"

"What the fuck are you talking about?" I seethe, shifting my head from side to side to dodge the occasional fist she swings towards my face. "Who is him?"

"G-Gunner." She stutters before the fight falls from her and she begins to sob.

What the fuck?

She thinks Gunner was the one to save her?

He didn't even show up until afterwards.

My head is spinning from this, but I don't correct her. Now isn't the time.

She's angry and she's heartbroken and all Zoe needs right now is to vent and let her anger out.

If that has to be at me, then I'll take it. I can be a punching bag for her.

As her sobs turn into wailing cries filled with so much despair and agony, I tighten my hold on her and cup the back of her head, pressing it to my chest.

She lets me give her this comfort. The hug she clearly needed from her dad today but didn't get.

We stand in the mostly empty cemetery for a long while, me holding Zoe as she breaks. She needs this moment away from onlookers to let it all go. To feel the raw pain and release it from her lungs.

The ass I usually am isn't here right now. Not in this moment. He's lurking just below the surface, but for now, even he knows when to fucking stay quiet.

I don't say anything else. What the fuck can I say? I'm sorry your dad's involvement in the Cruz Kings got your family killed. I'm sorry you've been dragged into my world because your dad is good at helping the MC launder money.

Those words won't help her move on. They won't bring back her mom and sister. And they won't heal the pain slicing through her heart right now.

When her sobs subside a short time later, I pull back from Zoe, straightening my jacket before leading her to her car and notice Gunner resting back on his bike.

His head is tipped back, a smoke between his lips as he enjoys the summer sun, but as we approach, our footsteps crunching on the gravel, his eyes dart in our direction.

With my focus on Zoe, I get her situated in the passenger seat of her car before approaching my club brother, watching as he tosses his smoke butt on the gravel and grinds his booted foot over it.

"You driving her to the celebration of life thing?" he asks and I nod.

Leslie's teacher thought it would be a good idea to hold a casual event after the funeral for her school friends to gather, as well as the rest of the community who are still reeling from the double homicide so many witnessed. One look at Zoe and anyone can see she'd rather hide away in her sister's room and suffer in silence.

Hopefully the gathering won't take too long.

I eye Gunner as I stand before him, Zoe's words coming to the forefront of my mind.

She thinks it was Gunner who saved her.

Why the fuck does she think it was him? I get that she doesn't remember, but for some reason, she thinks it was him and not me who shielded her. I want to ask her more about it, but I've been going along with her thinking I wasn't there, and I'm not about to spark a fucking conversation about it the day she buried her loved ones.

I consider asking Gunner about it. He's been messaging Zoe. I have no fucking clue what they talk about, but maybe she's mentioned something to him.

Then again, if she mentioned that she thinks he saved her, wouldn't he correct her?

Fucked if I know.

My fucking head hurts.

Running my hand through my hair, I answer my club brother.

"She's a fucking mess. I can't believe her dad let her drive here today. What the fuck is wrong with him? Did you see how cold he was toward her at the service?"

Gunner nods. "Yeah. I thought maybe he was just fucking heartbroken, but when I went with Rocco to talk to him after the service, he smelled like a fucking brewery. He turned up hammered to his wife and kid's funeral."

"Fuck." I rasp, dragging a hand through my hair. "Can you get one of the prospects to come and get my bike and ride back with them to make sure they don't fucking scratch it?"

Gunner chuckles. "Yeah, man. I'll see you at the gathering later."

Nodding, I give my buddy a thankful fist bump and return to the car to drive Zoe to the reception venue hosting the event.

She's quiet during the drive, no more tears falling, her face pale and her expression showing a hint of anger the closer we get to the venue holding the after event.

Her expression hardens even more when I pull up and she gets out of the car, holding her head high and rolling her shoulders back as she enters, showing everyone that although she has lost so much, she is still the composed, classy Zoe Miller from upper class Santa Cruz.

I watch her through the crowd during the gathering, my eyes never wavering far from her white blonde hair and piercing blue eyes. They find mine often as she pretends to care about what people say to her, mingling and doing the right thing even though I'm sure she'd rather tell them all to leave her alone.

As the time passes, her attention draws away from me where I linger on the sidelines, to her father who has emptied a couple of wine bottles into his gut at this point, and is becoming rowdy. I catch Gunner's attention across the room where he stands near Rocco, and shoot him a frown, gesturing to Brian Miller and the scene he's likely to cause anytime now if he keeps downing alcohol like we are about to enter prohibition, in front of a bunch of his dead daughter's school friends.

Gunner reads my expression, speaking quietly to Rocco before they both move in opposite directions.

Rocco moves to Brian's side, and Gunner goes to the bar, likely telling them they need to close it down or cut Brian off. Since we practically own the manager of this establishment, by way of blackmail, I don't think there will be an issue with such a request.

I glance back across the room to find Zoe, but she's gone. My eyes dart around the space, but before I get a chance to go in search of her, a small hand wraps around my wrist and drags me into a darkened hallway.

"Princess." I rasp, relieved that she is safe, but pissed that she is grabbing me like this in public. No one fucking touches me like that, but the fury in Zoe's blue eyes has piqued my curiosity. "What are you doing?"

She remains silent as she continues to drag me up the hallway and into the coatroom before placing her dainty hands on my chest and shoving me back against the wall. Her strength isn't much, so when I hit the wall, it's because I've decided to go along with whatever this is to see how far she's actually willing to go. I'm intrigued, really.

"Now that all the formal stuff is out of the way, perhaps you would like to tell me why I woke up with the taste of semen in my mouth? Not to mention the remnants left on my cheek and mouth?"

I smirk. "I have no idea what you're talking about, but it sounds like someone got lucky."

Her mouth drops open in shock. "Someone did not get lucky! I know it was you. You're the type of pig that would do something like that!"

"Do something like what?" I play dumb, infuriating her even more.

"Like... like..." She huffs and stomps her foot, her cheeks flushing red with heat.

"Like what, Princess?" I lean down, hovering my face before hers. "Say it."

"You jacked off into my mouth."

The moment the words leave her lips, I can't hide my smirk. The action infuriating her even more.

"This isn't funny! You're such a filthy animal!"

The moment she makes to shove me again, I grab her wrists and spin her around, shoving her hard against the wall, taking my spot.

"I am a filthy animal," I hiss, leaning into her and pressing my body flush with hers. "And guess what Princess. I know for a fact you fucking like it. So don't stand there and pretend like you didn't play with your clit in the shower after waking up to my dried cum on your cheek."

She gasps and I take that moment to silence any more words from spewing from her mouth by claiming her lips.

I haven't kissed Zoe before. Our encounters have purely been about arousing certain body parts, so I'm not sure why I fucking kiss her, but I fucking do. If I had to take a guess, it's purely to shut her the fuck up, and even though I haven't kissed a woman in.. well... years, I find I like it more than I remember.

Zoe's lips part easily for me, her body relaxing as she fists the lapels of my jacket, pulling me closer.

Instinctively, I grind my already hard dick against her, and the minx meets the grind with one of her own.

Momentarily, a flash of my mom fucking my dad's best friend at his funeral shoots past my closed eyes, but then Zoe moans, and all thoughts of the day I witnessed that fall away.

With one thing on my mind, I quickly reach between us and work my cock free before gripping Zoe's thigh and pulling it up high, wrapping it around my hip.

The movement breaks our lip lock, and as her dark lashes flutter open, her blue eyes gazing up at me, I slip my hand past the fabric of her black dress and find her damp panties, moving the thin fabric aside.

Gritting my teeth, I position the tip of my cock at her entrance.

"You fucking love my depravity, Zoe. Don't act like you don't when your body so clearly gives you away." I slam home then, my stiff cock sinking into her molten heat as a soft cry falls from her parted lips.

"No." She pants, holding onto my shoulders now as I start thrusting. "I don't love it."

"Yes, you fucking do." I snarl, using my free hand to forcefully grip her chin and angle it up to me. "You fucking love knowing that I came into the room while you were sleeping. That I took my cock out and fisted it in my hand, pumping it over and over as I watched you sleep."

She moans, and her inner walls clamp tight, telling me that she does in fact like that idea. "You fucking love knowing that I pressed the tip of my cock to your parted lips as you slept," I thrust faster, remembering how much I fucking loved it too, "and drank down my cum as it shot from my cock into your mouth, even while you slept."

Zoe cries out, grinding her hips forward, chasing her orgasm, and I don't even try to muffle her cries, not fucking caring if anyone hears. I'm Grayson fucking Black, and if they have a problem with it, they can take it up with my fist.

Needing more momentum, I grip Zoe's other thigh, hitching her up to wrap her legs around me as I press her to the wall and pound into her, over and over.

With a need to dominate her completely and control her body, I reach between us, pushing through the fucking annoying fabric of her dress until I find her parted folds, accepting my thrusts, I then press my fingers to her clit, and build her pleasure.

"Admit it, Princess," I demand in a rasp against her ear. "Admit how fucking turned on you were when you woke to find that I'd gifted you my cum."

"Yes." She cries, right before she explodes in a convulsing orgasm.

Her cunt is so tight that it milks me quickly of mine, sending waves of pleasure through me as I shoot my cum deep inside her hot cunt.

Our pants are loud in the small space as we both slowly come down from our high. Instead of bailing quickly, like I normally do, I lean back and peer down at the bratty princess.

Her blue eyes are still lust drunk, her cheeks flushed a pretty crimson, and her full lips are puffier than usual. Probably from being kissed.

Before I know what I'm doing, I lean down and claim her lips once again. A soft whimper falls from Zoe into our kiss, and I fist her hair as I suddenly wish we weren't here at the fucking reception venue, and back in her room where I would have more time to defile her.

Slowly easing back from her addictive lips, I brush my thumb along them before pushing it inside her mouth.

"You loved waking up knowing I'd done something to you when you were asleep. Just imagine what other things I could do to you while you're out of it and can't fight me off."

Popping my thumb free of her lips, she lets out a deep breath, even as the walls of her cunt grip me again, telling me everything I need to know.

Zoe Miller is into somnophilia. Or, more specifically, being the recipient, meaning she is into dormaphilia, and fuck if that doesn't make my cock stiffen again.

Not wanting to lose myself in her heat in this fucking coatroom again, I reluctantly ease myself from her, and lower her feet to the floor.

"Take your panties off," I demand, and she frowns as she tries to brush down the skirt of her dress.

"What? Why?" she asks, and I raise a single dark brow at her.

"Don't make me ask twice."

For a long tense moment, she just glares at me, but then she concedes, bending to reach under her dress to peel the fabric free.

With a slap, Zoe throws them in my face, and I grin around the damp fabric before peeling it from my face.

"You do realize that I'm going to be leaking now that I'm not wearing panties."

I nod, flashing her a smile. "I fucking know, Princess. Why do you think I wanted your panties?"

Her lips part as an aghast look contorts her face, and I chuckle.

"I want to know my cum is going to be oozing down your legs while you talk to people. Now, be a good fucking girl and go back out and mingle with the guests. If you behave, I might just make you come in your sleep later tonight."

9

Zoe

Zoe 1.

Grayson motherfucking Black 0.

The wide smile making my cheeks hurt is downright maniacal, and not at all appropriate for being at my mom and sister's funeral. Or for what I'm doing in the bathroom.

After wiping myself furiously, I rolled up a wad of toilet paper that I gingerly placed between my thighs. I made sure it's big enough that I'll easily be able to tell if it falls down, which it won't as long as I don't spread my legs. Again. As long as I don't spread my legs *again*.

"What the fuck is wrong with you?" I hiss at my reflection in the mirror. "You don't even like the guy. Stop being such a horny bitch." My eyes glance down at the last part, which is more meant for my vagina. She clearly has a mind of her own, but right now, I don't agree with her life choices.

Ugh, whatever.

I splash some cold water on my neck and quickly wipe it away. I can't keep hiding out in here. With resolute strides, I exit the bathroom, only to run right into Gray.

He tsks at me. "Guess you don't want me to make good on my offer after all." That's all he says before he spins around and leaves me gaping at his broad back like an uncomprehending fool.

It takes me a few seconds for my brain to catch up.

"If you behave, I might just make you come in your sleep later tonight."

Why does the thought of him making me come while I'm sleeping both freak me out and excite me? I shouldn't want that at all, should I? But I can't deny that at least a part of me wants it, because the thought alone is enough to send a rush of heat through me, and make my nipples harden.

Ignoring him, I walk up to the bar and ask for a club soda. The bartender quickly pours a glass for me, and I slowly sip at the drink while looking around.

"Can I have something a bit stronger?" I sweetly ask the guy behind the bar who doesn't look like he's a day over puberty.

"Umm, I'm not sure." His eyes shift nervously around, taking in the surrounding people. When he comes to the same conclusion as me, that no one is paying attention, he gives me a sharp nod. "Okay, what would you like?"

My eyes quickly scan the bottles that are all neatly lined up behind him. "I'll take a vodka," I say with a shrug. "And Sprite." That way it'll look exactly like the club soda I just finished. "Oh, and can I have a slice of lime on the rim of the glass?"

I don't care that he's arching his blond eyebrow like my request is outrageous. It's not about me having a sudden desire to put him to work. I'm hoping the potent fruit will mask the scent of alcohol.

To his credit, the bartender doesn't question me. Instead, he focuses on the task ahead and quickly gets my drink ready. "Here you go," he says as he places the drink in front of me.

I'm just about to close my hand around the cold glass, when it's snatched from me. "Thank you," a woman says. I gape as she downs the entire thing. "Ahh, refreshing."

"Excuse you," I seethe.

"I don't need to be excused, honey. I'm not the one who shouldn't be drinking."

"What—"

Without missing a beat, she continues. "Besides, if you are going to break the law, don't you think it's tactless to do so at a funeral? And for what? Vodka? Come on. That's just sad."

My jaw is practically hitting the floor as I gape at the woman next to me. Her long, dark hair is hanging in wild curls around her shoulders and down her back. Unbothered by my obvious gawking, she drums her long, red nails against the bar.

"Look, I appreciate you getting a drink for me, but I have to warn you. If you keep looking at me like that, I might start thinking you want us to make out. And not only are you too young for me, but I'd eat you alive."

Her blood-red lips curve up on one side.

"You best close your mouth, honey. Gaping isn't an attractive look on anyone."

As she winks, the tear-drop tattoo beneath her eye glints.

Not liking the way she's speaking to me, I toss my hair over my shoulder and scoff. "Who even are you?"

She laughs cockily. "I'm not sure that matters." Then she straightens, and all amusement is erased from her face. "I know today sucks for you, and I'm sorry. But don't go make it worse by doing stupid shit, Zoe. The people here want to talk to you and your dad."

I shake my head. "They're only here because they feel like they ought to be," I say grimly.

"They want to offer up their condolences and, yeah, maybe some of them feel a sense of obligation. Stay away from those and focus on the people who really matter." She points towards a guy in the corner. "Him. He wants to talk about your sister."

My shoulders deflate as I look at Chris, Leslie's riding trainer. Shit, he looks so haggard I feel bad for trying to outrun how I feel.

I nod at the woman who looks dressed to kill in her leather. A part of me wants to thank her for setting me straight, but I don't. Instead, I make my way over to Leslie's former coach and join him at the table for four he has all to himself.

"Hey," I say as I pull a chair out and sit down.

"Zoe," he says, his voice gravelly. "How are you holding up?"

As soon as he asks, tears well up in my eyes, making my vision blurry. I want to tell him that I'm okay until someone *really* talks to me, but that's not a proper answer. I'm not doing well, no matter how much I wish I was. And I keep making stupid decisions all in an attempt at keeping my sadness at bay.

I still don't remember the night of the attack fully, or the following days, if I'm honest. There are so many things that don't make sense to me. Like, why wasn't Gray there to protect us? And why don't I remember? I know my dad's excuse of trauma is plausible, yet my gut is telling me that's not why.

Realizing I haven't answered him, I say, "I'm trying."

He gives me a weak smile and places his hand on top of mine. "That's all anyone can ask of you, Zoe." I nod weakly. "When you have time, will you come see me at the stables?"

"S-sure?" I don't know why it sounds more like a question than a confirmation.

"Leslie left some personal belongings in her locker that I think you'd want."

As soon as the words are out of his mouth, I lose the fight with my emotions. My shoulders hunch and I hide my face in my hands as I cry into my palms.

"What kind of things?" I ask. My voice is small and shaking as hard as my hands.

He looks at me through glassy green eyes. "Some spare clothing, and..." Trailing off, he swallows audibly. "Your graduation present."

At his words, I let out an inhuman wail. While I was completely caught up in Zoe-land, my sister not only thought of me, she either made or bought a present and even hid it from me in the one place I'd never think to look.

Unbidden, memories of Leslie begging me to come to the stables with her swim to the surface. I gasp, unable to breathe as I hear her voice in my mind.

"Come on, Zoe. I worked really hard to learn. I want you to come see me."

Cocking my head, I make a show of looking down at her. "I said no."

"Why not?"

Wrinkling my nose, I sigh. "Because it smells, Leslie. And because I don't care. Take your pick."

Ignoring my sister, I pick up my small handbag and leave.

I blink through the memory, confused why everything is upside down. It's not until Gunner comes into view that I realize the room is fine, but I'm lying on my back with big, fat tears trailing down my face.

Why the hell am I on the floor?

"Are you okay?" he asks, nervously.

"What happened?" I ask.

"You started crying and shaking so hard you fell out of the chair," he explains carefully.

He reaches a hand towards me, not budging as I try to bat it away while he crouches next to me, and pulls me up so I'm sitting. "Come on, Zoe." His words are low. "You need some fresh air."

I let him lift me up and carry me outside to one of the white benches. Rather than letting me go, he sits down and keeps me in his lap. His arms are wrapped around me, one hand gently rubbing circles on my back.

Closing my eyes, I try to breathe through the pain and vertigo. But I can't breathe. I mean, I can, but the air does nothing. It doesn't calm me down, it doesn't clear my head. It's as though there's a blockage stopping it from entering my lungs.

"I can't... Gunner... I can't breathe."

While tightening his hold on me, he croons, "You're doing fine, Sugar."

For some reason, that ridiculous nickname makes my lips twitch. "Sugar?" Turning my head, I arch an eyebrow as I look into his clear blue eyes.

I think he's going to kiss me when he licks his lips and leans closer. "Can you breathe now, Zoe?" he asks almost conspiratorially.

The answer is yes, I can. My guilt has subsided, making it easy to fill my lungs with air so I nod. I rest my head against his chest, enjoying the friendly embrace. Time has passed so quickly that I haven't had the time or head-space to give it much thought, but now I realize he might be the only real friend I have.

None of the people from school have done anything but send me obligatory hope-you're-okay texts. Not a single one has stopped by, or asked if they can do anything for me. But Gunner has. Hell, he's done more than that. He saved my life.

I pull back and look at him. Lifting my hand, I cup his stubbled cheek. "I don't think I ever thanked you for saving my life," I whisper.

"You don't have to thank me," he replies easily.

"But I want to," I say. "Thank you for being there that night. Thank you for saving my life, Gunner."

I throw my arms around his neck, squeezing him tight. Again, tears form and I sniffle while I let them fall onto the exposed skin on his neck.

Gunner hugs me back while whispering words of encouragement. It's a nice moment for sure, but it's broken as I feel him grow hard underneath me.

"I should go find my dad," I say as I struggle to get out of his lap.

Despite my efforts to touch his growing excitement as little as possible, I somehow manage to nudge against it at least twice. How fucking awkward.

When Gunner finally lets go of me, I'm quick to put some distance between us. I smile and give him an awkward wave before I head back inside. It's not Gunner's fault, and I'm not holding it against him. But that doesn't mean I want to sit on top of his hard dick.

"Wait a second," he calls after me.

I turn back, shocked when he holds up a rolled wad of toilet paper. There's no doubt it's the toilet paper from the bathrooms here, because it has flower imprints lining the edges.

"You dropped this." When I just gape at him, he continues. "I thought maybe you'd want to clean up a little before you go in there." He points over his shoulder.

"No, it's okay."

"Come on. You have mascara smeared all over your cheeks." Gunner stands up and comes towards me while holding out the wad of toilet paper with Gray's sperm on it. "Here let me—"

I slap his hand away as he lifts it towards my face. "I said no," I insist.

There's something off about the way Gunner looks at me. His eyes are no longer warm and caring, but rather cold and calculated. However, when I blink, he's back to looking like his usual jovial self. Phew. For a second, I could have sworn Gunner knows exactly what he's holding in his hands, but clearly my mind is playing tricks on me.

"Sorry," he mumbles sheepishly. "Just thought I'd help you, Sugar."

I force a laugh and quickly ramble an apology for my reaction. "That's sweet of you, Gunner. But I really should be heading inside."

Without looking back, I turn and half-run to where I see my dad slumping in a chair. Even though he's sitting by himself, four men from the Cruz Kings hover nearby. They're all wearing matching suits, which look so wrong on their big frames.

As my mind conjures up an image of Gray in his suit, I look around, equal parts pleased and disappointed when I don't see him anywhere.

"Can we leave soon?" I ask dad as soon as I reach him.

He looks up at me through red-rimmed eyes. "Zoe," he slurs. "Let's go home, baby."

I crinkle my nose as the stench hits me. Dad smells like he's been hitting the bar hard, so he's definitely not in any condition to drive.

"Yeah," I agree as I loop my arms through his and help him stand. "I'll drive."

Dad doesn't object, which is a first. He willingly gives me the keys. I clutch them in my free hand while we stagger towards the parking lot. It takes forever to get dad into the car, and if it hadn't been for the two guys trailing us, I don't think dad would have made it at all.

After falling twice, and getting his foot stuck once, they stepped up and held him between them, pushing him into the backseat.

"We'll follow you," one of them says, brusquely.

I open my mouth to reply, but Gunner joins us and beats me to it. "That won't be necessary, Slasher. I'll do it."

The guy—Slasher, apparently—lifts an eyebrow and looks at Gunner in a manner that makes it clear he's unimpressed. "Just following orders, man. VP said you should come find him inside."

Despite having his back to me, it's noticeable the way Gunner stiffens, which leads me to believe he isn't happy. "Zoe's my—"

The other guy interrupts Gunner. "Now, let's not argue in front of the pretty lady." He winks at me. "It might make her think you aren't willing to follow the orders of your VP. Is that the impression you want her to drive away with?"

While the second guy is talking, Slasher puts himself between me and Gunner while silently mouthing "Go." I pause for a second, but when I hear the loud snores from the backseat, I decide to leave them to do whatever so I can get dad home.

10

Zoe

As soon as we reach the house, the undynamic duo of
Slasher and the other one, help me get dad inside. When
they ask where they should put him, I point towards the
master bedroom, and they quickly drop him on the bed.

"Do you... umm..." I trail off as they both look expectantly at me. "Can I offer you something to drink? Or
eat?" I don't know why I'm offering. That's a lie, I do
know—it's what mom would have done.

Their eyes widen almost comically.

"No thanks," Slasher says.

"But thank you for offering," the other guy adds, completing Slasher's sentence.

Now that I look at the two burly men, I'm wondering if
they're related. The one who's name I don't know wears
an eye patch, but apart from that, they're very similar.

"I'm Slayer," eye patch-man announces cheerily.

Of course he is.

Wanting to make my mom proud, I hold my hand out to him. "Nice to meet you, Slayer. I'm Zoe."

"We know who you are," Slasher says.

"She's being polite, dipshit," Slayer sneers. "And we're being rude. We're sorry for your loss, Zoe. If you need anything..." He waggles his eyebrows playfully. "Anything at all, don't hesitate to holler."

I can't help laughing at his antics. Sure, he looks like a psycho, but there's something refreshingly down-to-earth about the way these two behave.

"Thank you," I say sincerely. "And thank you for all your help."

Slayer and Slasher bow awkwardly while they say, "You're welcome, Your Highness," in perfect unison. Even though it's clearly a mockery, I don't feel like it's at my expense.

As soon as the two guys have left the house, I go to get changed. I can't stand being in this dress for a second longer. Instead of heading to my impressive walk-in wardrobe, I raid my sister's normal-sized closet. I set my eyes on a pair of her pajama shorts and super-worn band-tees.

Since I don't feel like I can put Leslie's clothes on without showering first, I get some clean underwear from my bedroom before I make my way to the bathroom we used to share.

I quickly undress and start running the shower. As I pass the mirror, I quickly glance at my reflection. Huh, I thought Gunner said I had black streaks of mascara running down my cheeks, but I don't see anything. Either my tears have washed the traces away, or... surely he didn't lie. It's not that I don't think he would, but why be dishonest about something so inconsequential? He doesn't know me well enough to know it's been niggling at my vanity, thinking I was walking around like a raccoon impersonator.

As I step into the shower and let the hot water soak my hair, I close my eyes. I try my best to shut my brain off. I can't handle thoughts right now. Not any thoughts at all. To occupy my brain, I sing, which I'm horrible at. I can't carry a tune if my life depended on it, but that doesn't stop me from belting out from the top of my lungs.

Even though I want to, I can't stay in the bathroom-bubble forever. To postpone reality on the other side of the door, I do everything from shaving, shampooing and conditioning my hair, deep-cleaning my face, clipping my toenails, rubbing body oil all over myself, trimming my eyebrows, and even drying my hair. But despite my best efforts, I'm done.

I startle as there's a loud knock on the door.

"Zoe, are you almost done?"

"Yeah, I'll be out soon," I reply, surprised dad is up. I thought for sure he'd sleep until some time tomorrow.

With nothing left to do, I shove my phone in the pocket of the shorts and leave to go in search of dad. I find him outside by the pool. He has turned the pool lights on, even the twinkle lights that span from Leslie's window to a tree next to the pool house. The lights sway in the mild breeze, creating the illusion of lights dancing across the water. It's pretty.

"Come sit with me, baby." Dad sounds like he's aged ten years since he fell asleep in the car on our way home.

I take the seat opposite him, pulling my feet up under me.

"Is that one of Leslie's t-shirts you're wearing?"

Biting down on my bottom lip, I nod. "Is that okay?"

Dad's eyes turn glassy. "Of course it is. It's better to use her stuff than to get rid of it."

It's nice to sit with dad like this. Just the two of us, without all the people who constantly talk about one thing or another. The silence stretching around us isn't uncomfortable, and I welcome it like an old friend as I finally allow myself to think about my mom and sister.

I don't know why Leslie's death hits me the hardest, and a part of me is ashamed by that. Like I should miss mom more. But I already miss her so much my heart hurts, I just don't feel like we have any outstanding issues. With Leslie... that's a different story. I've behaved abhorrently, yet my sister was always forgiving, kind, and generous even.

"How are you really doing, baby?" dad asks, shattering the silence and penetrating my less than stellar thoughts about myself.

Inhaling deeply, I softly admit, "I don't know."

Dad runs a hand down his face. "We'll get through it, Zoe. Soon you'll be going to Harvard. And maybe... well, I've been thinking that maybe I should sell the house and move closer to you. That way you could maybe visit on weekends."

"You can't sell the house," I argue vehemently.

He gives me a sad look. "Zoe, this house is too expensive and too big for just one person."

"No," I almost shout. "I'll... can't I pay for the house? Or better yet, you can have the money. I don't care about that. But please don't sell the house."

I'm not having it. I absolutely refuse to let dad sell the house where we all lived together. No matter what it takes, it isn't an option.

This is the first time we're talking about the inheritance. I don't know what dad's reasons are for not bringing it up, but for me... it's uncomfortable. It was more than clear that he expected to receive everything, so I know he's disappointed. Even so, I'm still surprised he acted like that. I mean, he has his own money. Doesn't he?

The contents of mom's letter didn't make it sound like they were broke... or maybe it did? No, she only said he had to do work for the Cruz Kings to be able to afford their lifestyle, not that they were broke.

"It's not that simple, Zoe."

I'm just about to argue that it *is* that simple when dad's phone rings. He looks at the screen and curses under his breath.

"I'll just be two minutes, baby."

With those words, he walks back inside, closing the patio door behind him.

I don't get to wonder why he looked almost panicked before my own phone vibrates in my pocket. Pulling it out, I click on the notification of a new text.

Immediately, a video plays of Gray fucking me good in the coatroom. I watch as the video shows Gray sheathing his cock inside me, and it's clear to see the pleasure written all over my face.

My hand flies up to my mouth, and I gasp. "What the fuck?" I mutter as I desperately hold down the volume button on the side to silence it. I can't tear my gaze away from the depravity on the screen, and I hate the way my pussy clenches.

Like last time, the number unknown—literally. No numbers, the sender reads: Unknown Number.

Since both of Gray's hands are on my body, he's obviously not holding his phone while recording. But maybe... well, who's saying he didn't plant it in the coatroom ahead of time planning this? I remind myself that I'm the one who pulled him aside first, but I'm not sure that matters. He's done nothing but taunt and threaten me with the first video. A man willing to do that isn't above recording us while fucking.

No, this is my fault. I shouldn't have given in to him.

I'm pulled from my panicked thoughts when dad rushes back outside. I quickly exit the video and lock my screen before looking up at him.

"Zoe..." He looks like he's seen a ghost.

"Yes—"

"No!" Dad staggers as he stares at my forehead through wild eyes.

I get out of the chair and walk towards him. "Are you okay?" I ask lamely. It's a stupid question because it's obvious he's barely holding it together.

Dad grabs my arm and forcefully pulls me inside. "We're leaving," he shouts so suddenly he startles me. "Go pack your stuff. Only essentials, Zoe. We're leaving in five minutes."

"W-what?"

"Now!" he roars.

"But dad—" I don't know what to say, so I cut myself off. None of this is making any sense. "You're scaring me,"

I whimper when he shoves me towards the stairs while reiterating we need to leave.

"Is everything okay?"

I spin around, looking at Slasher who's now standing in the doorway with his massive arms crossed.

"What's going on?" he demands.

"Stay out of this," dad spits, wiping sweat off his forehead. "This is a family matter and you have no right to be in my house."

Slasher gives him a sardonic smile.

"You didn't answer my question."

He looks expectantly at me, so I swallow audibly. "Just fine," I croak.

Without another word, he walks back outside. However, he doesn't shut the front door behind him, and he positions himself directly under one of the lights.

Even though I know I should run upstairs and grab some belongings while dad's in the bedroom, I can't. I'm frozen in place by fear. I can't move, I can barely breathe. What the hell is going on?

I barely notice dad leaving. In fact, I didn't know he until he returns with a suitcase in one hand and the car keys in another. He carefully keeps to the side, so he's out of Slasher's sight.

Then he angrily hisses my name, and gestures towards the door leading to the basement. I nervously look at Slasher, but his face is turned away from the door and towards his brother. I take the opportunity to move closer to dad, and he yanks me with him while muttering angrily about me just standing there. All my pleas for him to tell me what's happening fall on deaf ears.

He bends and picks a pair of random shoes, practically forcing them into my trembling hands. "Put these on," he barks.

I try to hurry with the laces in mom's Converse, but dad loses his patience. Even though only one of the shoes is fully on, he grabs my arm and pulls me towards the car. I cry out in pain and panic as I stumble over and over.

"Forget the fucking shoes," he whispers. "Zoe this is dead fucking serious. We need to get to the basement now—"

The rumble of bikes has dad halting in his steps.

"Fuck!" He turns and runs back towards the patio doors. "Zoe come on."

The panic in his voice snaps me into action, and I follow him as quickly as I can. When I reach the garden, it's cast in darkness—dad's somehow managed to switch the lights off.

I stumble around blindly, calling for him, but I get no answer.

"Brian!" Gray's angry timbre causes me to whimper.

A sense of urgency takes me over as I stumble through the garden that has never seemed bigger. I don't even fucking know if I'm going the right way, and I daren't pull my phone out and use the light.

"Oh, Brian... come out, come out wherever you are." Gunner sing-songs from somewhere to my left.

I steer towards the right, hoping I'm almost at the pool house. My arms are outstretched, and I think I... fuck! I try to remain quiet as my foot catches on something and I fall to the ground.

"Over there. I heard something."

My heart beats wildly in my chest and I'm scared to even breathe.

As quietly as possible, I crawl forward. I could weep with relief when I finally feel the pool house wall against my hand. If I can just make it to the other end, then I can crawl through the hole in the hedge and...

"No!" I scream as the entire garden is suddenly bathed in light from multiple torches.

"There!"

As soon as that one word registers, I sprint as fast as I can towards the hole. Heavy footsteps fall behind me, I'm being chased. Fucking chased like an animal. Tears well in my eyes, but I can't focus on that. Just as I can't think about the branches whipping me and tearing into my skin as I run across the garden I've played in so many times while growing up.

Together with my friends, and even Leslie, we've played all the usual games. Playing tag in a garden like this is amazing as a child, plenty of room to run. But now, while I'm being chased, I hate it. And I hate every fucking tree, bush, and flowerbed I sprint past.

As I finally spot the hole, I run with renewed power in my strides. I'm so close I just need... I cry out as I'm being thrown to the ground, and all my air is forced from my lungs with the force of the fall.

The man standing above me isn't the same that fucked me so good only earlier today. No, this is Grayson Black the VP of the Cruz Kings. Lethal and terrifyingly angry.

"Where is he?" he demands.

Grayson

The silk of Zoe's hair is temporarily distracting as I fist it and drag her to her feet.

"Where the fuck is your dad, Princess?"

A whimper escapes her, and those big blue eyes that are normally filled with mirth at my very existence are now nothing but confused terror.

"Fucking answer me!" I hiss into her face, dragging her closer to hear another whimper slip past her plump lips. "You'd better start fucking talking!"

"He's gone." Gunner's voice drags my attention from Zoe's horrified expression and I glare at my club brother. "He fled on foot so he can't have gotten far."

"Call for more men. No one sleeps until we find the traitor," I yell through clenched teeth, and this time my words force Zoe to finally speak.

"T-traitor?"

I drag her flush against me, tugging her head back forcefully with the handful of hair still in my fist.

"Yes. Traitor. You and your old man have played us really fucking well, Princess. But the mistake you both made was thinking you could get away with it. You're going to regret ever thinking you could go against the Cruz Kings. By the time we are done with you and your dad, you'll both be begging us to send you to an early grave to join your mom and sister."

"W-what?" she stutters. "I-I don't know what you're talking about."

I chuckle, but there's no humor in it. "Sure you don't." I tug her away from me, shifting my grip from her hair to her upper arm and drag her towards the house.

"Ouch, Grayson. You're hurting me." She whines as she stumbles at my side to keep up, but I don't ease my grip.

I can't believe I've been played like this. Yeah, I knew her dad was acting suss, but never did I think that Zoe had the balls to distract us on purpose without us realizing her intentions.

A honey trap perhaps?

She's fucking good. I'll give her that. Not once did I think she was playing me, but while I thought I was tormenting her, the bitch was probably secretly fucking laughing at me.

Once inside, I shove her down hard, her thin body slamming into the timber floor in front of the kitchen island with a thud before I spin on my heel and upend the fucking antique looking dining table.

The crash makes her squeal, and I spin to face her again as she cowers, pressing her back to the side of the kitchen island like she's trying to push through the solid wall.

"Do you and your dad a fucking favor and just tell me where the money is."

"Money?" she whispers as tears stream from her eyes. "I don't know what you're talking about."

My top lip curls and I storm towards her again with my fists balled at my sides.

"Don't make me fucking hurt you, Princess. Just tell me where your dad put the money and you won't have to suffer!"

"I don't know what you're talking about." She cries, shaking her head. "Please, Grayson. I really don't know!"

As my fury begins to boil over, I find myself confused as fuck by how fucking well she lies. I can't even tell. Which pisses me off because a part of me thinks she really could be telling the truth.

"Then why run?!" I boom, and a vicious tremble starts to wrack her body. She starts to sob, fear contorting her expression, changing her whole fucking demeanor until all I see is a frail, terrified young woman.

"Answer me!" I boom again. "Tell me why I shouldn't just put a bullet between your eyes, right fucking now?!"

"P-please... G-Grayson... I-I don't k-know w-what's happening." She tries to swipe at her tears, but it's no use. They fall faster than she can wipe them away. "O-one minute everything was f-fine, and the n-next my dad is yelling at me to p-pack a bag b-because we have to l-leave." She hiccups through her tears, trying to ward off the waves of fear that keep assaulting her. "I s-swear I have n-no idea what is h-happening."

Sucking in a frustrated breath, I pace for a moment, dragging my hand over my head as I try to clear the rage from my head. I'm so fucking close to pulling my Glock on Zoe and pulling the trigger. But I know I'll regret it. Especially if I find out later that she's telling the truth.

"You say that one minute everything was fine," I snap, coming to a stop in front of Zoe, and dropping to my haunches. "What happened between it being fine to your dad telling you to pack your bag?"

Her blue eyes peer up at me through the fan of her damp lashes, and her lower lip trembles as she speaks.

"Dad's phone r-rang. We were out by the p-pool talking, a-and then his phone r-rang and he went inside to t-take the call."

"And while he was inside on the call, what were you doing?"

As if a switch is flipped, Zoe's scared eyes turn to anger, her gaze dark, shooting me a glare that tells me every bad thing she wishes would happen to me.

"I was by the pool, mourning my mom and little sister when your fucking message came through! Who the fuck do you think you are? Do you enjoy sending your conquests videos of you fucking them? Is that it?" She scoffs. "Do you think it would turn me on to see you fucking me in that coatroom?"

At first I have no fucking idea what she is talking about, but my brain catches up fast enough to figure out that she's received a new video. This one is obviously from today at the reception venue. And once again, she thinks I sent it.

And once again, I'm not going to fucking correct her.

"You'd do well to remember who the fuck you are talking to, Princess. Don't forget, you're the one with the traitor for a father."

She shrinks back at my words, the fire in her eyes dying out quickly, and fuck. I think I miss it.

The rumble of bikes coming down the road draws my attention from Zoe, so I stand and glance down the hallway to see a handful of headlights filter in through the window next to the front door. Zoe's whimper at hearing them sparks the possessive asshole in me that for some reason thinks it needs to fucking protect her.

I need that prick to get with the fucking party though, because this little beauty is nothing but a fucking honey trap.

I try to ignore Zoe as the loud rumbles shut off, and moments later heavy booted feet stomp up the front porch steps, right before the front door swings open with a loud thud.

"Gray!" Rocco calls, and I step out further so he can see me at the end of the hallway.

"Over here," I call, and Rocco's dark gaze locks with mine.

"Where the fuck is she?" he hisses, his feet pounding the timber floors as he makes his way to me.

"She's here," I call back, moving back in front of Zoe who is still cowering on the floor.

Rocco bursts into the room like he's on a fucking mission, his feet skidding to a stop as his eyes land on the timid frame of our club accountant's eldest daughter.

"What has she said?" he asks on a growl, his anger barely contained.

"She maintains that she doesn't know anything about the money, and that right before her old man demanded she pack a bag because they were leaving, he took a phone call inside the house."

Rocco's eyes narrow as he looks from me to Zoe, and then gestures his head across the room.

Following him to the far corner where we can still see Zoe, he steps in close.

"You believe her?"

I shrug. "Honestly, I can't tell. I have no idea if she's been playing me or not."

Rocco nods. "Gunner called. They still can't locate Brian. Until this matter is resolved, you aren't to let Zoe out of your sight. Stay here in the house with her. Let's see if Brian returns for his precious daughter."

I nod, already knowing this is what would happen. Brian was trying to get Zoe to run with him, so it makes sense that he might return for her.

"I'll put some guys on the perimeter too, and you should monitor the external security cameras. Gunner can help you so you can take a break now and then, but Gray, don't let her get in your head. She may be well trained in seduction and the last thing I need is my second getting knifed while he's balls deep inside the honey trap."

Rocco and I talk shop for a few more minutes, keeping our voices hushed so Princess can't hear, and then Prez leaves, taking most of the men with him.

Zoe hasn't moved from her position on the floor, but her tears seem to have dried up now, and her blue gaze remains on me as I pace the room again. My mind is racing, going over everything we spoke about, and wondering if there's something I missed.

It's been a fucking day. That's for sure.

It seems like days ago that I stood in that church and looked at the caskets of Astrid and Leslie Miller. But it was earlier today.

Such a long fucking day.

"Get up," I snap, my eyes feeling the exhaustion of the day I'd just been remembering.

Zoe's eyes widen a little, but she remains on the floor, curling in on herself.

"Zoe for fuck's sake, if you don't stand the fuck up, you're not going to like the way I make you."

That gets her moving, uncurling herself before she stands on shaky legs, never taking her eyes off me like she's preparing for me to attack.

"Get upstairs." When she hesitates, I ball my fists again, itching to palm my fucking gun and point it her way. "Don't fucking make me ask twice, Princess."

Slowly, as she eyes me, she walks towards the stairs. I follow close behind, hoping she can feel the heat of my body at her back just to remind her of the danger she's in.

Even though her slow pace is making my blood boil, I don't demand her to move faster. I should, but I don't, and I don't fucking know why. Maybe it's just hope being a bitch, making me want to believe that she has no idea that her old man just cleaned out the club's bank account. Maybe she really has no idea where he transferred the money. But unfortunately for Zoe, even if she doesn't know, we can still use her as leverage.

For now, she's ours to torment until this situation is resolved.

At the top of the stairs, I shove her shoulder to keep her moving towards her bedroom, and we enter the open door before I point to the bathroom.

"Take a shower."

She rolls her eyes. "I've already showered."

"Do I look like I fucking care that you have already showered. I told you to do something, Princess. So get the fuck in the shower. NOW!"

She flinches at the thunderous rumble of my voice, the trembles in her body starting up again as she moves into the bathroom that joins hers and Leslie's bedrooms.

As I lean against the frame of the door, she timidly peels her clothes off, her back to me as she does this, trying to hide the parts I enjoy looking at the most. Then she reaches into the shower cubicle, still smattered with water from the shower she claims to have had earlier, and turns the water on.

I'm silent as I watch her step in under the spray, and wonder if she'd be more likely to talk if I took a different approach.

"Prez said she's not admitting to anything yet."

Gunner's voice comes from behind me, and that possessive asshole in me stiffens, standing taller so he can't see past me to where Zoe's naked form washes in the shower.

Turning, I make sure I'm in his line of sight and nod.

"Get a dining chair from downstairs for me. And rope to tie Princess up."

Gunner's blond brows shoot up.

"You wanna tie her up?"

I nod. "Yes. I'm changing up the interrogation."

Slowly, my club brother nods. "Yeah, okay. I'll get that for you."

As Gunner leaves the room, he tries one last time to peer past me at Zoe showering, and I have to fight the urge to punch him and tell him to pull his fucking head in.

I turn back to watch Zoe. She's not doing anything but standing under the spray, and I can tell by the way her shoulders shake that she's crying. Silently.

Gunner returns a few minutes later with the things I need, and I thank him and suggest he keep watch on the lower floors before he walks out with his shoulders dropped low.

I don't know what his problem is lately, and I'll ask him as soon as things fucking settle down, but right now, we are on high alert, and I have to stay focused on trying to get to the bottom of those trying to ruin us.

I close the door behind him, hearing him take the stairs back to the lower level, and then I turn back to Zoe's bedroom.

She's been sleeping in Leslie's bedroom, but what I'm about to do shouldn't happen in her dead sister's room. It needs to happen here. In the princess' room, filled with the finest of furnishings, and an oversized wardrobe of designer clothes.

I drag the chair to the center of the room, facing the bed, draping the rope over the back, before moving to her bedside drawers, where I know she keeps her toys.

Pulling out a generous black dildo, and a smaller vibrator, plus her lube, I place them on the tall dresser, before returning to the bathroom.

Tugging the shower door open, Zoe gasps, spinning to face me even while her hands attempt to cover herself.

Gripping her upper arm, I drag her out before leaning back in and flicking the water off, and then I drag her into the bedroom.

"Hey. I need a towel." She complains, but I ignore her, walking her to the chair and stopping her to stand in front of it. "What are you doing?" She gasps, but I ignore her, taking the rope and securing her wrists behind her back.

"Grayson. What are you doing?" she asks again, fear lacing her tone, and still, I say nothing.

Moving slowly away from her, I watch her as she watches me, and I pick up the dildo I extracted from her drawer, before flicking the cap on the lube and lathering the black object in it.

"Gray?" she says warily. "What are you doing?"

"We are going to try a different sort of interrogation," I admit, and she frowns.

"What do you mean? I've told you everything."

I chuckle as I close the lube and toss it on the bed. "Maybe you have. Maybe you haven't. I need to make sure." I nod. "You understand."

Her blue eyes widen. "The hell I do. What the fuck are you doing?" She shifts back, her calves hitting the chair, forcing her to stop.

Keeping my eyes on her, I lower to my haunches, holding up the dildo, and using one hand, I pry her ankles apart, even as I graze the black object over her clit and through her folds.

"Gray," she whispers, her legs trembling, even as she parts them wider.

Ahhh, there she is. My hungry princess. Hungry for dick. Hungry to be filled. Hungry to be claimed.

Slowly, I ease the dildo inside her, seeing how her body trembles with lust this time, and not fear.

That will change soon enough.

Once her cunt is fully stretched around the dildo, I stand, watching her lust filled eyes as they watch me, and

I grip her shoulders, easing her back until her bare, still wet from the shower, ass meets the seat.

A gasping moan escapes her at the new position, the dildo pushing deeper as she basically sits on it, the chair forcing it further and locking it in place.

Then I take the remaining rope and tie her arms to the back of the chair, and her ankles spread apart to the front legs.

"Grayson," she whispers, and I smirk.

"You're at my mercy now, Princess. Tied to that chair, open for me, there's nothing you can do to stop me from doing whatever the fuck I want to you."

Her blue eyes broaden as fear flickers over her face.

"Why are you doing this?" she asks, and I shrug.

"I need the truth, Princess. This will ensure I get it."

I take that moment to move to the dresser and pick up the small vibrator and flick it on.

"Grayson, this isn't f-funny," she stammers, her eyes glazing over as she watches what's in my hand.

"Do I look like I'm laughing, Princess?" I ask, and she shakes her head.

"I've told you everything." She repeats.

"Time will tell." I lower between her legs, her eyes shifting between lust and fear, and I press the vibrating toy to her clit.

Instantly she stiffens, her lips parting as a squeak escapes her before her teeth bite into her lower lip.

"Does that feel good, Princess?" I ask, and her cheeks flush as her teeth dig in deeper.

"It's okay. You can let yourself enjoy this. I want to make you feel good."

She shakes her head as she tries to fight the way her body is responding, so I press the switch on the vibrator, increasing the speed.

This time, she cries out, her hips surging forward as her body takes control.

"That's it, Princess. Let yourself feel good."

Her lids fall shut, and she throws her head back as she does just that. Even as I circle her clit with the vibrating toy, she pushes her hips up trying to seek friction before she grinds down on the dildo filling her.

"Yes," she pants, and I grin.

"That's it. Take what you need," I urge, seeing how quickly she is rising, ready to explode.

It's only a few seconds later that she does just that. Her body surges as the ripples of her orgasm consume her, and she cries out in pleasure.

That is, until her cries change.

"S-stop." She pushes past her gasps, her blue eyes connecting with mine.

"Where's the money, Zoe?"

It's at that moment that Zoe understands what's going on here.

"I-I already t-told yo—" Her hips grind up on their own as her body responds again, even while she looks like she's in pain.

"You told me something that I'm not sure I believe. Just tell me what really happened and I'll stop."

"G-Gra-!" Her words are cut off as she starts convulsing again, her body no longer her own, but a tool for me to milk.

The tremors that wrack her body send my already hard cock into a stone fucking rod that aches with need I can barely refrain from chasing. But the club has been drained of every fucking cent, and Zoe is the closest thing we have to knowing where the fuck all the money went. So I ignore my own need, and focus on how her body still can't get enough, even though her mind is refusing.

I make her come three more times before she starts crying. It's then that something snaps in me, and I fucking throw the vibrating toy hard against the wall where it falls to the floor before slowly dying.

"I-I d-don't k-know." She sobs, her body falling lax on the chair, the only thing keeping her up is the way she is tied to it.

I quickly untie her. Ankles first and then the top half, catching her before she hits the floor as she tumbles from the chair.

Cradling her to my chest, I carry her trembling body to the bed, and lower her down.

"No. No." She starts fighting me as she tries to sit up. "I need to sleep in Leslie's bed."

"Not tonight, Princess," I hiss, and her blue eyes plead with me for something I'm not going to give her. "Let's not taint her room with this," I suggest, hoping it will calm her, and it does, her sweat covered brow furrowing.

"You d-didn't c-care about that w-when you jerked off i-in my mouth while I s-slept," she snaps in a stutter, and I can't help it. I fucking grin.

"You're right. But that was different. Things are different now." I lean over her legs and slowly part them. "Open wider for me."

She tenses, and I shoot her a raised brow before she obeys.

"I'm going to pull it free now. Then you need to sleep."

Her chin quivers, even as she nods, and I grip the base of the dildo, now slick with the remnants of her orgasms, and I slowly ease it free.

Zoe doesn't say anything else to me after that. I tuck her in and sit on her small vanity stool, watching her as she watches me, and for a long time, we simply stare at each other.

My cock is still as stiff as a fucking board, but I make no attempt to ease the pain it's causing. I don't fucking deserve it after what I did to Zoe tonight.

I've always known I was a monster, willing to do whatever it takes to protect my club and the members, but never have I tortured anyone through pleasure.

Even as sleep takes Zoe, I watch her while loathing myself for what I did, and know deep down that I tortured her for nothing because I'm pretty fucking sure she's telling the truth.

12

Zoe

I awake to the sound of a not-so hushed argument. That answers my question of whether or not I've been sleeping at all. My body and mind sure don't feel like it's had any rest. I'm exhausted, scared, and just so overwhelmed with everything going on.

Reaching for the water bottle on the floor, I greedily drink the stale liquid down. I fucking hate waking up with the taste of Grayson's cum in my mouth. Okay, that's a lie. I... nope. I'm not going to analyze that shit. I'll stick with hate and plead the fifth while pretending my body isn't responding to the thought of him sneaking in here and... fuck's sake. I'm not doing a good job at not thinking about it.

Every day I have to remind myself of my new reality because if I don't, it seems like the plot of some over the top teen drama. Honestly, even with the reminder, it doesn't feel like my life.

Unlike the other mornings, or evenings, or whatever the fuck time it is when I awaken, I don't cry. I'm not sure I have anymore tears left to spare. Or maybe I should find a way to make it happen. Surely Grayson will let me go if I shrivel into the empty husk I feel like.

My head is pounding, my throat raw, and my eyes are so puffy I can barely see anything. Or maybe it's because my room is hidden in a cloak of heavy darkness. It doesn't matter. Nothing matters anymore.

This isn't some fucking fairy tale. There's no red cape for me to wear. No glass shoe that magically fits me, and if I let my hair down, no prince will use it to scale the walls to free me. I'm well and truly trapped. Not that I want any man in here—prince or otherwise. After what Grayson's put me through, I'm wondering if solitude is a favor rather than yet another punishment.

"Let me in there to talk to her."

I recognize Gunner's voice.

"No."

And Grayson's.

"Come on, man. She shouldn't be alone," Gunner insists.

I cringe as Grayson deadpans, "She has no one left."

He isn't wrong. Everyone has left me.

Mom is dead.

Leslie is dead.

And dad... oh God... dad just took off—he fucking saved his own fucking ass while leaving me at the mercy of Grayson fucking Black. I swallow back a snort at the thought of him showing me any mercy. He's treating me like enemy number one, all because he thinks I know something I don't.

"You know that's not what I meant," Gunner argues.

"Don't go feeling sorry for the fucking rat." Grayson's voice is eerily calm. "The rodent isn't your problem. Don't let me hear you feel sorry for her again."

"For fuck's sake, Gray. You're taking this too far." The angry lilt to Gunner's voice surprises me.

"Careful, Gunner," Grayson thunders. "Your desperation is starting to show. I already told you we're not going ahead with the plans, so calm the fuck down before I'm forced to think you're insulting your VP."

Even though a part of me wishes Gunner could get past Grayson, I'm glad he's being sent away. Not even his easy jokes can help me right now.

I wince as I sit up on my bed, my inner muscles crying out in pain from overuse. Night after night, day after day, Grayson uses my body against me. Not leaving until I'm a sobbing mess, begging him to believe me.

Dad would never steal money from anyone, it's not like he's some kind of lowlife petty criminal. Just as I think that, the contents of mom's letter pops up in my mind, like an unwanted jack in the box. She warned me about dad living above their means, didn't she? But... no. No. Dad wouldn't do something like that. Then again, until a few days ago, I wouldn't think that he would ever leave me either.

I stand on shaky legs and stumble my way to the closet. The only good thing about being in my room is that I know it well enough I don't need light. I quietly feel my way to the wall, and then I slide my hand down until I touch the carpet. With a sense of urgency, I roll it back and find the loose floorboard. There's a reason it's a cliche to hide things under a floorboard, it's because it works.

Sighing in relief, I close my hand around the crumpled up piece of paper that is mom's letter. As I hold the letter, I wonder if I should tell Grayson about what happened in the lawyer's office. Surely, they'd have no choice but to believe me then.

I shake my head, already knowing I can't and won't do that. While this letter proves my innocence, it incriminates my dad. I might be pissed that he's left me here, but I still can't do that to him. He's my dad—my only close family to still draw breath.

Without making a sound, I slide the floorboard back. I almost leave the letter, but then I think better of it. In the dark, I can't see if I'm smoothing the carpet perfectly, and if I'm not, there's a chance Grayson will notice. The letter isn't safe there anymore.

Now that my eyes have grown used to the darkness, I can make out the shapes of the furniture. None of them are safe, though. Sure, Grayson, Gunner, Slayer, and Slasher have already ransacked my room twice, but I don't trust they won't do it again.

My blood runs cold as new voices join Grayson's and Gunner's outside the door. I don't know who they are, or what they want. But what I do know is that anyone can burst in here at any moment. I need to hide mom's letter quickly.

With no more secret hiding places, I decide that my best option is to hide the letter in plain sight. As quietly as possible I make my way back to the bed and reach for the box of tissues I know is on the floor. After emptying the box, I hide the letter at the bottom and refill it.

I'm almost done when my door is shoved open with no warning.

"Well, well, well. Looks like someone is done with her beauty sleep," Grayson says with mock concern in his tone.

When he switches the light on, I scurry under the covers like a cockroach caught out in the open.

"Aww don't be like that, Princess," he drawls. "Why hide when you know it won't do you any good?"

He's right, and I hate my first instinct was to hide. I can't fight him, but I can... ah, fuck it. I'm not kidding anyone here. There's fuck all I can do, and not only does he know—he revels in my helplessness.

When I don't move, he clucks impatiently. "I've warned you about making me repeat myself. It won't end well for you, Princess."

The coldness of his tone causes a shiver to run down my spine. I swallow and lower the cover, blinking against the harsh light from the ceiling. Since I'm still clutching the box with tissues, I pull a few out so it doesn't look out of place in my hands.

After making a big show of wiping under my eyes, I fix my gaze on him. I don't talk, I silently await his command.

"You really should open the curtains and let some fresh air in," he says conversationally like he didn't just threaten me. "On second thought, Slasher can do that while you shower."

Before I can think better of it, I shake my head. Grayson's obsession with watching me shower is as disturbing as it's belittling. Especially when he begins to bark orders of where he wants me to wash myself.

"I'm going to pretend you didn't just shake your head at me," he smirks. "Hurry up. We don't have all day."

"N-no!" My voice is filled with gravel from barely using it when I'm not screaming at him.

My cheeks burn as I remember screaming his name as I came on his fingers last night. Jesus. It's fucking with my head that he can wring such intense orgasms from me when all I want to do is stab him.

I squeak as Grayson closes the distance between us and wraps my long, blonde hair around his fist. "Do you want a chance to take that back?"

Stubbornly, I shake my head. I know I shouldn't provoke him, but I'm already in it now. What more can he possibly do to me?

Grayson releases my hair and grabs my shoulders instead, using his hold to force me out of bed. As soon as my feet touch the floor, he pushes so hard my knees buckle and I land on my knees with a startled cry.

"Crawl to the bathroom."

The cold command hits me like a bucket of ice water.

"W-what?" I stammer as I turn my head to look at him. Surely I didn't hear him right.

Grayson pinches the bridge of his nose and exhales audibly. "For someone who got such a high GPA you're not all that bright, are you, Princess? If you stopped rebelling and making me repeat myself, you'd make it much easier on yourself."

Unable to stop myself, I snarkily ask, "Or is it easier for you if I behave? What's the matter, Grayson? You don't like forcing me?"

My head snaps up as someone laughs. "She's feisty." Slasher makes a big show of sticking his hand down his pants and rearranging himself. "If you're not going to break her in, I call dibs."

The deranged fucker winks at me.

Grayson crouches down next to me and whispers, "Now look what you've gone and done. You're making it look like I can't handle you. Would you like for me to give you to Slasher, Princess? He usually only plays with his brother and the two of them..." He trails off and licks his lips. "I'm not sure you'd survive their brand of kink."

Fear takes a hold of me at the thought of being passed around like some kind of toy. "Please don't," I whimper. "I promise I'll behave. I promise."

"Good girl," Grayson croons, patting my head with a derogatory smirk. "Sorry, Slasher. This pussy is all mine."

"What about her ass, VP?"

No. No. Not that. The vicious glint in Slasher's eyes makes it clear I'm way more out of my depth than I first thought. My smart mouth and academy-smarts won't save me here. Fuck, I'm not sure there is any saving at all.

I feel Grayson's eyes burn into my skin as he stands up and pats his leg. I know what he wants, and although I hate it, I crawl over to him.

"See that?" His question is aimed at Slasher. "As I said, this pussy is mine. All her holes are for that matter. So it looks like you and Slayer need to find yourself another girl to share."

With a chuckle, Slasher leaves my room. "Well, I still have dibs for when you're done with her." He calls over his shoulder as he disappears.

Luckily Grayson grunts for me to follow him before I have time to succumb to my thoughts, and like the fucking pathetic excuse for a woman I am, I crawl into the bathroom and shower while Grayson watches me like a hawk.

I hate the way his lustful gaze burns into me as I lather my tits and stomach in my body wash. The first few times he forced me into the shower, I tried to cover up, but I've learned my lesson. It doesn't fucking help—if anything, it excites the fucker even more. So instead of giving him a show of disobedience, I give him one of indifference.

My face is carefully schooled into a mask of nothingness as my hand glides down my flat stomach to the apex of my thighs. As I move my hand between my legs, I close my eyes. I can't stand seeing him while I do something as simple and natural as cleaning myself. I doubt I'll ever be able to shower again without remembering how mortifying this is.

"Hmm, maybe I should check if you've cleaned yourself properly," Grayson growls when I switch the water off. "You did seem to rush it."

I involuntarily shiver at his words. "N-no need," I stammer.

Fuck I hate how weak I sound. A part of me wants to stand up to him, to challenge him into doing his worst. But since I don't know what his worst is, I look down at the floor.

Grayson cups his crotch and rasps, "I can think of a need."

Forgetting about my plan to stay quiet and yield to him, I roll my eyes and huff.

Wrong fucking move.

His dark eyes smolder as his lips twitch in amusement as he takes my hand, yanks me out of the shower and roughly shoves me up against the sink.

His breath is hot against my ear as he menacingly whispers, "Don't fucking move."

Before I can fully comprehend his words, his hand is between my thighs. The tips of his fingers dance across my mound, all too easily finding my clit.

As he expertly works my pussy with deft fingers, I mentally curse my body for reacting to him. Fully naked and with his hand on my core, there's no way to hide the wetness or my hardened nipples. I bite down on the inside of my cheek, smothering the moan that's threatening to give me away even more. It becomes increasingly harder to keep quiet as he works two fingers inside my slick cunt.

"Mhmm, you're so fucking wet for me," Grayson rasps approvingly.

Grayson curls his fingers inside me, grazing that magic spot that has made me see fucking stars in the past. This time, my cheeks burn hot with embarrassment as my inner walls flutter in response to the movement.

I know he felt it, and I know he'll think it's because I want him. I don't. Regardless of how my traitorous body acts, there's no way for me to want him less. But even I can't fight biology, and that's all my reaction is.

Proving I'm right in thinking he misses nothing, Grayson growls, "Look at you, trying so hard to fight it."

I squeeze my eyes shut, refusing to look at his smug expression in the mirror.

"Open your eyes, Princess," he immediately commands.

Rather than doing as he says, I shake my head while trying to ignore the rush of pleasure washing over me.

"I won't let you come if you don't."

That makes it easy for me because that's the last thing I want. I don't want to come, and I definitely don't want him

to make me. Every single time I orgasm from his touch,
I'm losing a part of myself. And by now I'm scared I only
have a few pieces left, which means I'll fight to hang on to
the rest.

"Princess!"

Tears gather behind my eyelids, but they're not caused
by the smack he delivers to my ass, or the way he painfully
pinches my nipple while sucking on my neck. It's because... because... fuck. Fire erupts in my lower stomach,
and my legs shake as my pussy squeezes his fingers tight.

No.

No.

I won't come again. He won't... I can't...

"Please stop," I cry. My tears spill over and run down my
face.

"You don't want to come?" Grayson sounds genuinely
surprised.

"P-please... I'll do anything. I swear. I'll—"

Grayson slaps his hand across my mouth, making it
impossible to continue pleading with him. It doesn't stop
me from trying, but it does stop my words from being
heard. Instead, I'm just making nonsensical noises that
cause him to laugh heartily.

"Save it, Princess. You'll come because I fucking want
you to, and because you fucking want me."

There's a hint of determined madness in his voice,
which I'm not sure bodes well for me.

Grayson continues to play my cunt like his favorite fucking instrument. His fingers piston in and out while the
heel of his hand rubs my clit. Before long I'm a trembling
and crying mess, unable to stop what's coming.

My muscles tighten, which causes me to cry out in pain. At least I try to, but his hand is still muffling me. I try to bite him, but that only seems to make him more determined. As a last fuck you, I keep my eyes closed, refusing to give him the satisfaction of looking at him.

When I come, I know I'm close to moaning his name. In pure stubbornness and spite, I bite my tongue so hard I taste iron. Logically, I know I'm not getting to Grayson at all, he couldn't care less as long as he gets to pull my Pinocchio strings. It matters to me, though. The feeling of not surrendering completely is all I have left.

"Are you happy now, Princess?"

My eyes fly open, and a retort is on my lips. However, when I see the fleeting look of anger on his face, I smirk behind his hand. He might not want me to know I got to him, but I know I did. About fucking time.

Instead of answering, I wait patiently for him to remove his hand. Then, much to his surprise if his slack jaw is anything to go by, I get down on all fours.

Without needing any prompt, I crawl back to my room and get dressed in the outfit he picks out for me. A skimpy crop top that barely covers my tits, and a miniskirt.

Because he'd be so fucking predictable and pick an outfit like that.

Afterwards I obediently follow him into the kitchen where I do my best to swallow the food he puts in front of me.

"And here I thought you'd learned your lesson, Princess," he huffs when I take forever to chew.

I ball my free hand into a fist while chanting to myself that I need to bite my tongue and do as he says. "I'm trying," I say.

"Try harder."

My temper rises to the surface, and before I can stop myself, I push the plate with buttered toast across the table.

"What do you want from me?" I scream as I stagger to my feet in the ridiculously high heels I now wish I'd never purchased. "You're the reason I can barely sleep. It's because of you I can't eat or breathe. I can't fucking breathe when you're near me."

Without waiting for what I'm sure would be a scathing response, I kick my heels off and run into the garden. I don't stop until I reach the tree with the swing I used to love. Walking over to it, I sit down and begin to move. The old thing creaks, but I don't care. The wind on my face feels like someone is breathing new life into me.

I don't understand any of what's going on, and I don't want to admit how much it all scares me. Being held hostage in my own home is a sick kind of oxymoron. It's the place I've always felt safe and loved—special, even.

Now there are bikers treating it like their place all while throwing their weight around. It's sickening and... yeah, scary.

"What are you doing, Sugar?"

Gunner's voice pulls me from my thoughts.

"Look I'm sorry about Grayson. He—"

Shaking my head, I hiss, "I don't want to hear it."

There's nothing he can say that will help. Nothing he can do to ease my pain, so why bother with words that don't matter.

I'm surprised when Gunner walks behind me and starts pushing me on the swing. He keeps pushing me until I'm flying so high I can see the treetops.

When we were kids, Leslie and I were sure we'd be able to see the angels in heaven if we could get up that high, but we never could. Not on our own.

"I don't feel so good," I croak.

Gunner gently helps me slow down enough I can jump off the swing. I land on the grass with a soft thud, and without looking back, I walk back inside.

"Zoe?" he calls after me, but I ignore him.

The Cruz Kings might think I'm their enemy. They might come and take my home from me, but I refuse to let their presence sour my memories of Leslie. Since I can't stop myself from thinking about her in the very place where everything reminds me of her, I have to get them to leave.

As I ascend the stairs, I come face-to-face with Grayson. He doesn't look angry, he looks... no. He can't be looking worried. It has to be another mind game.

"Princess—"

I hold my hand up to silence him. "I want to speak to Rocco." My voice doesn't waver.

Grayson's face betrays nothing, but there's suspicion in his voice when he asks, "Why?"

Rolling my shoulders back, I jut up my chin and cock my hip. "Because I said so."

Without looking at my tormentor again, I slowly walk into my room. I don't bother slamming the door behind me, it's not like it would keep him out, anyway.

To my surprise, I hear Grayson call the club Prez. While he's still talking on his phone, he comes into my room. Once he ends the call, he looks at me with a mixture of disbelief and cockiness in his dark eyes.

"I hope you know what you're doing, Princess."

Pulling the tissue box closer, I pretend I can't see him. I look at the wall right behind him and swallow back the words I'm thinking.

I hope I'm right to show Rocco the letter.

I hope I'm right to buy my freedom by condemning my dad.

But what else can I do? I need to be free, and I don't see any other way. However, as soon as the Cruz Kings Prez sees what my mom wrote, he'll have no reason to keep me here.

13

Grayson

The moment Rocco steps through the door, Zoe's phone starts to ring. Gunner and I share a wide-eyed look before I dart to the kitchen counter where we have been keeping an eye on it in the hopes to see any communication come from Brian since the tracker in his phone and watch seem to have stopped working.

The name flashing across the screen is unknown, but I don't hesitate to answer the call on speaker, waiting quietly for the person on the other end to speak.

There's a beat of silence before Brian's hushed voice fills the room.

"Zoe?"

A quick glance at Rocco shows he understands who is on the call, and he waves a hand at me, gesturing for me to speak. So I do.

"She's busy right now."

Brian's gasp is audible, and some rustling sounds come through the line as if he's moving quickly.

That's all it takes for Rocco to drag Gunner closer to whisper an order, and Gunner's wide eyes dart out through the windows before giving Rocco a nod and quietly leaving through the back door.

"Are you running again, Brian?" I ask, and he grunts, while the rustling still meets our ears.

"Where is Zoe?" he snarls and I chuckle.

"I already told you. She's busy."

"You'd better not have laid a finger on her or—"

"Or what?" I hiss. "What the fuck are you gonna do Brian?"

The sound of a door slamming meets my ears before an engine starts up.

Rocco comes to join me at the kitchen counter, his eyes caught on the phone as Brian pleas.

"Please don't hurt her. She has nothing to do with this."

"Brian." Rocco's demanding voice causes Brian to curse, and I smirk. Rocco can seem like a teddy bear at times, but when the man is pissed off, he's fucking terrifying. "Where's our money?"

"It's g-gone." He stutters, his fear seeping through.

"Gone where?" Rocco hisses, his fist resting on the counter near the phone as he opens and closes his fingers, fighting for control.

"It doesn't matter. Just tell me my sweet angel is okay. Please don't hurt her."

"Hurt her?" I mock. "She hasn't suffered any pain by my hand."

Rocco finally cracks the smallest of smirks at the meaning behind my words before he returns his attention to the phone.

"We haven't hurt her... yet." Rocco leaves that dangling and Brian curses under his breath again. "But you see Brian. There's just one problem." Rocco leans down closer to the phone on the counter top. "We need our money back. Every last fuckin' cent. And if we don't get it back in the next twenty-four fucking hours, then we are going to introduce your daughter to so much torture, she's likely to die of fright before the pain even sets in. And then we will start leaving little gifts for you. Gifts in the form of her body parts."

"No," Brian whispers, and I chuckle.

"Yes, is the correct answer here Brian. Yes, we fucking will. So here's what you are going to do. You are going to trade places with her. We will let Zoe go if you hand yourself and the fucking money over."

"But I can't." He wails, causing the phone speaker to crackle.

"You have no choice, Miller," Rocco growls. "Meet us on the riverwalk, under the Cabrillo Highway overpass. 10pm tomorrow night. Make sure you have the money, or you can say goodbye to your last remaining daughter."

Rocco is the one to end the call, and for a moment, we both just stare at the phone, the screen now black.

"You think he'll show?" I ask, and Rocco's dark gaze meets mine. He looks tired. Older than when I saw him yesterday. I guess having the club's bank account cleaned out will do that. That money houses and feeds our men and women, plus most of the families. Now there's nothing, and everyone who looks to us for help will be let down when we can't help them.

"I don't fucking know. I get the feeling he didn't just steal the money for himself. My gut is telling me it's the Reapers. Disabling us financially means we can't help our community, and if we can't help them, then they will turn their backs on us and look for someone who can."

I nod. "Which is what the Reapers have been trying to do all along. Discredit us. Make us look bad so our community turns on us."

Rocco nods too. "Exactly."

"Shit," I sigh, my eyes glancing to the staircase that leads up to Zoe's room. I locked her in there earlier. I didn't like the spark in her eye when she demanded to see Prez. She's up to something.

"She still claiming to know nothing?" Rocco asks, and I turn my gaze back to his.

"Yeah. I've fucking tried everything but painful torture. I've been as fucking harsh as I can and still, she has nothing to tell us."

"I asked you the other night if you thought she was telling the truth. What does your gut say now?" he asks and I shrug.

"I want to think she knows something because we fucking need that money back, but..." I hesitate, raking my hand through my hair. I need a fucking haircut.

"But?" Rocco urges and I sigh.

"I think she's being fucking honest. I really don't think she knows what her dad did."

"So you don't think Brian had her mess with your head and dick on purpose?"

Fuck.

I keep wondering if she is a honey trap or not. Wondering if I'm thinking with my dick too much when it comes to the blonde goddess, but something has me doubting her ability to trap me and Gunner like that.

Sure, she's as smart as they come with an attitude to boot. But a master manipulator at seduction?

No.

Could she be?

Fuck yes. But she's still too green in that department.

"No." I shake my head, answering Rocco. "I don't think Zoe is a honey trap. I think she's innocent when it comes to everything that's happened with her dad."

Rocco nods. "Okay. Where is she? I'd like to know why she demanded my presence."

I smirk, gesturing for the staircase in the hall, and he grins back, taking the lead up to Zoe's bedroom.

Unbolting the door, something we added to some of the rooms the night Brian fled, I push it open to reveal Zoe, sitting on her bed in the same clothes I had her dress in earlier.

I was sure the moment I gave her space she would have them off and ripped to shreds. But then again, she'd have nothing else to wear. I cleaned out her wardrobe and drawers that first night too, leaving her at my mercy.

"Zoe." Rocco grunts as he steps into the room which has too many frills for a guy like my Prez to be comfortable in.

"Thank you for coming," she says formally as she stands from the bed. Her eyes shift from Rocco to glare at me, and I can tell by the angered look on her face that she is about to talk to me this time. "You may leave."

I chuckle, leaning against the doorframe and crossing my arms over my chest.

"Not a fucking hope in hell, Princess."

Her blue gaze darts from me to Rocco like she's hoping he will tell me to fuck off, but when he widens his stance and crosses his arms over his chest too, she knows he's not about to kick me out of the room.

Then she fucking rolls her eyes.

I bite the inside of my cheek as I fight the urge to laugh, knowing Prez is likely doing the same.

"I'm a busy man, Miss Miller. You'd do best not to waste my time," Rocco states and she nods quickly before moving to the tissue box on the end of her bed.

"I want you to read something," she says as she tugs the tissues from the box. "It's a letter my mom left for me in her will." Then she pulls a piece of paper out from the box.

Motherfucker!

How the fuck did we not check the fucking tissue box? And why the fuck would we even think to look there?

Zoe hesitates a moment, unfolding the paper, her eyes grazing over the words written from her dead mother.

Then she holds the paper out to Rocco.

Stepping forward, he takes it, not wasting another second before he's reading it.

When he's done, he hands it back to her.

Zoe crosses her arms over her chest and cocks her hip. "This is proof that I didn't lie. I don't know anything. It wasn't even until I got this letter a few days before the funeral that I knew anything was off with my dad." She scrunches her nose and glances towards her bedside table for a moment, her eyes studying the framed picture she has there of her with Leslie, her mom and dad. "Dad lost his mind when he found out mom didn't leave him anything in the will. I've never seen him behave so... so unhinged."

Pausing, she glances back at Rocco and inhales deeply, the action making her tits even more prominent despite her crossed arms.

"He has been acting weird since that day, but he never said anything to me about any money. I swear I would tell you." Her arms drop to her sides, and when she speaks again, her tone is laced with a stubborn lilt. "My dad isn't a thief. Whatever you say he's done, I find it hard to believe..." She frowns trailing off. "But maybe..."

"Maybe what?" Rocco urges, and her blue eyes fill with pain.

"Maybe I never really knew him." She shrugs, her voice just above a whisper as she fights her emotions. "If I knew where your money is or how to get it back, I would help you, if for no other reason than to get you all the fuck out of my house. But I don't know where your money has gone, and I have no idea where my dad is." Her lower lip starts to tremble, and I watch as she takes a moment to compose herself, quickly pushing her emotions back.

"Anyway, as you can see, I'm no good to you. I promise I won't report this to the police or anything. It's the least I can do since Gunner saved my life, but I can assure you there's no need for your men to be keeping me prisoner here or anywhere else. I'm not worth anything to you."

Oh, how wrong she is.

Nodding, Rocco unfolds his arms.

"Thank you for showing me the letter Zoe. I understand that you are hoping for your freedom but unfortunately, that's not going to happen."

Rocco turns to leave, and Zoe's face turns red in anger. "What!?"

The moment she takes a step towards my Prez is the moment I insert myself between them. Not that I think she could hurt him, but still, touching Rocco is off limits unless invited.

"Back off Princess," I rumble, winning myself a classic Princess glare.

"But I'm useless to you," Zoe calls to Rocco, leaning from side to side to try to see him around my frame.

"On the contrary." Rocco chuckles from behind me. "You are extremely valuable to us, Zoe."

"What? How?" Zoe cries, but Prez ignores her, slapping me on the shoulder.

"Have her ready to go by 9pm tomorrow night. Until then, keep her quiet and out of trouble."

"Will do." I nod, not taking my eyes off Zoe who now resembles a fish with her mouth opening and closing in shock as she tries to think of something to say.

I hear Prez make his way downstairs as Zoe remains in place looking stunned before her big blue eyes look up to meet mine.

"What's happening at 9pm tomorrow night?" she asks in a whisper, and I grin.

"We trade you for your dad."

While she stands stunned, I lean down and snatch the letter from her slack grip before dashing out of the room and bolting the door shut.

Moments later her screaming starts up followed by her small fists thumping on the door as she rages about me taking her mom's letter.

I should feel worse than I do about snatching it, but my need to know what's in it is a beast of its own, so I lean back against the door, feeling it rattle each time Princess beats on it, and I unfold the letter.

The first thing I notice as I read the letter is that Astrid really didn't think she would be leaving this earth so soon, hoping that Zoe would have graduated Harvard and met a nice man.

There's a huge fucking chance that Zoe will never make it to Harvard, and if she stays around here, she's not going to meet a nice man.

The part about Astrid wanting Zoe to look out for her little sister manages to make me feel... something. Leslie was a good kid. She didn't deserve to meet her end so fucking soon. And even though Zoe is a bratty snob at times, I'd never wish for her to lose her sister like that.

The next part of the letter is what's really interesting.

Brian Miller has been a problem husband it seems. The fact that Astrid fought to keep Brian from getting his hands on her estate tells me he's a money hungry man who probably wastes it, or loses it, without a second thought. Maybe even worse. Which would make sense as to why he agreed to work for my club. Straight and narrow professionals don't just decide on a whim to get into organized crime, which means Brian Miller came looking for it. To support his habits and lifestyle, apparently.

What habits?

Gambling? Drinking? Drugs? Whores?

The list could go on.

"Give me back my mom's letter!" Zoe's piercing scream draws my attention, and I fold the letter again as I turn and face the door, picturing her reddened cheeks flushed with anger, her curled lip, baring her teeth as she seethes at me.

It's enough to make a man hard.

"The letter is gone, Princess!" I call through the timber between us.

"What! No! It can't be gone!"

"It is. I just tore it up."

"NOOOO!" Zoe screams, and the next thing I hear is something hard crashing into the door.

"The fuck did you do to her?" Gunner's voice comes from behind me, and I shoot him a grin.

"Nothing for you to worry about. She'll calm down, eventually."

"I'll fucking kill you! You hear me Grayson Black?! You are fucking dead!"

"Jesus. I think you broke her," Gunner says with concern, and for a moment, I fear he may be right.

I slip the letter, still folded neatly in my palm, into my back pocket, ignoring the crashing of furniture from behind Zoe's bedroom door.

"Did you catch sight of Brian?" I ask Gunner and he shakes his head.

"He was definitely calling from close by, and I heard a car start up and speed off just on the other side of the treeline by the golf course, but by the time I got up to the road, the car was long gone."

I nod. It was obvious when Brian rang that he started running. It makes sense that he was nearby. Probably wanted to see if the coast was clear to come back.

"You going to interrogate Zoe again tonight?" Gunner asks, a dark glint in his eye, catching my attention.

"No. There's no need. She doesn't know anything and we trade her tomorrow. I think I've pissed her off enough for one day."

Even as I say it, a loud frustrated scream bellows from her bedroom, and Gunner's blond brows shoot up.

"Yeah. I'd say you're right about that."

Gunner and I return downstairs where we take call after call from my club brothers about possible sightings of Brian, before Marcie's Florist calls to say two Reapers paid her a visit. The fuckers had the audacity to tell Marcie that the club is broke and that we will start harassing local businesses to pay us protection money so we can make quick cash. Then the fuckers handed her a 1k stack and suggested that when the war comes to her door, she'll need to choose a side.

The motherfuckers are now trying to buy support right under our fucking noses!

What pisses me off even more is that Prez wants me to stay on babysitting duty instead of going to reassure our community that we have things handled.

The fuck!

How am I meant to stay fucking put when I have more to offer out on the streets? Even Gunner gets sent out, but I have to fucking stay here in the Miller house and watch over the brat.

Thank fuck she eventually calmed down. Her screaming stopped about an hour ago and I listened at the door to hear her crying until she fell silent.

Now in the dark house while my club is out doing what I should be doing, my frustrated mind keeps thinking about the feisty blonde upstairs, and how much I want to feel her cunt wrapped around my cock.

I do another lap of the lower level, checking that all doors and windows are locked, before I make my way up the stairs. I try not to make much noise, the anticipation of surprising the bratty princess keeping my steps light.

Unlatching the bolt on her door, I push it open to find her bedroom only lit by the faint glow coming from the cracked door of her wardrobe. It's enough to see that she completely trashed her room. Her furniture, which probably cost a small fortune, is mostly in pieces, and her walls are dented in places from the obvious onslaught she lashed out.

Fuck. Why do I like this so much?

The precious princess has a vicious side. I'm probably lucky I wasn't in the room when she set it free because I'm pretty sure she would have ripped my nuts from my body.

Of course it took taking away the letter her mom wrote to send her over the edge. It's a true cunt's act. Something she won't forget easily. Luckily I like tormenting her.

I round the bed, my eyes focused on where she lies on top of the sheets, sprawled out like she flopped back onto the mattress in exhaustion and passed out.

The sleep shorts she's wearing are gaping, showing me that she's not wearing any panties.

My cock fucking approves, stiffening with the need to slip those shorts aside and sink inside her.

Without second guessing myself, I free my dick from my jeans, palming it as I shift closer, standing in between Zoe's parted feet.

"You want me to make you feel good Princess?" I ask quietly, watching how her lids remain closed and her body remains still.

I smirk.

She always loves it when I make her feel good, even though she tries to deny it. Her body doesn't lie. Her wet cunt tells me everything I need to know each time I go there with her, and I know tonight will be no different.

Leaning forward, I slowly tug her tank up to reveal her perky tits, her rosy nipples pebbling harder as I graze my fingers over them, and a faint moan floats from her parted lips.

Slowly I glide a finger down her stomach and over her shorts, coming to the leg opening where I shift the fabric aside just like I imagined doing only moments ago.

Knowing I can't just stick my cock inside her because she needs to be primed first, I lower my head between her legs and graze my tongue up her center seam. Her silky skin is so hot down here, and when I repeat the move, Zoe moans again, parting her legs wider.

Well, if that's not a fucking invitation...

I grin even as I use my fingers to part her folds, my tongue finding her clit this time. I kiss her cunt like it's her mouth, feeling her nub swell as blood rushes to the area, and a moment later I feel the telltale sign of her arousal start to seep from her cunt.

She's slick and ready.

Like always, I don't bother covering my cock with latex. Zoe's cunt is the most pure one I've ever had. It hasn't been used by hordes like a Cruz Cunt, and I know she has that birth control implant in her arm, so I don't have to worry about knocking her up.

Pushing my jeans down further, I kneel on the bed between her thighs and line my cock up with her entrance. I know this will probably wake her, but she loves the way I make her feel, so I don't see her trying to kill me until it's over.

Running the tip of my dick through her folds and to her clit, Zoe moans again, her hand coming to her tit to graze her nipple, and that's when I slowly ease inside her.

Fuuuck. Her cunt is so fucking tight. Thank fuck she's drenched for me, my cock sliding in deep with ease and my eyes flick from where I disappear inside her, to her face.

Her lips have parted further, and her cheeks are flushed, but she still seems to be asleep, so I slowly ease out and sink back in.

In sleep, Zoe's body responds, her back arching a little as her fingers tweak her nipple, and I pick up my pace, not wanting to hold back anymore. I want to fill her with my cum.

I'm not gentle now, jostling Zoe's body on her messy bed and I know the moment she's awake, even though my eyes are trained on how her cunt swallows me whole.

Zoe's legs wrap around my hips and she starts meeting my thrusts, her moans turning to cries of pleasure. I risk a glance at her, my eyes locking onto her half lidded gaze as she watches me thrust from above.

"See how much your body wants me, Princess?" I ask her, but she doesn't answer. "Do you like waking up to me being inside you?" She bites her lip this time like she's trying not to answer me, and I chuckle. "Answer me Princess, or I'll stop."

"Yes." She pants, picking up her pace as she tries to grind her clit on my pubic bone.

"Yes, what?" I snap, stopping my thrusts and using a firm grip to stop her hips from moving.

"Yes, I like waking up to you being inside me."

I don't know how she does it, but her words are laced with truth and venom, and it makes me fucking grin.

"That's a good little Princess." I tease, releasing her hips so she can move again.

"Do you want me to fill you with my cum?" I ask, even as my fingers press to her clit.

The one thing I've learned about this little firecracker, is she tends to be honest when she's chasing her orgasm. So when she nods and says, "Yes please," I'm helpless not to give her exactly what she wants, and with some extra friction on her clit and a few more thrusts, she explodes around me, milking me dry.

14

Grayson

Despite knowing she has no hope in hell of successfully fleeing from us, Zoe still struggles in my grip as I lead her down the riverwalk surrounded by Cruz Kings. She even pretended to hate that she had to sit on my knee in the pickup Rocco drove us in with the rest of the guys on their bikes.

I would have totally bought the whole I hate you act she has going for me if it weren't for the fact that when I started playing gently with her hair, she seemed to melt into me.

Her lids even fluttered closed for a few moments as I brushed my fingers through her silky strands, before running my hands gently over her shoulders and down her arms where goosebumps traveled over her skin.

If you ask me, they were good goosebumps.

"You're hurting my arm," Zoe snaps, shooting me a glare as we walk, and I offer her a smirk in return.

"You love the way I hurt you. Stop pouting."

Her mouth drops open in a gasp while the guys chuckle around us. That makes her snap her full pink lips shut as if she's just remembered they were there, and fuck, she even steps closer to me.

I guess she hasn't seen this many of the Cruz Kings in one place before.

We're not fucking idiots. We know Brian could have contacted the Reapers and set up a trap, so while we have plenty of cover around me, Prez and Princess, we also have men hiding in strategic places along the river and overpass.

The Reapers have taken so much from us already. We aren't going to risk losing more.

As we approach the overpass, it's easy to see, even in the darkened space, that Brian isn't there.

"You think he will show?" Gunner asks Rocco who just shrugs.

"He's been nothing but a fucking coward so far. It stands to reason that he won't change."

"Not even for his daughter?" Gunner asks, and Rocco glances back at Zoe who is now looking too scared to speak.

"I'd like to think so." Rocco tugs out his smokes and slips one free. "What do you think Zoe? Do you think your old man will hand himself over to save you?"

Zoe nods quickly, jutting up her chin, her dark lashes blinking quickly as she prepares to lie.

"Of course he will."

Rocco smirks as he lights his cigarette and nods. "I hope for your sake he does." He mumbles past the cancer stick before turning his attention to the other men. "Fan out a little but keep your eyes and ears open."

A few grunts respond as our pack grows thinner, and as Slasher slinks closely past Zoe, she all but hides against my side.

"How long will we give him, Prez?" Gunner asks, and Rocco shrugs.

"Not too long. He knows better than to keep me waiting."

As if Brian heard Rocco speak, the phone in his hand starts ringing. Zoe's phone.

She stiffens next to me as Rocco reads the screen and then shoots her a glare as he answers the call on speaker.

"You'd better be calling to say you are nearly here." Rocco barks and Zoe takes a step forward, her lips parting as if she's about to speak.

Quickly intercepting her, I slap my hand over her mouth and drag her back against me while she struggles in my hold, once again thinking she's strong enough to overpower me.

As if.

"Is Zoe there? I need to know she's alive," Brian demands, so I nod at Zoe when she looks up at me, and something like relief washes over her.

"Dad. I'm okay."

Her voice is strong, reminding me of the girl who walked with confidence even as she fell apart at her mom and sister's funeral.

"Zoe honey. I'm sorry about all this. I never wanted you to be caught in the middle." Brian tells his daughter, and

I frown at Rocco, wondering why Brian doesn't just show his face and say that to Zoe in person.

"It's okay, dad." Zoe reassures him, right before Rocco glares at the phone.

"Now that you know she's okay, you need to show your face."

"I-I'm not coming."

"What?!" Zoe shrieks.

I gotta be fucking honest. I didn't think Brian would risk his daughter's life like this, and by the way Zoe stiffens against me, she didn't expect that either.

"And why is that?" Rocco snaps, tossing his half-smoked cigarette to the ground as his face contorts in anger.

"I-I can't. The money is gone. I can't get it back. If I try, the Reapers will kill me, and if I hand myself over to you empty-handed, you will kill me."

"Dad!" Zoe yells. "They will kill me! What are you doing?"

The glare Rocco shoots Zoe's way even makes me want to recoil, and she snaps her mouth shut as her body starts to tremble. It takes a lot to send Rocco over the edge these days, but cleaning us out of cash will do it.

"So instead," Rocco sneers, "you're happy for us to send Zoe back to you in pieces? Because you know we will have our fucking fun with her first, right? She will be used in every way imaginable, and even some ways unimaginable before we finally start chopping her up."

Zoe's breathing quickens at Rocco's words, her tits pressing rapidly against the arm I have wrapped over her chest to hold her close to me. I want to tell her not to believe Rocco, but shit, I can't be sure he doesn't mean it.

We are no fucking saints, that's for sure, but doing the things he just suggested goes against the very thin layer of morals we have.

But fuck. We are now financially crippled. If we can't get an influx of cash soon, we are fucked.

"P-please don't hurt my Zoe. She's done nothing wrong. P-please." Brian sounds like he is fucking crying, but his tears mean nothing if he's willing to sacrifice his daughter for his own worthless life.

"She's fucking dead!" Rocco roars causing Zoe to whimper which earns her a glare and a gesture to me to get her the fuck out of here.

I glance at Slasher and Slayer, one look making their feet move my way, and I pass Zoe off to them and lean in to speak quietly.

"Take her to the pickup. Don't fucking leave her until I get there. Got it?"

"Wait! No!" Zoe yells, panic etched across her face as her blue eyes plead with me. She struggles against the hold my men have on her, Slayer's hand covering any further verbal protests from Zoe before he carries her off, her screams muffled by his palm.

Rocco swings his arm wide, pointing down the path, and our remaining men understand, knowing he is sending them away. Gunner looks back as he walks and I get the feeling from the hint of anger in his expression, that he's pissed to be sent away.

"You don't understand." Brian cries through the phone, and I can tell by the way Rocco's lip twitches that he is seconds away from completely losing it. "I had no choice. They were going to kill Zoe."

That gets my attention.

"What do you mean?" I bark, and Rocco looks at me in confusion.

"A-after the funeral, they called me. They said I had to transfer all the money, and if I didn't do it in the next ten minutes, then Zoe would die." Brian sobs, "I didn't want to believe them, and when I ended the call and went back out to the pool where Zoe was sitting, I saw it."

When Brian sobs again, not telling me what I fucking need to know, I almost lose my shit this time. "Fucking saw what?!" I yell, wishing Brian was here so I could introduce his face to my fucking fist.

"T-the red laser thing. On her head. T-they were going to s-shoot her right there by the pool."

"Fuck," Rocco mumbles quietly as this information has me reeling.

"How do you know it was from a gun?" I snap.

"I didn't, but it was the only thing I could think of and I wasn't willing to risk it."

"But you risk her life now by not handing yourself over," I bark and he sobs again.

"I know you will treat her right," Brian says and my brows shoot up as I lock eyes with Rocco.

"What the fuck, after everything we have threatened, makes you fucking think she is safe with us?" Rocco snaps.

"Because she's worth something to you if she's kept alive and well."

That piques our interest, and we both step closer to the phone.

"Explain," I hiss through clenched teeth. This is giving me a fucking headache.

"Zoe's inheritance. It's a lot. Like six times what I stole from you. You can have it all, but you have to wait until

Zoe turns twenty-one. That's when she gets access to the entire trust. In the meantime, a monthly income will go into her bank account. It's not much for the club but you can use it to feed and clothe her. Make sure she's in good health. And then after her twenty-first birthday, you can empty the trust and send Zoe away. Just please don't hurt her."

Brian starts sobbing again and Rocco and I stare at each other trying to wrap our heads around this information.

"It's a good deal, except for one thing." Rocco snarls, and Brian stutters.

"W-what?"

"We need fucking money now, Miller. We have mouths to feed. Children to educate. We aren't just a pack of thugs. The money you stole wasn't just mine. It's the entire club's."

"I-I... sell my house. Everything we own. Sell it and take the money. There's about eight thousand in Zoe's bank account right now. Take that and I will try to get some more money to you soon."

"Eight fucking grand won't go far Miller," I add and Brian sobs again.

"Please. That's all I can offer."

"I need evidence," Rocco snaps. "You'll understand we can't exactly take your word for it."

"I can email you a copy of the will and trust deeds now. Plus the bank records that show the balance. I can't touch any of it. Astrid made sure of that, but in less than three years, Zoe can."

"Send them through," Rocco hisses, glaring at the phone like he's ready to smash it to pieces.

"O-okay," Brian mutters, and we wait quietly while he does that.

Rocco doesn't have to say anything for me to know how he's feeling about this. Six times what we had in our account is a lot of fucking money, but we have to wait three fucking years to get it.

"It's sent." Brian's voice draws our attention again, and Rocco opens his phone email, waiting for the files to come in.

A moment later, Rocco angles his phone screen towards me, and we do a quick read through of the will, and trust deeds before confirming that the trust account has more money than we could have ever hoped to have.

"Everything looks legit," Rocco grumbles.

"So, do we have a deal? You'll keep her safe? You won't let the Reapers get her, and you won't turn her into a pass around?"

Rocco chuckles. "I don't think you have that much fucking bargaining power Miller. You were the one that fucking stole from us. You owe us big time. Zoe's services will do the job until we can access the trust."

"What? No! Please don't do that."

"It's either that or we revert to the original plan. You decide." Rocco deadpans and Brian sobs.

"F-fine. Just p-please treat her r-right. She's innocent in a-all this."

"Oh, don't worry." I interject. "I'll take good care of your little princess."

"You'd better find us some more money if you want to live to see your daughter walk away in one piece from us in three fucking years, Miller."

"Yes. O-of course."

Rocco hangs up then, no longer patient enough to deal with Brian's sobbing.

"Fucking idiot thinks we have a deal that somehow sees him still fucking breathing," Rocco snaps, slipping Zoe's phone into his pocket. "The only freedom coming his way is the freedom you get from dying. Keep a team looking for him. I'm not done with that prick yet."

"What about Zoe?" I ask, and Rocco sighs, raking a hand over his head.

"She belongs to the club now, but I don't want her to be a pass around or a Cruz Cunt. Miller was right when he said she's innocent in all this, but the idiot never thought that perhaps because of Zoe's connection to the man that stole from the club that she will be a target. Bringing her in isn't going to sit well with some, especially if we don't allow them to get their claws into her."

"You're right. She isn't safe with us either."

Fuck. The thought makes me feel sick. I don't fucking know why. Perhaps because she has lost so much already, and now she's basically been gifted to an MC.

Rocco stares at me for the longest time, and I shift from foot to foot as uneasiness seeps into my gut.

"It needs to be you."

"What?" My brows hitch at Rocco's words. What the fuck has to be me?

"You need to be the one protecting her."

"The fuck man! I'm not fucking babysitting the brat!"

Rocco chuckles. "Why not? Isn't that what you've been doing before all this? Babysitting her. Playing with her? Don't act like you don't enjoy tormenting her."

"I never said I don't enjoy tormenting her. But three fucking years, man. I can't fucking babysit her for three fucking years."

Rocco shrugs. "It's either that or you stand back and let them have their way with her however they see fit."

I growl, my fists balling at my sides as red starts to tint my vision.

"That's what I thought." Rocco chuckles. "At least for now until things settle down, the brat belongs to you. Let's make that clear so the guys keep their distance. And in the meantime, we need to get our lawyer to help us sell the Miller house and get the money."

I nod, not liking this one fucking bit.

Zoe Miller just went from a plaything for me to torment, to a thing I need to fucking protect. There goes all my fucking fun.

15

Zoe

Like sharks smelling blood, the Cruz Kings circle me as soon as we arrive at the clubhouse. The not-so welcome committee of twenty or so people, all scowl at me with anger and something akin to hate in their eyes. One even spits in my direction.

"Why the fuck is she here?" a woman gripes, glaring daggers at me like anyone could have any doubt as to whom she's speaking about.

Even though their words slice through me, I do my fucking best to hold my head high while wearing an expression of indifference.

Don't let them see.
Don't let them see.
Don't let them see.

I mentally repeat the words like a fucking chant.

"Yeah, we don't want her here." Another whines.

The women all make derogatory comments, calling me every dirty name under the sun. Some red-headed bitch looks me straight in the eyes while slowly, dramatically, moving her index finger across her throat.

Jesus fucking Christ.

For some reason, I get the urge to laugh at the absurdity of it all. Luckily I'm smart enough to lock that shit down. If someone bothered to ask me, I'd agree with the women. I don't want to be here either. Then again, I'm pretty sure I've been brought here to be killed.

I'm scared, of course I am. And it's not like I don't feel the emotion, I just don't have anymore fucks to give.

No one is going to come for me, dad proved that when he didn't show up to swap places with me.

A person can only give so much before numbness starts setting in, and I'm at the end of my fucking tether. The worst has already happened, so I don't even know why I can still feel fear and mortification. There's nothing more that can be taken from me. My soul is already broken—shattered into a million pieces that can never be put back together.

Moving my gaze across the onlookers, my eyes fall on the woman I saw at the funeral. This time there's no kindness on her face. Her expression is one of hardness, and in her eyes is the promise of retribution. I want to tell her to do her worst. Since I don't think she needs the prompt, I look away without saying anything.

"Enough!" the woman's voice slices through the noise.

"Come on, Mama C. Can't she just go into the hole so we don't have to look at her?"

Another snickers. "Yeah, it's not like she'll want to be around people like us, anyway."

TEMPTED BY A KING

A smile splays across Mama C's lips before she schools her expression and looks at the two women who spoke up.

"That's enough. Get the fuck back to manning the bar. Once your shift is over, you come find me." There's a finality in her tone making it clear she's in charge.

"But Mama—"

She lifts her hand, which is enough to silence the one who wanted to argue.

"Not. Another. Word."

Shit, Mama C knows how to land a punch with her words alone. I'm in awe of the respect her mere presence commands.

Now that she's made it clear that there's nothing more to be said, the women disperse and go back to their duties. My eyes follow them, and it's only now I'm paying attention to what they're wearing.

My breath hitches as I take in their barely there clothes. One of the women, a pretty redhead, is wearing a pair of knee-high leather boots, latex booty shorts that show the bottom half of her buttocks, and a see-through fishnet tee over her black bra.

The other one serving a pint of beer next to her, is in a similar outfit. With the exception of wearing a skirt instead of shorts. My eyes narrow as I realize the clothes Grayson forced me into the other day are very similar to what these women are wearing.

Lord give me fucking strength. I'm nothing like these women, and no amount of clothes will ever change that. For one, they actually look happy. For two, they have each other. And lastly... they're fucking free.

Missing nothing, Grayson smirks, "Those are the Cruz Cunts."

My brows furrow at the name. Did he really just call them cunts?

As though he can read my mind, he clarifies. "The Cruz Cunts are the women who hang around here. They live and work here. Unlike you, they're actually worth something. Do you know why?"

Since I don't want to answer his question, I bite down on the inside of my cheek. The pain momentarily distracts me from the hate that's emanating from everyone in the room.

When I take too long to say anything, Grayson wraps his hand around my hair and pulls until I'm forced to look up. His almost black eyes sear into my blue ones. I shiver from the nothingness and anger in his orbs. It shouldn't even be possible to portray both, yet he manages perfectly, and it chills me to the marrow of my bones.

"What's the matter, Princess? Cat got your tongue?" Grayson sneers.

I shake my head as much as his grip allows me to move.

"Then fucking answer me."

Something stirs in my chest, and as soon as I recognize the feeling, I wish it would dissipate. Hope is a dangerous thing. But Grayson wouldn't have any reason to ask me questions and show his dominance if he was going to kill me, would he?

"No. I don't know why they're worth something," I whisper.

The words burn like acid in my throat. As fellow human beings they're automatically worth something. I should have said that instead of making it sound as though I need a reason to... value them.

One of the women scoffs loudly enough for me to hear it. "I don't have a gag reflex. Makes me pretty fucking worthy."

"Sure does, honey," one of the men laughs.

Grayson's chuckle is low, dark, and so fucking sexy.

Ahh, no. No, I need to stop thinking about the sinfully hot package this devil is wrapped in. Grayson's sexy exterior doesn't make up for his rotten interior. Not by a long shot.

"Because," he says, dragging the word out and tightening his hold on my hair. "Around here, you fucking earn your keep, Princess. Nothing is free."

By now we've gathered an even bigger crowd, I can hear their amused snickers and scathing whispers all too clearly. I try to look around, but Grayson's hold on my hair restricts my movement. Though, not enough to avoid seeing the angry looks on the Cruz Kings' faces.

Fuck.

If looks could kill, I'd be nothing but a pile of ashes from the fury burning in their eyes. Their hostility is rolling off them in waves, threatening to consume me whole. I loathe to admit that it scares me, which is why I'm not fighting Grayson.

Being humiliated by him like this hurts my pride, but that's a small price to pay for the miniscule semblance of safety his proximity gives me. Or maybe I'm merely hoping he's going to keep me safe.

The truth is that I have no idea what's going to happen to me. I don't know why I'm here instead of back home. All I know is that dad didn't show up, instead opting to leave me at the mercy of the very men who now look like they're eager to take a bite out of me.

As sick as it is, a part of me is glad I'm not left on my own. I know the second my head isn't spinning, preoccupied with other things, I'll succumb to the hurt of dad leaving me to these fucking vipers without a care in the world. But for now, my fear is overshadowing the lingering pain. Talk about going from bad to worse.

"I-I can work." I lick my dry lips and clear my throat.

The hope in my chest goes from stirring to fluttering. Yes, maybe that's it. If I can prove myself useful, I might get to live.

Grayson throws his head back and lets out a roaring laugh. "Did you hear that, guys? The princess wants to work."

Trepidation and fear causes me to shake, my legs damn near buckling at the sound. He just said I had to earn my keep, and I can. I'm not useless. I can cook, clean... I can... oh, fuck. Fuck. It's only now dawning on me what he's hinting at.

Fighting his grip, I shake my head, grinding my teeth as it feels like my hair is about to be yanked out by the root.

"Not that," I hiss. "I-I—"

Grayson interrupts me with a growl. "You'll do whatever the fuck we tell you to, Princess. There's a debt that needs to be paid."

When the onlookers don't just voice their agreement, but also suggest lewd ways for me to repay what my dad stole, Grayson tells them all to fuck off.

After releasing my hair, he drags me to the back of the property where we walk up seventeen creaking stairs—yeah, I'm counting. It helps keep my mind off the things I actively avoid thinking about.

Upstairs we're met by a corridor with six doors, three on each side of the hall. I curiously eye the doors we pass on our way, but Grayson is in too much of a rush to let me get a proper look at anything. Once we reach the end of the hall, he pulls a key from his jeans pocket and unlocks the door.

Without a word, he shoves me inside. My foot catches on some clothes on the floor, and I stagger to regain my balance. My arms shoot out in front of me, and I accidentally knock something off a shelf. My breath hitches as I turn around just in time to see the cup shatter on the floor.

"Fuck's sake," Grayson growls. "That was my favorite cup."

My eyes dart up to his face. I can't tell if he's serious or not.

"R-really?" I stammer.

He rolls his eyes and mutters something unintelligible under his breath. If I were to guess, my money is on him cursing me out for merely existing.

The thing is, I can't even blame him for his hostility towards me. My dad has stolen from his club. I might not know a lot about what it means to be in an MC, but I know never to cross them. Now, my family has done just that. And I'm the sacrificial lamb—I just wish I knew if I'm here for the slaughter, or to... I don't even know if there are any other options.

Even though I get the club's dislike of me, my understanding only goes so far. I've never personally done anything to Grayson, yet he goes out of his way to hurt and humiliate me. So even though it might be horror movie stupid, I can't keep my mouth shut.

"What exactly is your problem with me?" I hiss.

Grayson smirks and rakes a hand through his tight curls. "You're fucking kidding me, right? You might be stupid, but you're not dumb, Princess. You know what my issue with you is."

I shake my head. "I don't, actually. Whatever it is, it started before my dad... well, before he did what he did."

Even though it makes no sense, I refuse to speak the words out loud. It's not like it changes anything to skirt around what he's done, yet it seems like it'll be real the second I speak the words. And I'm not ready for that yet.

Denial isn't as bad as I used to think. As a matter of fact, I think it's going to be my new lifestyle. At least, if I actually have any life to live.

"Where do you want me to begin?" Grayson asks as he slowly stalks towards me. "You walk around acting like your shit doesn't stink. Like everyone is fucking beneath you. Do you even care about anyone but yourself?"

His heated words cause me to flinch back. They're too close to the thoughts I've had myself, and I don't like that. I know I'm not a good person. I know Leslie was the good one. Self reflection is a bitch, one I've avoided for most of my life. But look at where that's got me. I took my family for granted, something I'll never do again.

Then there's the small matter of my dad fucking giving me up. Surely, he wouldn't do that if he actually loved and cared for me. So yes, I know I'm worthless. I don't need Grayson or anyone else to spell it out for me.

If I'm ever free... no. Not if. When... when I'm free again, I'll never waste a second. I'll do the cliché things like dance in the rain, and ride so many rollercoasters I throw up. In other words, I'll live life to the fullest.

Without saying anything else, Grayson disappears into another room, and when I hear the toilet flush, I'm guessing it's the bathroom.

The first thing I notice when he reemerges is that he's changed his tee. Instead of the black one he wore before, it's now a dark green one stretched across his impressive chest.

"What are you going to do with me?" I ask when he sits down on the queen sized bed.

"Don't know yet," he answers gruffly.

What kind of fucking answer is that?

I know I'm pushing my luck, but I can't leave it alone. I have to know what the Cruz Kings are planning.

"A-are you going to kill me?" My voice cracks.

Grayson cocks his head to the side while penetrating me with his dark, smoldering eyes. "Does my answer matter to you?"

There's no menace in his tone, only curiosity.

My breath hitches, and a shiver of something I can't put my finger on runs down my spine.

"Yes," I breathe. "I want to know."

The way he slowly nods has me wondering if he understands more than he lets on. Maybe he truly does see and get the turmoil inside me. I want to snort at those stupid thoughts because there's no way he can when I'm not even sure I fully get it... get me.

My thoughts and feelings are all over the place. One minute I'm numb, the next I'm angry. Then I'm indifferent, sad, desperate... well, that's it, really. I refuse to acknowledge the flutter of hope I felt earlier.

"I'm not going to kill you, Princess."

Rather than sighing in relief, I wait for the 'but' that's sure to follow. His tone and facial expression are much too grim for good news.

Grayson straightens and licks his lips. "I won't lie to you. Staying here isn't in your best interest—"

"So why am I here?" I ask, interrupting him.

"Why the fuck do you think you're here?" he explodes. "You're here because your dad has proven himself to be a spineless, lying, fucking coward. So Rocco wants you here where we can keep an eye on you."

I sag with relief, which I know is odd considering his words. But I've heard what he isn't saying. If Rocco thinks I'm an asset, they'll keep me safe. And if my safety is guaranteed, then maybe one day I will get to dance in the rain.

Grayson scowls as he notices the change in my mood. Unease grows inside me, tamping down the relief I just felt. I just can't catch a fucking break here.

"What?" I hiss, intending on getting him to tell me everything.

He narrows his eyes, studying me leisurely. His dark gaze takes everything in from my shoes to the top of my head. A calculated smile splays across his lips and mirth dances in his eyes. I'm pretty sure whatever is going through his head doesn't bode well for me.

"Here's the thing. You saw how people reacted to having you here, and you heard what I had to say. I wasn't lying when I said everyone has to earn their keep, and in your case, I don't think I need to spell out what the men will want from you."

I unconsciously take a step backwards not liking the bite in his tone.

"No," I growl. "I'm not going to whore myself out for my dad's sins. I have money, Grayson. I have almost twelve grand. I know it isn't much but..."

He arches a dark eyebrow. "Twelve? Your dad said eight. Show me," he demands.

Out of habit, I reach for my phone in my back pocket. Only when it's not there do I remember I haven't had it since dad ran away the night of the funeral.

"I need my phone," I deadpan. "Or a computer so I can log into my online bank."

Grayson chuckles. "How stupid do you think I am? You don't need either of those. Tomorrow we'll go to the bank and withdraw the money."

I nod eagerly. "Is that... I mean, will that be enough money to buy my safety?"

With a huff, he moves past me, only pausing when he's opened the door. "No, Princess. Because the only one who can give you the safety you want, is me. And I'm not interested in your money."

"So what do you want?"

I scream in exasperation when he just smirks before slamming the door. Then I scream at the door as he locks it from the outside.

I fucking hate Grayson Black.

16

Zoe

Restlessness is the reason I bend down and carefully gather the shattered parts of the porcelain cup I accidentally knocked over. I carefully study the pieces, most of which are big. Then I try to stack them, but of course they fall apart all over again. If I'm to have any hope of saving this—favorite or not—I need some glue.

After looking through the... apartment slash room twice, there's no glue to be found. I've found lube, crusty socks, dirty plates, and food I'm surprised hasn't managed to crawl out of here by itself yet. But no fucking glue.

The place is nice, kinda. I mean, it's a pigsty, but I wouldn't expect differently from Grayson. He's the kind of guy who seems to think room hygiene is beneath him. Now, his personal hygiene is a different story. Even when he's sweaty, he smells of... nope. Not going there.

Unwilling to give up completely on the project, I place the broken pieces of the cup on one of the few plates I found. Then, because I have nothing better to do, I start tidying up.

I gather all the obviously dirty clothes in one pile, fold the clean stuff, and place everything in between in a maybe pile. Afterwards, I change the sheets, throwing the dirty stuff on top of the correct pile.

By the time I make it to the kitchenette, I find myself humming the Ghostbuster theme song while filling the sink. Christ, who knew that domestic chores are good for the mood. I sure as fuck didn't. But when I'm done washing and scrubbing, I'm actually singing the words out loud while drying the cutlery with the tea towel I found in one of the drawers.

When I go to put the plates away I realize I've done things in the wrong order. The cupboards are so dirty I can trace the pattern left after running a finger over the darkened surface.

"Fucking pig," I mumble with zero heat.

I quickly empty all the cupboards and drawers, and after rummaging around under the sink, I'm armed with lemon scented cleaning products and rubber gloves.

"Take that!"

I talk to myself while aiming the nozzle at the surface in front of me. As I wash down one thing after another, I'm wondering if I've missed my calling as a cleaning lady. Maybe I'm getting high on the cleaning fumes, but there's something fulfilling about the menial task.

The way the dirt and grime disappears in front of me is satisfying, and when every drawer, shelf, and cupboard shines spotlessly, I feel like I've just cleaned my future.

I'm not happy about my current situation, far from it. I guess I'm just no longer feeling as hopeless. All I need to do is find a way to help, like I'm doing right now. I'm not naïve enough to believe I can clean my dad's debt away with a few squirts from a cleaning bottle. But maybe I can help by giving my monthly allowance from mom's trust to the Cruz Kings.

"That's it," I say excitedly.

Harvard is fully paid for. Maybe if I explain my idea to Grayson and Rocco, they'll allow me to call the administration office. I need to find out if a meal plan and dorm has been included. If not, I'll get a job to pay for it. That way, every cent can go towards paying the MC.

And in the meantime, I'll offer to work at the bar, clean... anything. Hell, I'll even donate all my clothes to the... my nose scrunches in distaste at the name for the women here. Cruz Cunts. It's crude and derogatory. But whatever—they can still have all my stuff. Clothes, shoes, bags, purses, wallets, makeup, perfumes.

I'm so excited by my newfound positive outlook, that I'm eager to run downstairs right away. Except, I'm locked in. I refuse to let that temper my spirit. Rather than sulking, I walk over to the dresser and rummage through it until I find a pair of boxers, and a black tee that looks big enough that I can use it as a dress.

Then I head for the bathroom, which, ironically, is a lot cleaner than I am. The room is small, quaint even. Tiles line the floor and walls, and everything from the toilet to the overfilled laundry basket is white. It's a shame there's no washing machine here, or I could get started on that mountain as well.

As I shower, I'm wondering if this is really where Grayson lives. Even though I have no obvious reason to think differently, there's something about the small place that just doesn't fit him. I could just be overthinking it, though. Just because I've never seen him dressed sloppy, doesn't mean he can't be a slob in his home.

I wonder who else lives up here. Obviously there weren't enough doors in the hall for all the Cruz Kings, but there might be more rooms elsewhere. It strikes me as odd if they all live here. The place just doesn't seem big enough to house all of them and the Cruz Cunts.

While washing the soap off my body, I relish in the fact I'm alone for this intimate act, a luxury I've definitely missed.

Once I'm done I use Grayson's towel to dry myself before I get dressed in his boxers and tee. Since I don't have a spare bra, I put the same one on again before I leave the bathroom.

Entering the main room, I freeze as I hear the lock click. I turn expectantly towards the door, but no one comes in. Huh, that doesn't make any sense. I wait for what feels like forever, but Grayson doesn't enter.

My stomach chooses now of all times to let out an embarrassingly loud growl, reminding me I haven't eaten all day. That could be why Grayson came to let me out, and if that's the case, I shouldn't make him wait.

I only hesitate briefly, but I tell myself I'm being stupid. He wouldn't unlock the door if it wasn't safe here.

Earlier I almost bought his indifference regarding my safety, but now that I've had time to think, I'm pretty sure it's an act. He might be a fucking jerk, that's not the same as outright putting me in harm's way, though.

I walk over to the door and push the handle down, and sure enough it opens. There is no one else out here, but as I reach the stairs I'm met by the heavy bass from the music playing. It's so loud it's practically making the steps vibrate.

Back downstairs, I discreetly pull the tee further down. It's reaching my mid-thigh, but rode up as I walked down the stairs. My outfit isn't going to win any fashion accolades, but it's clean and covers what needs covering.

Now I wish Grayson had waited for me upstairs, because the tee has the skull with a crown on the back, and I'm not sure the others will be okay with me wearing it. However, I only have to walk through the doors to be where the party is, and how hard can it be to find Grayson and Rocco in there?

I don't make it that far before someone puts their hand on my shoulder and spins me around. I don't recognize the man I come face-to-face with, but his gaze causes gooseflesh to erupt and a shiver works its way down my spine.

"What do we have here?" he slurs. "The Princess all on her own. I'm guessing no one cares about you since VP left you to walk around alone. And in one of our club tees," he tsks condescendingly.

"I-I..." Words fail me.

"Shh you don't need to speak," the man growls.

Before I can react, he slaps his hand over my mouth and forcefully shoves me up against the wall. My back hits the brick with so much force, air is forced out of my lungs, and my head bounces off the unforgiving material.

I try to cry out, but his hand muffles any sound.

"Ahh, such a bad girl. Hasn't VP taught you only to speak when spoken to?" The man gives me a wicked grin.

Stars dance in front of my eyes, but I desperately try to blink them away. As the man moves closer, I lift my knee, intending to hit him in the groin. Anger distorts his scarred face into a scary grimace.

"You fucking bitch," he bellows.

Then he backhands me so hard my head snaps to the side. I try to sink my teeth into his hand so I can scream for help, however, finding purchase is impossible.

The man moves one hand to my throat, squeezing until my vision blurs.

"You're going to fucking regret that you stupid bitch," he roars.

He throws me to the side. As I skid across the floor, I open my mouth to scream, but before I get the chance, the man is on me again. I swing my arms wildly, kicking my feet with all my might.

This man is no stranger to forcing himself on women, the malicious glint in his eyes tells a story I'm not sure his club brothers know. Or maybe they do, it's not like I know them well enough to make an educated guess.

Crawling on top of me, he forces his knees on my arms while firmly planting his ass on my thighs, making it impossible to move.

"Get off me you fucker," I scream before he clamps his hand over my mouth again.

I thrash as one of his hands trails up my exposed thigh, but no matter how hard I fight, I can't get free. When he reaches the top of my leg, I clamp them together like my life depends on it. Sadly, it very well might—or at the very least, my sanity is riding on my ability to stop him from touching me.

Tears stream down my face, and my breathing becomes ragged as I fight with everything I have. But no matter how much I buck, he remains where he is.

His sinister smile stretches from ear to fucking ear as he runs his fingers across my mound.

"Oh, how I'm going to love fucking you." He chuckles to himself. "And if the rumors are true, you're already familiar with Cruz King cock. Is that right, Princess? Do you know how to take a dick like a good girl?"

I freeze in place from his words. Those aren't baseless accusations or wild guesses. The certainty in his eyes makes it clear he's heard about my trysts with Grayson.

Anger and mortification courses through me, giving me extra strength. To think I came down here because I wanted to make things right, and now I'm being fucking assaulted.

The man roars as I finally succeed at sinking my teeth into the meaty part of his hand. I bite until I taste blood, and only then does he let go of my mouth. I don't waste any time, as soon as his hand is gone from my mouth, I scream as loudly as I can.

"Help!"

The words 'I'm being attacked' are on the tip of my tongue, but then I remember a documentary I once watched. At the time it seemed ridiculous, now, however, it might save my life.

"Fire!" I scream. "Help me. The house is on fire."

I barely manage to get the words out before I hear footsteps coming closer. My attacker doesn't seem to have noticed the sound, though. He fists my hair and slams my head down into the concrete twice, before he... disappears.

There's an angry roar, followed by the sound of fists meeting skin.

I stagger to my feet, and without even looking back, I run back up the stairs to Grayson's room where I crawl into the corner behind the bed. From here, I can watch the entrance.

My heart beats wildly in my chest, and it takes me a long time to get my breathing under control. It's then I realize how fucking stupid I was to run back up here. Why didn't I try to leave?

I barely manage to finish my thought before the door is slammed open. I whimper and reach for anything to use as a weapon. My hand closes around a fucking lamp of all things.

"Are you okay, Princess?" Grayson asks frantically.

I stare at him, dumbfounded and confused. "You came," I whisper.

"Princess?"

"You came," I repeat a bit louder.

Grayson holds his hands up as he slowly moves closer. It's almost comical that this man who's responsible for so much of my pain is now acting like he cares.

"Look at me, Princess," he coos.

Why is he saying that when I'm looking right at him? It doesn't make any sense.

I gasp when he touches me, his hand gently cupping my chin.

"You might have a concussion. You need to stay awake, Zoe."

His use of my name causes me to giggle hysterically. I don't even know why I'm laughing, it's not funny. Or maybe it is, I can't tell.

"Look at me."

I do.

"Did he touch you?" Grayson growls.

My vision becomes blurry as more tears fall. "He tried," I admit.

I yelp as Grayson wraps his arms around me and picks me up. With slow steps he walks us over to the worn-out leather couch, where he sits down. When I scramble to get out of his lap, he places his hands on my hips to keep me in place.

"Let me go," I scream, startled by his firmness.

"No," he retorts. "I need to..." He pauses like he's trying to find the words. "Just let me fucking hold you and make sure you're okay."

My fear is forgotten as I laugh. "You don't fucking care about me, Grayson. You've made that abundantly clear at any turn, so why pretend now?"

He completely ignores my question and instead asks one of his own. "Are you hurt?"

I snort. "No more than I was before I came here."

Maybe he's right and I have a concussion. That's the only explanation for thinking he flinches at my words. Grayson doesn't fucking care, so my mind must be playing tricks on me.

"I care," he admits after a lengthy silence.

"No, you don't," I argue.

He chuckles softly. "From one human to another, trust me, Princess. I fucking care." Then he ruins it by adding, "It's my job."

Actually, I take that back. He didn't ruin it, he saved it. Because if he wants me to believe he cares, it would mean he'd been body swapped. That's the only logical explanation.

"I'm fine," I say sourly. "He didn't have time to do anything. I'm not bleeding and no bones are broken. So can I go to sleep now?"

Grayson shakes his head and sighs loudly. "I'm afraid not. As I said, you could have a fucking concussion. Don't you ever listen?"

I can't help smiling at his words. This is the Grayson Black I know and hate.

"Fine," I huff. "Can I get off your lap and go to the bathroom?"

His hands immediately fall away from my hips, and I rush to the bathroom before he changes his mind.

When I return to the room, Grayson has opened every cupboard and drawer in the kitchenette.

"What the hell?" he asks surprised. "Did you... did you fucking clean, Princess?"

I go to nod, but even moving my head a little hurts. So instead, I say, "Yeah. I got bored."

He whistles softly. "Can't say I expected that."

For some reason, the lack of bite in his words rubs me wrong. I need him to say and do stupid shit so I can be mad at him.

"Well, I figured I'd try to butter you up so you don't sell me to the highest bidder," I hiss.

Grayson laughs. "Trust me, Princess. If I gave you to someone, it would be for free. No money would change hands because of your fine ass."

"Fuck you," I spit back.

He makes a show out of adjusting himself. "Right now? Are you sure you're up for it?" he rasps.

My breath gets caught in my throat as I look into his smoldering eyes. No. Yes. Maybe... ahh, fuck. I'm not sure. My nipples strain against the fabric of his tee.

"After all, you are wearing my shirt." He slowly walks towards me. "Normally, only your Old Lady or the Cunt you're fucking wears your clothes. Since you're not my Old Lady, you're the—"

I interrupt him. "Yeah, yeah, you've fucked me. Big fucking whoop. What are you? Twelve? Get over it."

With slow, sauntering steps, Grayson closes the distance between us. Before I can protest, he scoops me into his arms, cradling my head almost reverently against his chest. I wind my legs around his waist while he carries me over to the bed. He gently lies me down while crawling on top of me. He rests on his arms while nudging my legs apart with his knee.

"Tell me if you don't want this, Princess," he rasps.

"I get a choice?" I ask, surprised.

He kisses his way up my neck before biting the shell of my ear. "Tonight you do. I don't trust that he didn't touch you, and I'm sure as fuck not going to take advantage of you."

I'm so surprised by his admission that all I can do is blink.

"Princess," he prompts.

His hand runs down my torso and disappears under his shirt, inching closer to the V of my thighs.

"Tell me to stop," he groans as he reaches my pussy.

I want to say just that, so I'm just as surprised as him when my mouth takes on a life of its own and says, "I want you, Grayson."

A part of me wants to stop him, but as I recall his words from earlier, I quickly decide not to. He didn't want my money in exchange for safety. Surely that means that this is what he wants. I can give him this, my body. As long as it keeps me safe, what does it matter? Using my body is a small price to pay, especially when it's with a man that actually knows what he's doing.

My admission of wanting him seems to awaken something inside Grayson. He immediately fuses our lips together, wasting no time before invading my mouth. While our tongues battle, he rubs my pussy outside the boxers I've borrowed from him, and before long I'm a panting mess.

"Grayson," I cry out as he swirls his finger around my clit. "P-please."

"Tell me what you want, Princess," he rasps.

Words are too hard to form, so I lift my hips instead, trying to get him closer. He takes the hint and dips his hand inside the shorts, immediately cupping my pussy.

"You're so fucking wet," he groans into my mouth.

I whimper as he slides two fingers between my folds, painfully slowly working them inside my cunt. Keeping his lips on mine, he greedily swallows every moan, whimper, and pant leaving me while his fingers move in and out of me.

"Come for me, Princess," he rasps, and fuck, I do.

My entire body tenses, my pussy squeezing his fingers tightly as he curls them, reaching that magic spot inside me.

While he continues to fuck me with his fingers, I move my hands down to his jeans. I quickly undo the button and pull the zipper down, eager to feel him in my hand. With impatient and jerky movements, I push his pants and boxers down. Then I wrap my hand around his hard cock.

"Ah, fuck. Princess."

The rawness of his voice makes me smile.

I tighten my hold until he makes a guttural groan. Swiping my thumb across his slit, I use his pre-cum as lube, spreading it down his hard shaft.

While I work my hand up and down, I try to pull his shirt off with the other. I want him naked. Picking up on what I'm trying to do, Grayson removes his fingers and gets off the bed. I shamelessly watch him rid himself of his clothes, all while drinking in his magnificent body. For all his flaws, not a single one is linked to his body.

"Your turn," he rasps.

After pulling the boxers down my legs, he kisses his way back up. Reaching my pussy, he groans and inhales deeply before licking my sex from top to bottom. I arch my back and try to move my hips closer, needing more of him.

"More," I whimper.

I'm rewarded when he uses his tongue to circle my clit while spearing my cunt with two fingers. His large hands cradle my thighs as he moves my legs over his shoulders.

"Smother me with your thighs, Princess," he rasps.

I cry out when he sucks my clit between his lips, grazing the sensitive nub with his sharp teeth.

"I said," he groans. "Smother me with your fucking thighs."

As my legs clamp shut, squeezing his head, he begins to work me in earnest. His fingers piston in and out of my drenched cunt while his tongue laps at my clit. It doesn't take long before I'm a shaking and screaming mess.

"Grayson... I... I... oh fuck!"

"That's it, Princess. Take what I'm fucking giving you."

He bites my clit again, quickly licking the pain away and within minutes I come on his tongue. My moans and cries are nothing but primal sounds that I didn't even know I could make.

When I come down from my high, Grayson has moved further up the bed, looking down at me with my juices glistening on his chin and cheeks. I can't explain why I reach my finger out and trace the outline of his lips, or why I suck that finger into my mouth to taste myself after. But fuck, the almost feral look in his eyes makes my pussy clench around nothing.

I push myself up and pull the borrowed shirt over my head, discarding it on the floor. His gaze immediately drops to my bra covered tits. As he slowly licks his lips, I shudder in anticipation. Then I move my hands to my back and quickly unclasp the hook, throwing the bra the same way the shirt went.

Reaching for his cock, I close my hand around it again, slowly moving up and down. His eyes roll back as he groans my name and thrusts into my hand.

"If you want me inside you, you best let go," he rasps. "Otherwise my cum will soon be all over your pretty hand."

Without waiting for my answer, he reclaims my lips and slaps my hand away. I feel the crown of his dick as he lines himself up against my core.

"Oh my God," I moan, loving the way he's stretching me as he slowly feeds my pussy his cock.

Grayson is the kind of man who effortlessly commands your full attention, and with him here, the events of tonight are almost forgotten. I don't think about the man who wanted to hurt me, how can I when the Cruz King between my legs is making me see the good kind of stars.

He palms my tits, pinching, plucking, and pulling at my nipples while thrusting into me. I move a hand between us, rubbing my clit while he fucks me. My other hand is on his stomach, loving the way I can feel his muscles contract.

"Fuck. Zoe."

I wrap my legs around his waist, tilting my hips so I can meet him thrust for delicious thrust. The new angle makes it so he can grind his pubic bone against my clit, and I move both my hands to his sculptured ass.

Seriously, poems should be waxed of the pure perfection that is Grayson's ass. Hard, round, and oh so fucking delicious. I almost want to sink my teeth into it.

My body begins to shake as another orgasm teeters on the edge. I'm so close I won't need much to drive me over the edge.

Grayson leans back down, once again fusing our lips together. Kissing him is like... it's unlike any other kiss I've ever experienced. I can feel it in every cell of my body when our tongues are locked in a battle for dominance.

"I'm so fucking close," he pants.

I bite down on his lower lip, not licking the sting away until he hisses out my name. Then I dig my nails further into his ass, spurring him on.

"Oh... fuck... Gray..." I scream as pleasure slams into me like a freight train.

My pussy pulses and squeezes him so hard I force him over the edge with me.

"Princess," he moans into my mouth while ropes of cum paint my insides.

Afterwards he lies down beside me. He softly kisses my cheek before rolling to his back. He's quiet for so long I almost think he's fallen asleep.

"Are you awake?" I ask tentatively.

It's probably stupid of me to ask because if he is sleeping, I won't get an answer. And if he isn't, he might remember he doesn't want me to sleep.

"Mhmm," he replies.

I hate what I'm about to ask, but seeing as what happened tonight, I need to know for sure.

"Now that I gave you... that we've... I mean, that's what you wanted to keep me safe, right?"

The bed dips as he suddenly sits up. "What?" he asks, confused.

I'm so nervous I rush the words out. "Earlier you said you didn't want money for keeping me safe, so I just assumed you wanted my body. But I need to know if what we just did was enough."

Grayson's expression morphs into thinly veiled anger. "Are you telling me you just had sex with me as a payment to be kept safe?"

Incredulity is written all over my face as I look at him. "What the fuck did you expect?" I snap. "You're a fucking piece of shit. I hate you."

"Keep telling yourself that," he huffs.

I continue watching him as he gets out of bed. With angry movements, he pulls his jeans back on and runs a hand through his tousled curls.

"I'm not lying," I shout, angered that he clearly doesn't believe me. "You fucking took my mom's letter. The only thing I had to really remember her by. And you took it and... and..." I angrily swipe at the fresh tears forming and trailing down my cheeks. "So yes, Grayson. I fucking hate you."

For a second he looks taken aback, maybe even ashamed. But the expression morphs into cockiness so quickly I can't be sure I'm right.

"The answer to your question is yes. You just bought yourself one week of my protection."

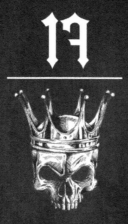

Grayson

Leaving Zoe behind in my shitty apartment has me feeling uneasy while I'm not at the club, but I have work to do, and I can't fucking watch her all the time despite the protection she paid with her body. She's locked in. She can't get out, and no one can get in except for Mama C, who is the only other person aside from Rocco and Gunner that I trust right now, and since the latter two are with me, Mama C is back at the club making sure none of my club brothers, or the Cruz Cunts, even attempt to get to the princess.

"Cain. Good to see you." Rocco nods to the Diamond Crew chapter President before leaning in to give him a half hug, half slap on the back.

"Well, well, well... look what the cat dragged in. You fuckers really are in deep." Cain observes dryly, which doesn't match the gleam in his eyes. He looks almost

excited about our misfortune. Fucker. He turns his attention to me and Gunner. "If it isn't the double G's.
Wish we were meeting under better circumstances, guys.
Like maybe one of those moments that goes on a postcard
reading 'wish you were here'."

I nod. "Me too. Is Dante joining us?"

"Via video call." Cain nods before gesturing to the passage that leads to the back of Dirty Diamonds Strip Club.

We follow behind, ignoring the chicks dancing on stage.
Well Rocco and I do. I'm pretty sure Gunner gets a good
fucking look.

Taking a seat at the small table in the back room, Cain
angles a laptop towards us, and Dante's face appears. The
last time I saw him, he got his niece off in front of us—not
that I knew it was his niece at the time—and even though
that was only around five or six months ago, he looks
different. The mean son of a bitch is actually smiling. I
guess that answers any questions about how he's doing.
Living in nightmare suburbia while playing house seems
to agree with him.

"I didn't think I'd be seeing your ugly mugs so soon."
Dante smirks, and Rocco rolls his eyes before responding.

"How's things in New Jersey? Is Storm keeping you
outta trouble?"

Dante's smirk turns from teasing to almost sinister.
"More like she is *the* trouble. I think sometimes she forgets how fucking old I am."

We all chuckle, while Cain nods, knowingly.

"She hard to keep up with, old man?" I tease. "Is her
youth reminding you of how old you are?"

"Nah. Fuck. More like she makes me feel more alive than ever." Dante admits before cringing. "Although my body aches in places I never thought possible."

"You should take up yoga or something." Gunner snickers and we all laugh.

"Can you imagine that brute in a yoga class?" Cain adds, and Dante frowns.

"Shut up. I'm limber. I could do yoga if I wanted to."

"And I could be a fucking ballet dancer if I wanted to." Cain teases and Dante glares through the screen.

"You're too fucking mean to be graceful."

Cain nods. "A ballet dancer with a ten-inch blade then? I could wear one of those tutu things and point my fucking toes as I kill."

"You've put way too much thought into this." Rocco grumbles, and we all laugh once again before Dante turns serious.

"What have you fuckers gone and gotten yourselves into?" Dante asks, teasingly, his smirk familiar, and fuck, I miss the guy.

Dante is the leader of the Diamond Crew, a gang that he started with his Australian friend and Rocco by his side. Mama C came on earlier as well, and Gunner was only young, his mom joining as one of the crew whores.

My appearance in the club came five years later as a result of Rocco taking me under his wing after my dad was killed in front of me, and my mom went off the rails. I learned how to be a man in the Diamond Crew with Rocco as my mentor and Dante being the man I looked up to like he was a big brother.

Parting ways was a strategic move. The Diamond Crew had grown considerably, having syndicates across the US and another in Briarwood in England, so we broke off to create an MC that links to the Diamond Crew, allowing the empire to expand through different avenues.

"You already know," Rocco rasps, looking nothing but pissed off. "I know you read the messages I sent."

Dante nods. "I gotta be honest. I didn't think the Reapers had the smarts to pull off something like this. Makes me wonder if they've brought in a consultant."

I nod. "I've been wondering the same. And this is obviously something they've been planning for a while. It surprises me that we didn't catch wind of it earlier since they love boasting about themselves so much."

"Agreed." Rocco nods, but doesn't offer any more.

"Rocco, man. I know what you're thinking, and you need to fucking stop," Dante adds. "None of this is your fault, and I know you hate having to ask for help, but this is exactly why we agreed to branch out into other areas. No one knows that the Diamond Crew and the Cruz Kings are affiliated the way we are. We are there for each other to fall back on when times get tough, and this is one of those times, so stop thinking you're asking for a handout, and let me help my mate."

Rocco nods, emotion swirling in his eyes as they dart down to his lap, momentarily showing his vulnerability in this.

"So they cleaned out the whole account?" Cain asks, and I nod.

"Their puppet was the accountant we brought in. Brian Miller." Gunner adds. "I guess he was taking too long to do what they wanted, or recanted on what he agreed to, so the Reapers hit his family, taking out his wife and youngest daughter."

"The oldest one is still alive though, right?" Dante asks and the three of us nod.

"When he still refused to do what they wanted, they threatened her life too, which is when he went ahead and drained our bank account. Then he tried to run," Rocco explains before sighing. "It's a fucking mess."

"So the girl is still with you? The accountant traded his life for hers?" Dante asks having the information already from the messages Rocco sent him.

"She's still with us," I grumble and Cain chuckles.

"And here I thought you were like the pussy whisperer," Cain laughs. "She giving you grief, man?"

"Something like that," I snap and they all chuckle this time.

"So why is she still alive?" Dante asks, and I glance at Rocco wondering why Dante is asking that. Hasn't Rocco shared the part about Zoe's inheritance?

"She's a nice piece of ass. We will keep her until she's no longer useful," Rocco explains and Dante nods, even as he frowns.

"You know where I stand on trafficking. This better not be that."

My brows shoot up, and when I glance at Rocco, his are mimicking mine.

"The fuck, man. You know we aren't into that shit." Rocco hisses. "She's a bargaining chip, and Gray is in charge of protecting her. No one else will so much as touch her."

Dante and Cain both nod, while I feel a little fucking insulted that Dante even suggested we might be into the very shit he's been trying to stop. We were in the Diamond Crew once too. We followed Dante because he's the only motherfucker that has any fucking morals on this side of life we all walk.

"I had to check." Dante offers. "We may be running as different entities these days, but I'd like to think our goals are still the same."

Rocco nods, but doesn't offer our old leader any hint of a smile. "Of course they are. This is why we parted, to divide and conquer."

Dante seems happy with that response, meanwhile I'm still baffled as to why the fuck Rocco didn't tell them about Zoe's inheritance.

I glance at Gunner, who looks none the wiser about any of it and remember that he wasn't around when Brian made the deal with Rocco. He still thinks that Zoe is with us until we can trade her for her low life dad.

"So you need a cash injection, and fast?" Dante asks and Rocco nods.

"Unfortunately."

"Even though we are here for you, I can't just hand over such a large amount and get nothing in return."

Rocco nods again at Dante's words.

"I figured that. What can we do? Want some extra protection? Want us to pick up some runs for you. Help you double your services?"

Dante shakes his head. "Nah, nothing like that."

"Your women." Cain chimes in this time, gaining everyone's attention. "We are short staffed here at the club. We need some fresh meat on stage and in the booths. Give us some girls to roster until you can pay back the loan."

"You want our Cruz Cunts on your stage?" Rocco asks and Cain and Dante nod.

"And in the booths." Dante reminds us and I frown.

"We don't whore our girls out."

"Well, we need flesh in those booths. The girls will get paid good money to work the booths on top of the tips they get from the poles. And when word gets around that they are on my stage, we will get more horny fuckers coming in. So it's a win win. We get more business and the girls get paid."

Gunner and I share a look while Rocco remains impassive.

"Deal," he says before standing. "We appreciate your help."

Dante nods, and Cain stands too.

"I'll have the money transferred into your account within the hour."

"Please tell me you've changed the passwords so Brian can't steal more fucking money."

Rocco grins this time. "Yes, of course we have. Thanks, man."

We say our goodbyes, and as we leave the club, I can't help but feel unsettled.

Firstly, Rocco kept a huge fucking secret from Dante, and secondly, Mama C is going to fucking flip when she finds out we agreed to have the Cruz Cunts offer services in the booths.

When we get back to the club, the men are in party mode, fucking drinking down beer like we have plenty of fucking money to buy more, while the Cruz Cunts get spit-roasted, with Slasher and Slayer seeing which girl they can make gag first with their cocks down their throats.

Jesus fucking Christ, I'm exhausted.

Rocco disappears to his apartment, so I decide to do the same, my mind on Zoe, but I stop in my tracks when I notice Gunner frowning at me.

"What's up?"

He shrugs. "You going to see Princess?"

I nod. "Yeah, I wanna make sure she hasn't trashed my apartment." I lie.

Gunner nods. "You want company?"

I don't know what it is, but knowing the only reason he wants to come with me is to see Zoe, fucking pisses me off.

"You wanna see her?" I ask, and he hesitates, his hands shove in the pockets of his jeans which looks fucking ridiculous with the bush blond beard that makes him look tough as shit.

"I guess. Not much else to do."

Fuck. I don't want him in my apartment with Zoe. I don't fucking know why other than I want her sweet cunt to myself.

"If she's awake, I'll send her out to find you." I lie again, because fuck, I'm not sending her out. If she's awake, then she's going to be busy on her knees.

Even as I think it I realize I'm fucking lying to myself now. I'm too exhausted to fight with Zoe. The push and pull we have is fun, but fuck, I just want it to be easy for once.

My eyes dart to the Cruz Cunts. They are easy. I'd only have to snap my fingers and three of them would come and service me at once.

So why aren't I doing that?

"Yeah. Okay. Thanks man." Gunner nods, and I can tell by the way this beard shifts that he's smiling under it.

Jesus. I'm a fucking prick lying to him like that.

Turning my back on my buddy, I ignore anyone that calls out to me, trying to gain my attention, and make my way to my apartment.

Stepping inside, I can tell Zoe has been cleaning again. I can't say I hate it. I've never had anyone clean for me since leaving my mom when I was fifteen. It's nice to have no clutter, and it no longer smells musty like it did.

No.

Now it smells like her.

Fuck.

My dick is instantly hard, so I go in search of what I need, finding her curled up in my bed, sound asleep.

I strip immediately, leaving my clothes in a pile before I slip under the covers and press myself to Zoe's back, spooning her.

She's wearing my t-shirt again, and fuck I love that she wears it. I don't fucking know why. There's just something really hot about a chick wearing my clothes.

Of course if one of the Cruz Cunts wore my shit, I'd fucking flip, but I'm not going to bother reading too much into it right now.

As I pull her back, pressing my dick into the valley of her short covered ass, I snake my hand around to her front until I'm pressing my fingers to her core before slipping them under the fabric.

It's hot between her legs, and I don't mess around with taking it slow or gentle, because she will wake up soon, and when she does, she's going to be as ravenous as I am to sate this need.

I cup her pussy while sliding my other arm under her, shifting her so her legs fall open.

"Gray?" She breathes, half asleep, and I nip her ear, loving that she calls me that instead of my full name as I inhale her sweet scent as my free hand cups her tit.

"Shhhh." I whisper, "Go back to sleep."

She nods gently before falling lax again, and I wait a few long drawn out moments before I start working on her clit again.

She's so fucking drenched, her pussy primed already, so I quickly toss off the sheets to give me a better view and pull up my t-shirt that's hiding her creamy flesh before I work the leg of the fabric aside, guiding my straining cock to her heat.

Hitching her leg up on mine, I part her enough to get the access I need, and then slowly sink inside her.

Another small moan escapes her, and I return my fingers to her clit, as I slowly ease my cock in and out of her. I've never fucked so slowly before, or so gently, but fuck, there's something teasingly satisfying about doing it this way.

Zoe's chest pushes forward as I tweak her nipple, and I kiss her neck as I look down the front of her body. She's fucking perfect. Her creamy skin is flawless and her tits are just the right size, while her cunt is nothing but heaven.

The slow teasing strokes work me up quickly, and I can feel Zoe's hips moving every now and then, enjoying the ride.

"Come for me," I whisper in her ear while picking up the pace of my fingers, and just like I commanded, she shatters around my dick.

I rub faster on her clit, creating good friction, trying to draw out her climax, and as I do, her slickness turns into a small gush, right before my nuts tighten and a tingle rushes over me as I come hard.

A whimper escapes Zoe as I keep working on her clit, and a moment later she convulses around my cock for a second time.

Fuck. That was different, but good, and all I know as I let the exhaustion of the last few weeks catch up with me is that right now, there's no other place I'd want to be.

18

Grayson

Ducking quickly as a glass narrowly misses my head, I shut the door to the back room usually used for closed door parties and poker, and take stock of the situation.

"What the fuck were you thinking?" Mama C hisses as she stalks towards Rocco, who for the most part looks calm about the tornado coming his way. "Why the hell would you agree to that?"

"Cara, honey. I didn't have much of a choice." Rocco takes a step back as she nears, finally showing that he's still fucking pussy whipped by this queen.

"Oh, no, Rochus," she scoffs as she points a claw-like nail to his chest, using his full name. "Don't pretend like you even fought hard to take the booth services off the table. You fucking agreed to my girls not only stripping, but providing services in the fucking Dirty Diamonds booths?!"

"Can I say something?" I ask, and they both swing their furious glares my way.

"NO!" They yell in unison, and I have to bite the inside of my cheek to hold back my grin.

These two were fucking made for each other.

"Well, I'm going to anyway, if for no other reason than to prevent a bloodbath. I'm too fucking tired to clean that up."

Mama C finally cracks a smirk.

"We gotta play nice with Dante and Cain if we want the handout. Nothing is for free, and unless we can figure out something else, it's the quickest way to get a cash injection."

"Think of a different way!" Mama C turns her snarl to me. "I'm fine with them dancing on stage. They'll like that part, but I'm not asking them to go into the booths for free."

My brows hitch and I lock eyes with Rocco who looks fucking exhausted. "You didn't tell her?"

"She hasn't exactly let me finish telling her the ins and outs of it." He sighs, and Mama cocks her hip and crosses her arms over her chest.

"Tell me what?"

"The girls get paid for booth services plus the tips from the poles. So they'll walk out with their own cash to do with as they please." I advise and her frown deepens.

"It's still whoring, Grayson. You can wrap it up and put a fucking bow on it all you like, but it's still asking them to whore."

"Have you considered that perhaps they might be happy to do that?" Rocco interjects and wins himself another death glare.

TEMPTED BY A KING

"I hope you like fucking your hand, Rochus, because that's the only way you're going to be getting yourself off from now on." Mama deadpans and Rocco's face falls while I smother my laugh with my hand.

"Shut the fuck up," Rocco hisses at me, and I suck my lips in, holding my hands up in surrender.

"Don't take this out on Gray. You're the fucking president. You call the shots around here. This is on you." Mama reminds him and he turns a heated glare at his woman.

He's never claimed her as his Old Lady, and Cara has never wanted to be that, but for the most part, they are together. It's been that way ever since I can remember.

"That's right. I am the fucking president. Perhaps you have forgotten your place?"

Oh shit.

Rocco just went there.

I'm not a fucking idiot.

That's cue for me to fucking leave.

Backing up as they glare at each other, chests rising and falling with heavy breaths, I can see that they are moments away from that bloodbath I was afraid of earlier, or, a fucking porn scene.

I make it out the door just in time to hear one of the poker tables get upended.

"What the hell is going on in there?" Slasher asks as I press my back to the door.

"It's hard to tell. Could be a murder scene." I chuckle and he grins.

"A murder scene after she fucks him senseless." Slasher grins and I nod.

"Most likely."

The heavy beat of music coming from the main club-room meets my ears and I look past Slasher down the hallway to overhear Beth, one of our younger Cruz Cunts make a remark about Zoe.

"I guess living the rich life teaches them how to make cocktails. Has anyone told the bitch that we don't bother with those frilly drinks here? We only like the hard stuff."

Slasher stiffens, overhearing Beth's words too, and his lips thin.

"Want me to shut her up by sticking my cock in her mouth?"

I shake my head, my mind going back to that night so many weeks ago when Gunner suggested shutting Zoe up the same way. That's when it all began, this fucking obsession with messing with her. Making her bend to my will. Forcing her to feel the pleasure I can milk from her.

"Is Zoe in the clubroom?" I ask, changing the subject before I let Beth's words piss me off too much.

"Yeah. Gunner is showing her how to work behind the bar."

Fucking Gunner. I asked him to watch her for like five minutes in my room, and he goes and brings her out into the lion's den where everyone wants a bite of her.

"He put her behind the bar?" I ask to clarify, and Slash-er nods.

"She's trying to teach Tex how to make cocktails."

My brows hitch. "And how fucking well is Tex taking that?"

Tex refuses to let any of the guys behind the bar, and only on occasion lets a few select Cruz Cunts invade his space, so the fact that Zoe is behind the bar and is still breathing must mean he likes her.

Fuck.

No matter how pissed any of my club brothers are that Zoe's dad is the reason why we are all strapped for cash, they will still want a piece of her. A piece I don't want them to fucking touch.

Pushing past Slasher and ignoring the loud moaning coming from the back room, I make my way into the main room, my eyes going straight to the bar that lines the far wall, to the blonde goddess that looks very fucking out of place here surrounded by dirty bikers and Cruz Cunts that are barely wearing any fucking clothing.

To my surprise, Zoe is teaching Tex how to make some sort of concoction, and he's listening attentively, not staring at her the way the others are. Gunner is sitting at the bar sipping on some sort of purple liquid in a fucking cocktail glass. I didn't even know we had glasses like that here.

"She may not be everyone's favorite person right now, but she certainly demands attention just by being in the room," Slasher says from behind me just as another crash sounds from the back room.

I nod. "Yeah. Too much fucking attention."

Slasher chuckles, brushing past me. "If she's going to be around, you'd better get used to it."

I grunt in response, staying at the mouth of the hallway to stop anyone else from going back there should they try. Not that a Mama C and Rocco clash doesn't happen publicly on occasion, but there's no need for onlookers if everyone is currently none the wiser.

I lean my shoulder against the wall, watching the room as the Cruz Cunts get up to their typical antics, and my club brothers take full advantage of it.

When Sasha, Rose and Alana drop to their knees in a row, I subtly cast my gaze across the room to see if Princess is aware of what's about to happen. She's busy explaining something to Tex when the cheers in the middle of the room draw their attention, and I watch as her blue eyes widen right before her cheeks redden and those plump lips part.

I can imagine a small gasp falling from those fuckable lips, and I bet if I were to slide my hand into her panties, she'd be wet.

As if she's known I've been standing here the whole time, Zoe's gaze darts to mine, and I can't hold back my smirk, knowing how uncomfortable she must be right now. Then I gesture my head to where Munroe, Stretch, and Titch have their dicks buried deep in Cruz Cunt mouths.

This time Zoe's eyes widen with disdain at my invitation to join the group in the center of the room, and I throw my head back laughing, knowing how much that would freak her out.

Hell, I would have been shocked if she agreed to it. Not sure what the fuck I would have done then since I really don't like the idea of these horny fuckers seeing her like that.

It's one thing to know Gunner watched that time at the pool house, but now, something has changed.

I'm not sure why. Probably because she's been through so much already.

Who fucking knows, but the idea doesn't sit well with me.

I realize then, that all has fallen quiet in the back room, and a moment later I hear the door swing open and turn to see Mama C strutting towards me.

"Who won?" I snicker as she passes me, but I still see her eye roll. She doesn't stop, beelining for the bar.

I guess fighting and fucking can make a woman thirsty.

"She's gonna put the offer to the girls about the booths," Rocco mumbles as he comes to stand next to me, still doing his fucking fly up. "She won't make them, but if they want to, then that's their prerogative."

Tilting my head towards my Prez, I raise a brow. "What if none of them want to?"

He shrugs. "Then I guess we need to start recruiting new Cunts that will happily offer that service for them."

"If that's the case, are you gonna toss the current girls?"

He shakes his head, his dark gaze meeting mine this time. "Nah. They're club property. We look after what's ours."

I nod in agreement, happy to know our honor code is still intact.

"The Miller girl has certainly stirred everyone up," Rocco gestures his head towards the bar. "Have you told her that her old man gave her to us?"

I shake my head. "Nah. Not something she needs to know right now."

"I agree. In fact, if we need to keep her around and fucking alive for the next three or so years, we may need to consider how the fuck we can keep her here without her feeling like a prisoner, otherwise those three years are going to feel really fucking long."

I turn fully towards Rocco now, curious as to where he's going with this.

"You and Gunner had a bet going before the attack on her family, didn't you?"

"Yeah." I nod. "How the fuck do you know about that?"

Rocco chuckles. "Gunner was drunk and told Tex one night. I believe the bet was to see if you could get her to fall for you."

Fucking Gunner. When the hell did this even happen?

"I would have fucking won too. But then her mom and sister got killed, and priorities changed."

Rocco nods. "Well, change them back again."

I flinch back like the fucker just slapped me. "What?!"

"Let's be honest. She gets wet over you no matter how fucking shitty you treat her. Making her yours will shut her up and stop her from trying to fucking run if she finds out about the deal we made with her old man. Hell, you, this," he gestures to the clubroom, "can be her new family. But she's gotta want it."

"I'm not fucking making her mine," I snap and Rocco's brow shoots up.

"It will keep the Cunts' claws in and stop these horny fuckers from thinking she's a pass around. Unless you're cool with her being passed between the men. I'm sure they'll fucking like it."

"Fuck off, man. You're not playing fair."

Rocco steps up into my space, crowding me against the wall. "You need to remember who the fuck you are talking to. Unlike Cara, you don't have the pussy to fucking make speaking to me like that acceptable."

I roll my tongue, trying to keep my anger at bay. "Funny. I thought I was talking to my buddy. My fucking mistake." I shove Rocco back and he lets me, letting his smirk show.

"You need to figure out a way to make her yours, or at least make sure the others know she's not fair game. Because the way they are eyeing her, she's gonna be fighting them off again tonight."

"You're the Prez. You can just declare her off limits."

He nods at my comment and then shrugs. "I could. But then they would want to know why, and I can't tell them about her trust fund and the trade we did. And yes, I know I could tell them that's just the way it is and to mind their business, but I will lose their trust doing that."

"Of course. So you will keep their trust by lying to them, anyway?"

"Listen, Gray." Rocco sneers past gritted teeth. "Until such time as you are in my fucking shoes, you'd do best to fucking do what you're meant to do. And support me. Besides, we still don't know who the rat is in our ranks, so the less information we share with everyone else, the better."

Rocco and I have come to a head before. It doesn't help that before the Cruz Kings, we were friends. Yeah, he was more of a big brother but still, we were closer to equals, which sometimes blurs the lines with the roles we play now.

He's never really played the Prez card on me as much as he has lately, and I know he must be feeling the weight of the world with the Reapers breathing down our necks.

I shift my gaze from my Prez to Princess behind the bar who is actually smiling right now. She's talking with Gunner, and a slither of jealousy seeps its way under my skin.

She never smiles like that for me.

"Figure something out." Rocco slaps me on the shoulder then and steps into the clubroom, heading to the bar where Mama C is shooting down some whiskey.

Fuck.

I rake a hand through my curls, eyeing the crowd in the center of the room as more club brothers line up to get their cocks sucked.

I could really use a fucking release right now. It would be so easy to go over there and fist Sasha's black strands and shove my dick so far down her throat until I come.

Deciding that Sasha really isn't who I want to lose myself in, I start weaving through the tables when Rose, one of the Cruz Cunts, steps in my path, eyeing me like I'm her next fucking meal.

"Hi Gray. Wanna party with me tonight?"

"No," I grunt, dodging her touch as I pass by.

"Oh, come on. Mama primped me herself to make me ready for you." Rose's sultry voice does nothing for me except make my fucking blood boil as she rushes to step in my path again. "It's been so long since I've had you in my bed."

I force myself to remain still as she runs a sharp nail up my arm, pushing her tits against my chest as she leans in.

Instinctively, my eyes flick over to the bar, only to lock onto the heated blue gaze of my princess.

Well would you look at that. Zoe is jealous.

"Not tonight," I grunt, returning my gaze to Rose, shooting her a lethal glare.

"Come on, Gray. I'll let you piss on me." She whines and my brows shoot up.

Water play hasn't really been something I've gotten into, and I know it's not something I want to do with this Cruz Cunt, or any.

"Hard fucking pass!" I snap, and she recoils a little.

"Enough!" Mama's authoritative voice slices through the loud atmosphere, and a hush falls over the room. Even those balls deep in Cruz Cunt mouth.

Rose shrinks back, stepping out of my path and when Mama C nods to me, I continue forward, closing the distance to meet her and Rocco at the bar.

The five-foot-nine, dark-haired woman is impressive. There's no other way to describe her. Mama C oozes confidence, and where some of the girls here are just that, girls, Mama is all woman. Her hourglass figure is always dressed in tight leather, and she generously shows everyone what they can't have.

"Thanks, Mama." I offer her a warm smile, glad to see she doesn't look as furious as she did earlier in the back room.

"Hmmm." She shoots me a sideways glance. "I wouldn't have to step in if you'd just show them some attention. You've been..." She shoots a glance over her shoulder at Zoe who is stacking glasses in the dishwasher at the far end of the bar. "Preoccupied."

"Busy." I counter, and she shrugs.

"Either way. Your absence is noticed by them all."

Rocco chuckles into the beer Tex just slid over the counter to him, and I shoot him a glare.

"Protecting the club is more important than rubbing their cunts and egos," I snap, and Mama grins.

"True." She turns in her chair before looking past my shoulder. "Come here, Rose."

This angle gives me a better view of Mama's face and my eyes land on the teardrop tattoo she proudly displays beneath her left eye. She's done time. Killed in jail. And she makes sure we never forget how well she can take care of herself.

When Rose reaches us, Mama slips off her barstool and places her hands on her hips, staring Rose down through cold gray eyes. "We. Do. Not. Beg," she states in her no-nonsense tone. "If the VP doesn't have time for you, you leave him alone. You don't fucking pester him like a common skank. You're a Cruz Cunt, girl. Have some dignity."

"I-I... I'm sorry, Mama." Rose keeps her gaze downcast as she apologizes to the club's matriarch.

Mama's eyes soften, and when she speaks again, her Latina heritage bleeds into her accent. "You're a good girl, Rose." Mama reaches up and cups Rose's chin, lifting it until the girl locks eyes with her. "Rejection is never fun. Take the night off to lick your wounds, and come and see me tomorrow, and we'll talk."

Rose nods, even as she frowns in disappointment. She knows she's being punished for being a fucking pain in my ass, getting vanquished to her room so she can't party with anyone else either.

Jesus, Mama can be a harsh bitch.

I fucking love her.

Mama turns back to me when Rose shrinks away, disappearing out of the room.

"I waxed her crack for you, you know. My efforts are wasted on you, Grayson." She points her long black talon-like nail to my chest and both Rocco and I chuckle, winning us a glare from Mama.

Shooting her a wink, I quickly win her back, and she grins.

"It's never a dull moment with you around, Mama." I chuckle and she rolls her eyes.

"You're lucky to have me around." She deadpans, retaking her barstool.

I nod, because we are all fucking lucky to have her around. Also, she scares most of the club brothers which works well so they don't typically step over the line too often with the Cruz Cunts.

A few years back some of the prospects had a bet going on who could tame her, something they all lived to regret when Mama spiked their drinks and single-handedly hung them from the rafters of the garage. Each of them had letters carved into their stomach, forming the words MAMA KNOWS BEST.

Fucking epic.

"How about instead of turning your snobby nose up at us, you show us how rich girls suck dick?"

Alana's irritating screechy voice draws our attention, and we spot her at the other end of the bar, egging Zoe on.

"How about you go back to doing the only thing you're good for, and I'll watch the men watching *me* as they cum down your throat?"

Zoe's retort gets a mixture of cheers and reprimands right before Alana screams and tries to climb over the bar to get to Zoe.

Fuck.

I can't hide my grin because Zoe's come back was fucking good, and I'm glad she can stick up for herself.

"See what I mean," Rocco mumbles in my ear. "They all want a piece of her, Gray. You need to decide if you're happy for that to happen."

Gritting my teeth, I just can't say the words he wants to fucking hear. I can't fucking make Zoe mine, nor do I want to be tied down like that.

How the fuck I ended up being the protector of the Princess is beyond me.

One moment I'm using her body to take her attitude down a notch, and the next, my Prez is demanding I fucking claim her.

Fuck. Fuck. Fuck.

Even as I fight against myself, I read the room and the fact that the men and Cruz Cunts are closing in, and I know if I don't get Zoe out of here right fucking now, she'll find herself in a situation like she did the other night.

When Alana slips free of Munroe's grip and manages to get her dainty frame on top of the bar, I move.

In one swift leap, I'm over the bar, rushing towards Zoe, who has now backed up against the back counter, armed with a broom. Her eyes are darting wildly around, knowing she's in danger, but the moment she sees me coming for her, she drops the fucking broom and closes the distance.

I'm not sure what she was expecting, but by her squeal when I bend and pick her up, slinging her over my shoulder like a sack of potatoes, that wasn't it.

"Back the fuck off!" I hiss at Alana, pointing a stern finger at her as she still attempts to come for Zoe even while she is slung over my shoulder.

Tex intercepts the out-of-control Cruz Cunt, and I turn on my heel, ignoring Mama's and Rocco's smug fucking smirks and I, once again, save the princess.

I wonder if she will remember this time?

19

Zoe

"Really? You're still not talking to me?" I hate the amusement in Gray's voice. "You know, it's rude to ignore people."

I'm glad my back is turned to where he's leaning against the bar, so he can't see the way my mouth opens, immediately wanting to say something, anything.

"Come on, Princess. What's it going to take for you to speak to me again?"

I pretend not to see him as I turn around and begin to wipe the bar down. Tex keeps telling me not to bother until the end of the night, but I have to. It irks me to see the spillage just pooling there. Which is fucking stupid with everything going on around me.

At one end of the bar a couple are fucking openly, and right next to them Slasher and Slayer are busy snorting shit up their nostrils.

Grayson laughs. "Speaking of my cock, it's almost time for your next payment."

Speaking of... no one was fucking speaking about that.

My body visibly tenses as I fail to hide my reaction to his words.

"Fine," I say coldly. "Do you want to do it right here? Should I lift my skirt up and bend over?"

Please say no. Please say no.

For all the bravado I try to display, I'm anything but. Constantly being on guard while openly hearing others talk shit to and about me is exhausting. I miss my home. I miss my family—even my fucking piece of shit dad.

No longer amused, Grayson grabs my arm and none too gently pulls me towards him. "Did you just mouth off to me in front of my guys?" His voice is hard and unforgiving. "Do you think that was smart, Princess?"

I want to tell him that being smart isn't high on my list of things to aim for. That ship sailed a long fucking time ago. If I was a smart person, I would never have gotten involved with Grayson to begin with. That was my first stupid thing to do. The second one was not being quicker when dad told me to run. If I'd only listened, I wouldn't be here now. I wouldn't live in fear of being attacked whenever I walk by a dark corner.

Having learned my lesson, I stick as close to the Cruz Cunts and Mama C as possible. I know the other women don't like me, and that's okay. But at least when I'm around them, I'm not alone. And that has to count for something. Right?

"I asked you a question," Grayson says, drawing my attention back to him.

Even though I know I should play nice, my temper gets the better of me. "I haven't made a fucking smart decision since the first time I let you into my body," I hiss venomously.

"Ooh, burn, Gray." Slasher's grin is so wide it reminds me of the Joker.

Fuck.

Now that we have an audience, it'll be all the worse. Shit, why can't I just act like I have a sense of self-preservation and be obedient? I suck so hard.

Out of the corner of my eye I notice Mama C and Alana talking, both of them looking in my direction. I wish I could read lips, then I'd know if they're secretly planning on holding me down while Grayson has his way with me.

Fucking Alana.

I wouldn't put it past her to do something like that. To say she has it out for me is like saying that Mardi Gras in New Orleans is a small event.

My breathing hitches as Grayson moves his hand from my arm, slowly trailing it up until he can wrap it around my throat. My eyes widen and my palms grow clammy as he squeezes. It's not uncomfortable, not really. But it's enough to demand my attention, and, much to my dismay, my inner walls flutter and my folds become slick.

The fuck happened to mind over matter? Whenever Grayson touches me, my body betrays me. Longing for the rush he gives me, all while my brain tries to fight him. Clearly, my mind isn't the winning fighter at all.

Grayson moves closer, trailing his lips across the shell of my ear. He nips and licks the skin before whispering, "I'm beginning to think you enjoy riling me up, Princess."

I shudder in his hold, and my eyes flutter closed.

"Can you two move just a little to the left?" Alana asks as she moves around the bar. "I have work to do, and I really don't want to accidentally touch your naked body." She sneers the last part in my direction.

"I would say 'get a room', but you already have one upstairs." Mama saunters towards us. "Or maybe you could keep it in your pants for now." She arches a brow as she locks eyes with Grayson.

"Mind your own business," he almost growls.

"I'm minding all of our business," she clarifies. "I need Zoe to do some work, and you need to stop distracting her."

Grinning, Grayson licks the length of my neck. Goosebumps arise as he blows on the wet skin. "Later, Princess," he rasps. "You'll pay for that smart mouth of yours."

I don't know why Mama keeps her eyes on him, it's almost as though she wants to make sure he leaves. But he does, and as soon as he joins Rocco and Gunner near the back, she turns to me.

"Breathe," she urges me. "Alana, get her a drink."

I'm surprised when the Cruz Cunt hands me a glass of water. Narrowing my eyes, I look at her. "Did you spit in it?"

Rather than taking offense, she throws her head back and laughs. "I think I might like you," she declares with a wink.

Despite not getting a straight answer, I quickly down the water. I feel better now that Grayson isn't here crowding me, studying me. I don't understand how my body can like him so much when he puts me on edge every time he's near. It's like his mere presence brings out my fight or flight instincts, which begs the question, why do I keep fighting him instead of just shutting the fuck up?

My skin prickles and when I look behind me, I immediately notice several of the Cruz Kings watching me. One even holds his hand up, his index and middle finger creating a V that he sticks his tongue through.

Fucking ew.

"You have to stop letting them get to you," Mama offers. "The more they know they bother you, the less chance you have of them leaving you alone."

"Just like fucking playground bullies," I snap.

My words cause both women to laugh.

"Exactly like that," Alana adds. "You're the new shiny toy around here."

Feeling attacked, I cross my arms over my chest. "I'm not here by choice."

She cocks her hip and juts her chin out. "And we're not whoring ourselves out by choice. Whether it's fair or not, you're here because your dad fucked us over. If you want to place fault, blame daddy dearest."

I hate that her words sting. But even more, I hate how right they are. My dad is the reason I'm here. He had the chance to save me, he just happened to think his own life was worth more than mine.

Wait... did she say they're whoring themselves out? When I ask, Mama sighs loudly and pinches the bridge of her nose like this isn't something she's happy about.

"A deal was struck, and my girls are the ones who have to help create a new cash flow. Grayson is going out of town on an errand, but if you really want to know, I'll ask Gunner to take you to Dirty Diamonds tonight. It might help you to see it for yourself."

I mentally repeat the name. I've never been there before, but it's impossible to grow up around here without hearing about this place. The guys at Santa Cruz Prep often talked about the club, and the things they got to do to the women working there.

My hands become clammy as I realize the Cruz Cunts are doing those things now because of my dad. Shit. Shit. Shit. I'm not okay with that, but I also don't know if there's anything I can do about it.

"Okay," I agree. My voice is as small as I feel. It's not that I want to go, not really. But I kind of feel like I have to. "I'll come tonight."

Mama and Alana look at me with begrudging... respect. Or maybe that's a stretch.

"Well, can't say I expected that. Good for you," Alana says reluctantly.

With a loud banshee-like scream and a low grunt, the couple at the end of the bar are finally done. I can't stop watching them as they sort their clothes. He tucks himself back in, while she openly discards her thong and pulls her denim skirt back up. Then she clasps her bra back into place, not bothering with her top.

Christ, a show like that and it's only early afternoon.

Despite my better judgment, my mind conjures up images of Grayson taking me like that—here. Maybe not on the bar, I think I'd prefer the shadows. Half hidden, but so people still knew exactly what we're getting up to...

I shake my head, all sorts of disturbed by those images. I don't want that, especially not with him. Maybe if I masturbated more my body would stop acting like that around him.

Remembering the reason I left Grayson's room the night I was attacked by one of the Cruz Kings, I clear my throat and look nervously at Mama.

"Can I speak with you alone?"

She arches a perfectly styled eyebrow while nodding slowly. As she leads us into the room where her and Rocco were fucking loudly last week, I notice the way people part for her. It's not like she's a leper they're scared to touch, or an outcast they can't wait to take their anger out on. Those are reserved for me, it seems. No, the way they get out of her way is respectful.

Just as she's about to close the door behind us, it's forced open, and Rocco comes into view. The club prez is a scary motherfucker. The brutal scar on his face and his cold eyes are the stuff nightmares are made of. At least, my nightmares.

"What's going on?" he asks.

Despite the bite in his tone, he looks at Mama with so much love I feel like an interloper for witnessing it.

"Zoe wanted to talk with me," she answers him easily.

He turns to me, kicks the door closed and crosses his big arms over his even bigger chest. "Anything you have to say to my woman, you can say to me."

Mama huffs and rolls her eyes, but doesn't ask him to leave.

I nervously take a step back and wring my hands in front of me. Fuck, he doesn't make it easy to get the words out.

"I ahh..." Trailing off, I lick my dry lips and swallow audibly. "Maybe my monthly allowance could help you out. That's what I was thinking. And... yes." I stumble over my words, and I'm not even sure they come out in the right order.

Mama laughs, but unlike the way the Cruz Cunts laugh at me, she doesn't sound condescending or scathing. That helps ease my nerves.

Squaring my shoulders, I dare meet Rocco's gaze. "What I mean to say is, I'm going to be receiving a monthly allowance. I want to give the money to the club, to help out."

Rocco looks like he doesn't quite know what to believe.

"Why would you do that?" he asks brusquely.

It's a good question, one I'm not sure I entirely know the answer to. I feel guilty and maybe even partially responsible, that much is true. But beyond that, I don't have an answer for him.

"The money means nothing to me," I sigh. "I've already lost everything. Material goods are the only things I have left, and it's not like it's doing me much good here." I can't keep my bitterness out of my tone.

I try my best not to fidget as Rocco studies me, but it's hard when he looks like my words have angered him.

"We can look into that," he finally says. "Thank you for the offer."

He doesn't sound thankful at all. In fact, he sounds like I'm an idiot for suggesting it, and right now, that's exactly what I feel like.

Mama clears her throat and places her hand on Rocco's impressive biceps. "He might not sound like he means it, so let me say it with feeling." She winks cheekily at him. "Thank you for the kind offer, Zoe."

Rocco grunts something that sounds like her being a pain in his ass, but I don't dare ask him to repeat it. And since I've said what I had to say, I look expectantly at Mama. I don't want to walk back out there alone, but I'm also not sure it would be a good idea to ask for her help with Rocco here. I'm sure the Prez can smell fear just like dogs, and if he can, he'll know I'm reeking from it in his presence.

Luckily, Mama comes to my rescue. She practically pushes Rocco out of the door, telling him we need some girl time. This has him smiling wide.

"If you're going to have a pillow fight in your underwear, I want pictures."

They both laugh loudly, and it's so infectious I almost smile. Almost.

"You need to toughen up, girl." Mama glares at me like my presence is offending her. "Don't let Rocco or the others know they're intimidating you."

"But they are," I say with no hesitation.

Mama nods. "I'll give you the same advice my not so dear mom gave me many years ago. Fake it until you make it. That's the only way."

From the way her face tightens, I so don't want to know what that advice was in regards to. So I just nod, wondering how I can heed her words of wisdom. How the hell does one act confident when they're placed amongst a group of sharks?

"They're not bad guys. Not really," Mama says as she sits down. "But they'll break you like a twig if you let them. Grayson especially."

My eyes widen. "D-do you mean..." I don't know how to articulate my thoughts, so I end up just leaving the sentence hanging in the air between us.

"I don't mean literally," she scoffs. Her eyes twinkle like she's amused by me. "Or maybe I do... it's hard to say with that guy. A strong man needs an even stronger woman. If you continue to let him carry you off like some kind of a fucking damsel in distress, no one will ever respect you. They might fear him, but you need them to leave you alone even when he isn't around."

Swallowing, I look around the room, but my mind is too preoccupied with all the ways I could get hurt here to take in the decor.

"Couldn't you just help me?" I ask.

Surely it would be easy for her to help protect me when Grayson isn't around. Or maybe instead of him, since I very much doubt she'd want my pussy as payment.

"I could." She stands back up and stretches lazily. "But you haven't given me a reason to."

My jaw goes slack, and I ball my hands in anger. "What the hell does that mean?" I demand. "What do I need to do to get some help? It's not even my fucking fault I'm here."

Amusement dances in her eyes as she takes me in. "There's the fire. Hold on to that."

"You didn't answer my question," I growl, beyond frustrated she's not giving me a straight answer.

"I did," she sing-songs. "But you didn't like the answer, which is why you're now acting all prissy. But if you need me to spell it out for you, it's simple really. I don't help those who won't even help themselves."

What. The. Fuck.

I can't believe this woman. She has everyone eating out of the palm of her hand. She's the undisputed Queen B, yet she won't help me. Whatever positive thoughts I've had of her just turned bad. Decaying within my brain in record time.

Fuck this place. Fuck her. Fuck Rocco. Fuck Grayson—fuck them all.

Rather than hang around to let her humiliate me further, I go to leave. Before I manage to open the door, she calls, "Gunner will take you to the club. Be ready in thirty minutes."

I flip her off over my shoulder, and then I practically run away—too scared my sass is going to earn me a punishment from her. I've seen her dole those out, and it never looks fun.

After I was attacked last week, Mama punished the guy by tying him to the rafters and then she fucking whipped him. Not only that, the onlookers didn't even try to stop her. They all stood there, nodding like it was the most natural thing in the world.

In case I thought she did it for me, when she was done, she made it clear that she won't tolerate any woman being harmed under her roof. As I think about that while walking back to Grayson's room, I realize how stupidly naïve I was to ask Mama for her protection. Like everyone else here, she doesn't care about me.

I'm really glad no one can hear my thoughts while I get changed. I'm hurt, scared, angry, and betrayed. No matter where I look, there are people ready to devour me. Even the ones giving me lustful stares want to hurt me, like Grayson.

This is all getting to be too much. I need to stop trying to think of ways out because every time I do, I get even more disappointed when it doesn't work. So what if they have no money and have to whore themselves out? I didn't fucking take their money so why am I the one paying for my dad's deceit?

In my time here I've heard whispers about the Cali Reapers, who are apparently synonymous with the devil. I'm sure they're not good guys, but from one particular conversation that I listened in on, I don't see what makes them worse than the Cruz Kings.

The Reapers hurt innocent people, well, so do the Kings.

The Reapers take things that don't belong to them, well, so do the Kings.

That's all I've heard, but it's enough to know that the Reapers aren't fucking worse. They might be the same, but that doesn't mean they're beneath the Kings.

I haven't asked for much, yet I'm denied every single request out of spite. And if it's granted, there's a heavy price I'm not sure I can continue paying.

As a heavy knock sounds on the door, I'm pulled from my thoughts. Before the next knock can sound I rush to the small kitchenette, desperately looking through the drawers for anything I can use as a weapon. My heart beats so wildly it feels like it's going to jump out of my chest, and my breath comes out in heavy pants.

"Open the door, Zoe."

I sigh with relief as I recognize Gunner's voice.

Looking down at my hand, I frown at the spatula I'm clutching for dear life. What the hell did I think I was going to do with that thing? Slap someone? I mentally curse at Grayson for removing everything that can be used as a weapon. All because I threw a butter knife at him when he demanded I give him the thong I was wearing so he could, and I quote, "Sniff it whenever he wanted to."

"Coming," I shout to Gunner as I gather my things.

My things... what a ridiculous notion. I don't have anything that's mine. The bag I'm carrying is Mama's, and all it has in the inner pocket is a fucking tampon.

As soon as I open the door, Gunner pulls me into a hug that I eagerly return. "Long time no see," he drawls. "How's my favorite royalty?"

I can't help laughing at him as he waggles his eyebrows while doing an exaggerated bow.

"I thought I was your 'Sugar'," I laugh while making air quotation marks around the nickname.

Taking my hand, Gunner slaps his other hand over his cheek. "You're so sweet you gave me a toothache."

Laughing like this is beyond freeing. Whenever I'm alone with him, the air around me doesn't feel suffocating, it feels like it should.

Gunner doesn't stop trying to make me laugh during our short drive to the club. He even makes us sing along to the radio, and his off-key singing has me in stitches. As we arrive, my cheeks and stomach hurt, but in a good way. It's like the knot I've been carrying around for weeks is gone, disappearing into nothingness.

When we arrive, Gunner wraps his hand around my shoulder. "Stick close to my side, Sugar." He urges. "If you think the men back at the clubhouse are bad, you don't want to tangle with the ones here."

I shiver, the warning bells in my head blaring in full force. I shouldn't have agreed to come here. Why the hell didn't I just say no? I might hate the Kings, but right now they're the devil I know.

Gunner licks his lips as we enter the club. His eyes are glued to the women on stage, and I gasp as I recognize some of them. In the back of my mind I hoped Alana was joking, but I should have known better. And now I have the evidence in front of me, because several of the Cruz Cunts are busy working the poles.

Fuck, now I feel guilty all over. Sure, it's not much different from how they act at the clubhouse. But it's not the same because back there it's their turf, this is someone else's.

"Do you want a drink?" Gunner shouts over the music, and I nod.

He leads us to the bar where he quickly orders one vodka with lemonade and a whiskey, before finding us a table towards the front.

One drink turns to three, and before I know it, I'm slurring my words. Christ, I'm not usually a lightweight. At Cassie's parties the drinks were always like eighty percent alcohol and twenty percent lemonade, so it made sense I was drunk after no more than three drinks. Unlike the ones I'm having now. They're so watered down I can barely taste the alcohol.

Then again, in those days I also ate and slept like a normal person. Now, my stomach is often twisted in too many knots for me to be able to eat. And forget getting a proper night's sleep. If Grayson doesn't wake me up with his tongue, fingers, or cock, I'm so on edge even the smallest creak wakes me up.

"F-fiddle me t-this," I slur, making it sound like the word has three S at the end.

Gunner cocks a light eyebrow while running a hand over his beard. "Fiddle what?"

I giggle. "I don't know. Can't r-remember."

His blue eyes darken and my eyes are glued to the top of his tongue as he licks his lips. "Do you want me to fiddle you, Sugar?"

I snort laugh at him and slap his hand away when he playfully runs it up my arm. My breath hitches as he reaches my collarbone. Fear curdles in my stomach like sour milk, scared he's going to wrap his large hand around my throat. Like Grayson does.

Shaking my head, I refocus. This is Gunner—my friend. He's nothing like the son of a bitch I share a bed with.

Gunner leans closer, he's so close I can smell the whiskey and stale tobacco emanating from him.

"If you ever want me to fiddle you, you only have to ask once."

The seriousness in his tone makes me uncomfortable. Sensing my change in mood, he leans back and roars with laughter. I eye him nervously because something about the laugh seems forced—off.

"To a night out," Gunner says, clinking his glass to mine.

"To having fun," I giggle, letting my suspicion go.

It takes me several attempts to make my glass touch his, which has us both in tears. I'm so focused on my task, I don't notice the music has stopped or the hands reaching for me.

"It's time, Princess," one of the Cruz Cunts sneers.

Her friend easily jumps off stage and before I can even process what's happening, she's pulling me towards the stage.

"You better hope you can make enough tips to make tonight worth it," she hisses in my ear just as the music starts up again.

"N-no," I stammer as I almost trip over my feet. Turning towards Gunner, I scream for him to come help me. But he isn't looking at me and the music is drowning out my screams.

With no one to help me, it's too easy for the women to pull me up on stage. As soon as I'm there, the spotlight hits me so I can't see a fucking thing. It's quickly dimmed, though, making it impossible not to notice how many people have gathered in the crowd.

Christ, how did I miss that almost the entire club is here? When Gunner and I arrived, the crowd was sparse, but now... fuck.

My breath hitches, and it takes me too long to realize the song has started. The girl next to me is already moving, gyrating her hips and palming her tits to the beat of the music. When I don't move, three of the cunts swarm me, pulling at my clothes.

"You're wearing too many clothes," they laugh.

One of them pulls a knife from her knee-high boot, using it to cut my skirt until it falls from my hips. Despite my screams and attempts to get away, the crowd cheers, chanting my name like they're here for me.

Oh, fuck... are they here for me?

My stomach plummets as I realize this is what Mama C meant. She wanted me here, dancing on stage with her beloved Cruz Cunts. Fuck, how could I have been so stupid? What the hell was I thinking agreeing to come here?

Realizing she played me has anger stirring to life. Looking down at myself I'm glad I wore my black lingerie set. It's one I bought just before my graduation, and for some reason, Grayson packed it when he went to get me some of my clothes from home.

Which he did... yesterday. Obviously, he was in on this as well.

Knowing that even the ally I had to bribe with my body has turned on me, is the last straw. The alcohol pumping through my veins is making me reckless in my anger. If it's a show they want... I'll give them a fucking show.

Giving myself over to the music, I move my hips while sliding my hands down to my ass.

As I spread the globes, I no longer feel embarrassed or awkward. I feel free. Because even though I don't really want to be doing this, I am. But only because I'm choosing to. Christ, even in my drunk mind that makes no sense.

Now that I'm dancing, the Cunts let go of me, focusing on the onlookers instead. I mirror one of the girls, getting down on all fours, rolling to my back and spreading my legs. The movement makes me dizzy, but I don't give up.

20

Grayson

The last fucking thing I wanted to do today is chase down more Reapers, but the moment Cain called with word of a couple of Reapers in his district, Prez sent me to go to Cain and investigate.

The intel was good, and I took my frustrations out on the two fuckers who have now been beheaded, their bodies burned to a crisp and buried, while their heads are on their way to be delivered to a known Reaper hang out up the coast near San Gregorio.

Cain and I end up at Dirty Diamonds and find it packed, mostly with Cruz Kings, and I remember the Cruz Cunts are having their debut on stage tonight. I try to see what's happening up on stage, but every motherfucker is on their feet back here, blocking my view.

"It sounds like your Cruz Cunts are a hit." Cain chuckles, nudging my shoulder with his.

"Yeah. Fucking sounds like it." I nod, still trying to see through the crowd.

Between two men who aren't Cruz Kings, I get a glimpse at the left side of the stage. Alana and Rose are up there, shaking their bare asses in a twerk, and I frown.

Has this crowd never seen a stripper twerk?

Then the crowd parts more, and I fucking stop breathing.

"Isn't that the girl you—" Cain's words cut off as I see fucking red.

Suddenly, all the noise of the room slips away, and I have tunnel vision for the bratty princess who is palming her black lace clad tits as she straddles Sasha, mimicking riding her face.

My feet fucking move before my brain can comprehend what I'm doing, and I shove through the crowd, upending table after table to get to that fucking stage. The squeals of Beth and Rose penetrate the vortex I'm trapped in as I leap onto the stage and they scramble out of the way.

Zoe's blue eyes widen, and she stands quickly from hovering over Sasha before she staggers back a few steps as I come for her. She holds up trembling dainty hands in front of her as if they will fucking stop me.

"The fuck are you doing!" I hiss, gripping her upper arm and tugging her to my chest.

"I-I..." Her words fail her, and I know she's realized that nothing she says can justify her being up here flaunting herself like a fucking whore.

"You want to be a whore? Is that it?!" I seethe, and she flinches back like I've slapped her before shaking her head quickly.

"Gray." Sasha starts as she stands, but the bared teeth and hiss I send her way has her ducking her head and rushing off the stage.

"Let her dance!" someone yells, and I store that fucking voice in the back of my brain for later, because that fucker is going to meet my fucking fist.

Spinning her to face the front again, the lights are hot and bright as they shine down on us, and I wrap my arm around her from behind, gripping her throat as I press my lips to her ear and speak just loud enough so she can hear.

"If you want to be a whore, let's make you one."

A shiver ripples through her, but I ignore it, my anger fueling me on as I see so many eyes watching us. Gunner is towards the back, not looking fucking bothered which surprises the fuck out of me. I thought he liked Zoe. Why would he let her get on fucking stage?

"You wanna see her perform?" I call, and the crowd starts cheering.

"Princess, tell them whose whore you are!" I yell so they can all hear, and even as Zoe stiffens in my arms, she answers.

"Y-yours." She clears her throat, before repeating it with more confidence. "Yours."

"That's right," I call, "and are you allowed to touch anyone other than me?"

What the fuck am I doing?

"No," she states loudly, almost like she's fucking proud.

"And is anyone else allowed to touch you?"

"No."

Fuck. What am I doing up here? Claiming her?

Fuck, even as I think it, I grin and nip at her ear.

"You want to strip so fucking much, then get your fucking bra off. Show them your perky tits."

My words are for her, but I can tell by the way Slasher's brows raise in the second row that he heard.

Obviously not expecting me to say that, Zoe stiffens, and I feel her body start trembling.

"W-what are you doing?" Her words are slight.

"I'm giving you what you want, Princess. You want to dance and strip, then fucking do it."

She shakes her head, sinking back into me like she is hoping I'll hide her, and I watch as her eyes dart to the onlookers before glancing up to the side at me.

"B-but you are meant to protect me. That's why you had me admit that I'm yours."

I chuckle at her words, her blue gaze filled with worry as she peers up at me.

"You mean when I asked you to admit that you're my whore?"

She frowns, but nods, and again, I chuckle.

"That's right, Princess. You're my whore. So start fucking acting like it and take your clothes off."

Her bottom lip starts to wobble, and an odd feeling stabs the center of my chest, so I try to push it back, and start fucking helping her along.

"I said, strip," I hiss, gripping the strap of her bra and tugging it forcefully off her shoulder, the cup coming away with it to expose her tit.

A gasp flies from her mouth and I ignore her reaction, palming her handful as the crowd cheers and hoots.

"Please Gray." Zoe's sob draws my attention to the side of her face again, and I watch the first tear roll down her cheek. "Don't do this here in front of them. Take me back to your room."

Narrowing my eyes, I lean down to her height and press my nose to her ear.

"It's too late for that, Princess. You were the one that decided you wanted to act like a whore. Now fucking accept your fate."

"You're a monster!" she snarls, trying to pry herself away from me, but my grip on her is too firm for her to succeed.

"Yeah, well. I never fucking used to be. But now I'm your fucking monster, so get on your knees and let's give them the show they came here for."

I spin her then, only to come face to face with the princess I first met who lived up in her ivory tower, turning her nose up to everyone below. Her eyes are hard. Her lips are thin. And her cheeks are flaming.

As we glare at each other in a stand-off, two parts of my brain are at war with each other, and I fight to remain on that stage.

Prez wanted me to claim her. I guess this is one fucking way to do that. Deep down I know it's not the way I would choose, but here I fucking am, unleashing the beast inside me in front of a crowd, and showing Zoe Miller that she can't turn this beast into a prince.

"What if I refuse?" she asks, jutting up her chin and swiping at the tears that pop free every so often.

"Don't you get it, Princess? If you're mine, I own you. Club property. VP property. I can do whatever the fuck I like with you."

"You're going to regret this, Grayson Black," she hisses and I shrug.

"Maybe," I admit. "Now, get on your knees, whore."

I push her shoulders down hard and she goes without any resistance as I free my dick from my jeans. I've never been one to care much for having an audience, but Zoe needs the full experience since she got up here in the first place. So I fist my cock and slap her cheek with it, her blue eyes flaring with a level of anger that I know I'll pay for later.

"Open your fucking mouth."

Her lips part, and I hold my breath as the bright spotlight makes her exposed tits glow, and then, she fucking spits on my cock.

Lip curling, I forcefully fist her hair, tugging her head back as I grip her chin painfully hard, forcing her mouth open.

"You're going to suck my cock like a good fucking princess, and once we are done, if you do a good fucking job, I'll eat your cunt until you cream down my throat."

Heat flares in her eyes, and I'm reminded of how much she loves this shit. Pretending that she doesn't fucking want me when she does. A bit of dubious consent. But as quickly as it shows itself, it disappears, and her blue gaze turns cold.

There's a brief moment where I consider that perhaps enough is enough. I should just fucking walk away from Zoe. I should take the Cruz Cunts to my room back at the club and have a fucking Zoe free party and just fucking forget about her elite white-collar pussy. But then I pick up on the shouting from the men in Dirty Diamonds, and my blood runs cold.

"If you won't claim her I will. I'll fuck her with every sharp object I can find and then send her back to her daddy as punishment for stealing from us."

Something in me snaps.

I release Zoe's chin before pulling my gun free of the holster under my cut, aiming it at the crowd. Shouts and screams fill the air as the Cruz Cunts and whichever fuckers in here aren't from my club run for cover.

"She is fucking mine!" I roar. "No one will touch her! No one will harass her! If they do, they will meet their fucking death!"

The crowd falls silent, and I shift my aim from the audience to press the nozzle to Zoe's temple.

"Hurry up, Princess. I won't fucking ask again."

With her whole-body trembling now, Zoe's eyes completely glassy as tears stream from them, she leans forward, mouth open, and takes me into her mouth.

The crowd cheers, and whistles ring out, but I zone all that crap out as I keep my eyes locked on Zoe's watching her haphazardly suck my cock.

I release my grip of her hair and pinch her nose which gives me more access to fill her mouth further as she struggles to breathe. Her mouth is like heaven. Molten heat that calls to my fucking soul. Or dick at least. I don't bother taking my time, deciding that hard and fast is the best course of action here, and I start fucking her mouth with abandon, not caring each time she gags.

Her body goes rigid, her natural reflexes kicking in as she tries to pull back, but I hold her in place and fuck her mouth over and over, relentlessly, while ignoring my brothers sitting in the audience in my peripheral as they fist their own cocks, loving the show.

The gagging noises falling from Zoe shouldn't turn me on as much as they do. That's fucking sick, yet the beast inside me goes harder wanting to push her over the edge so she knows what getting treated like a whore is really like.

She starts slapping my leg, so I pull my dick free as she gags again, nearly losing the contents of her stomach. I'm not into puke fucking, but I know some of the guys in this club are. They love making the girls hurl on their dicks, even going so far as shoving their fingers down their throats to induce it.

But fuck that. I might be trying to teach Zoe a lesson right now, but I won't do *that* to her.

"That's a good little whore," I hiss in her face as I release her nose, letting her breath, but only for a moment. "Choke on my dick."

Then I pinch her nose again, her lips parting automatically to try to breathe, and I slam in, causing her to jerk.

Over and over, I thrust, her slopping gagging sounds even louder this time as she relaxes into it, accepting my dick and the way I abuse her throat.

As I look down at her blue eyes, tears streaming from them, not just from crying, but also from her mouth being used in such a brutal way, I have the urge to move the aim of my gun and press it to my own fucking head.

I can't believe I'm doing this. Not only will she hate me and never speak to me again after this, but it's quite possible that I won't even be able to live with myself.

The need for this to be over takes control of me, and I break our eye contact as I throw my head back, letting my anger push my orgasm to the surface.

The moment my balls tighten, I look back down at my whore and tug myself free of her mouth, wrapping my hand around my shaft as I continue to pump.

"Keep your mouth open, whore," I snarl, and she does, tipping her face up to me, knowing what's coming.

She looks so fucking beautiful down there, drool dangling from her chin, dripping down onto her rising and falling partially bare chest and rosy nipple.

My climax slams into me hard, and with a roar, hot jets of cum shoot from my cock, landing on her tongue, chin, cheeks, and eyelids, with the last burst shooting over her exposed tit.

"Was that to your satisfaction?" Zoe asks, trying to hide the way her body won't stop trembling by wrapping her arms over her chest.

Slowly, I shift the barrel of my gun from her temple and holster it, before tucking my dick back in. I ignore the cheers and some clear telltale sounds of fucking happening in the audience. I'm pretty sure this club hasn't seen *this* sort of action before.

Towering over Zoe, who remains looking up at me from her kneeled position on the stage, I nod and answer her. "It was as good as any whore."

Her lips thin, and a sob escapes her before she speaks again.

"I really hope that was worth it, Gray. I really hope you're prepared for the repercussions."

It's hard to tell exactly what she means, and I don't bother asking, because all I want to do is get her out of this fucking strip club and back to the safety of my room.

The thing is, my room might be safe for her, but I have a really fucking bad feeling, that it won't be safe for me anymore. From now on, I'll be sleeping with one eye open.

21

Zoe

I can't breathe.

I'm lying on the floor, curled into a ball as I hug my knees as tight as possible to my chest.

I can't breathe.

The door opens, and the creaking has me wrapping my arms protectively around my head. If I can't see them, maybe they can't see me. Or maybe they'll see the pathetic mess I am and leave me alone. I'm good with either, as long as they leave me be.

Of course I'm not that lucky.

"Zoe?"

Although it's out of character for Alana to speak so softly to me, I recognize her voice.

"Have you eaten today?" she asks.

Through my arms I sneak a peek in her direction. She's approaching me much like someone would a wounded animal. Her arms are stretched in front of her, and the palms of her hands are facing me.

A wounded sound reaches my ears, and it takes me surprisingly long to realize it's coming from me.

"Go away," I whimper. "P-please just leave m-me alone."

My breathing is labored, making it a struggle to speak at all. It hurts my throat where I fear a ball of needles has taken up residence. At least that's how it feels when I swallow and talk. Not that I've done a lot of talking the last few days.

I've still worked my shifts at the bar, but since Grayson violated me like that, I don't think I've said much if anything at all.

Panic rises inside me as Alana crouches in front of me. "I just came back here to tell you that Sasha is covering your shift, so you can hide as long as you want."

"T-that's..." I pause as I try to find the right words.

"The least she could do," Alana finishes for me.

I shake my head, that's not what I wanted to say. But I let it go because I've lost my train of thought, and, frankly, it doesn't matter. Nothing matters anymore.

Trying to ignore the way she looks at me with concern in her eyes is harder than it should be. But then again, I can't let my guard down around here. I think I've finally learned my lesson. Too bad it took being pulled up on stage to realize just how little I matter.

Sitting down next to me, Alana runs her fingers through my hair. While toying with the strands, she tells me about her mom.

"Whenever I was sick, she used to give me a scalp massage and braid my hair. Even when I broke my wrist, she was playing with my hair like the motion had healing properties." She laughs softly to herself and shakes her head. "Of course it didn't actually help, but it made me feel better. Back then my hair was so long it reached my ass. My mom always told me that girls should have long hair, and I could never bring myself to tell her I envied a girl from my school who had short hair."

My heartbeat evens out, no longer erratic as I listen to her talking. It's soothing.

"When my mom died, I cut my hair and placed it in the casket. It seemed fitting to give her the part of me she loved the most."

Even though I want to ask what she means by that, I don't.

"My mom was a horrible, selfish bitch. She always hated me for existing. I don't know how many times she told me that I was the reason she couldn't model anymore, because being pregnant and giving birth ruined her body. So when I was five she began forcing me into beauty pageants."

Alana's voice hardens.

"When I refused, she'd beat me under my feet—"

I can't help asking, "Why there?"

She laughs scornfully. "Because it doesn't bruise. And she couldn't very well beat me anywhere the judges might see."

My mouth parts at the horrific answer. What the fuck kind of person even knows something like that?

"For years, I was her human dolly. Hers to dress up, hers to bend and do whatever she wanted with me. She was so high on my success in the pageant world, that she never considered what would happen if something happened to make me unattractive."

Giving up all pretenses, I slowly peruse the Cruz Cunt. She really is unnaturally beautiful. Her big brown doe eyes are as gorgeous as her porcelain skin you don't see often here where there's plenty of sunshine. Her slightly crooked nose is the only imperfection, but I like it—it suits her, like her dimples when she smiles. Alana's body is on the slimmer side, but her curves are perfect for her, and she knows how to work them to her advantage.

When my eyes land on the scar on her cheek, I ask, "How did you get that scar?" It surprises me that I want to know.

She turns her head to the side and looks at me. "I did that to myself. When I begged to be allowed to be a normal girl, my mom flew into a fit. She told me that if I quit of my own volition, she'd find other ways to sell my body."

I gasp in shock.

"So I went to the park where most of the alcoholics hung out. When I found a glass bottle I smashed it, using one of the shards to give me a way out that wouldn't require me to quit," she cackles at the last part. "Guess I won."

I don't know what to make of Alana's story, or where she's going with it. Though I'm pretty sure she doesn't want my sympathy, I can't resist wanting to comfort her.

"Did she let you quit?" I ask, forcing the words out.

Alana shakes her head. "Nope, but I got kicked out. The judges didn't want me there."

"Why are you telling me this?" I ask.

I chew on my bottom lip as I wonder if her story is an omen, a warning of what's to come. Maybe she's telling me so I won't be surprised when the Cruz Kings begin beating my feet.

She blows some of her short hair out of her face. "I honestly don't know. Maybe because I thought you could use a story to—"

Angered by her words, I interrupt. "I don't need a story to know there are worse things going on in the world. Despite what you all seem to think, I know the universe doesn't revolve around me."

I want to slap the smile off her lips. Pull my hand back and introduce my palm to her skin so fast and hard the sound ricochets around the silent storage room. I don't do it. Of course, I don't. My issue isn't with Alana or any of the Cruz Cunts, really.

Just like me, they're in a bad situation. That much I know. As much as I've cursed them out in my head, they don't owe me anything. But more importantly, they've taken nothing from me either. That's all Grayson.

Just like that, the numbness I've tried to wrap around me like an invisible blanket shatters and a sob breaks free as my brain assaults me with the memories of what he did to me. The sounds, the smells, the... oh, fuck. The taste of his cock.

My stomach churns, and bile creeps up the back of my throat. I leap to my feet so quickly the room spins, but I don't let it slow me down. I'm aware of Alana calling my name, though I ignore it. Reaching for the trash can, I manage to hold it up in front of me just as I throw up so hard it feels like it's coming out of my fucking nose.

Since I have nothing in my stomach, it's all water. Water and putrid stomach acid. While I dry heave into the trash can, tears freefall down my face. Mixing with snot, spit, and whatever else I'm expelling. Fuck me.

My legs give out from under me, sending me tumbling to the floor. I yelp in pain as I land on my knees, the trash can still firmly in my grasp. This is a new low for me. Too distraught to do anything but hide, cry, and exist—too weak to stand on my own.

I curl my hand into a fist and slam it into the hard, unforgiving floor. While I punch the floor over and over, I pour all my frustration, fear, and heartache into each punch.

Grayson stole me—took me out of my family home. Ever since meeting him he's done nothing but take. Well, I guess that makes me safe from him now because I have nothing else left. Even as I think that, I know I'm wrong. There's always a 'worse'. The fact that I can't see it means nothing, he'll find it.

"Stop it," Alana cries. She wraps her fingers around my wrist in an attempt to stop me. "Zoe, you need to stop."

I look at her uncomprehendingly. "No, I don't." My voice sounds as hollow as I feel.

Why the fuck isn't my hand throbbing in pain?

Before I can continue punching into the floor, the door flies open. As soon as Rocco and Grayson come into view, I force my eyes shut while throwing myself backwards. I need to get away.

Once again, my breathing turns labored, and I struggle to get oxygen into my lungs. I'm not even aware I'm trembling until Alana moves next to me.

"Breathe, Zoe. That's it."

Listening to her voice, I try to do just that, but I can't. The air is too thick, it doesn't belong in my body and I can't... I can't...

With my eyes closed, I imagine darkness taking over. I fantasize about it swallowing me whole, leaving nothing behind. For some reason, the thought calms me, or maybe it just numbs me. I'm not entirely sure. It doesn't matter, though, not when I can finally breathe without feeling like I'm choking on air.

"What the fuck is going on?" Grayson thunders.

The danger in his tone is unmistakable, and I know I'll be the one he takes it out on.

I ignore the part of me that wants to cower and hide away. The darkness will protect me. As long as I keep my eyes closed, I'm okay.

"You!" Alana screeches. "I used to fucking admire you. I used to look up to you, and now... fuck you, Grayson!"

Her reaction startles me so much I almost lose my grip on the darkness.

"Alana," Rocco warns. "Don't fucking forget your place."

She hisses like a rattlesnake coiled tight, ready to attack.

"Sasha tried to tell him," she volleys. "She tried to fucking tell him that she and some of the other girls dragged Zoe up on stage. She didn't go willingly."

"What?" Grayson sounds stunned, like he isn't sure he believes his own ears.

Not liking this conversation, I push myself closer to the wall. Hoping beyond hope that there's a trapdoor I'll fall through and disappear.

"Step aside," Rocco commands in his stern voice.

Alana begins to stroke my hair again, and it feels good. I think... maybe under different circumstances, we would have been friends. Or, at the very least, friendly. In this reality that isn't likely to happen, though. Especially since I'm pretty sure I won't survive the night, not if Grayson's mood is anything to go by.

"No," she spits venomously.

"What's going on here?" Mama asks.

Jesus fucking Christ, is the entire club squeezed into the small storage room? The thought makes me giggle.

"We got it covered," Grayson barks.

"Don't fucking take that tone with me," she sniffs, disdain palpable in every word. "The girls are mine, so don't you fucking take that tone with me when I'm asking what you're doing with my girls."

Rocco clears his throat. "Zoe isn't yours—"

"She's a girl under this roof, that makes her mine. Don't fucking start with me."

I listen to the swoosh of fabric and heels click-clacking on the floor, knowing it's Mama moving closer.

"Can you open your eyes, Zoe?"

There's so much concern in her tone I almost throw myself at her and beg for her help. But as I remember our last conversation, I know there's no point in even trying. She said she only helps those who help themselves, and I'm definitely not doing that.

Rather than using my words, I vehemently shake my head.

Mama sighs loudly. "That's it. Everyone out." When no one immediately moves, she shouts, "Now!"

As feet scuffle along the floor, I remember that Alana never finished explaining why she told me about her mom. So as soon as the door closes behind Rocco and Grayson, I ask, "Why did you tell me?" My voice is hoarse, making the words hard to hear. I clear my throat and try again. "Why did you tell me about your mom?"

Opening my eyes, I look at Alana who's still stroking my hair. "Because I want you to know that I know exactly how it feels to be forced to do shit." She turns to Mama. "Zoe isn't the one indebted to us."

I'm surprised by the fire in her voice, and the fact she's acting like she's on my side. No, I'm not falling for that again. It's a trick, I know it is.

"How are you feeling, Zoe?" Mama asks softly.

Forcing my gaze to meet hers, I try to smile. "Just peachy. Never better."

I know my tone doesn't match the statement I'm trying to sell, but I don't know what else to do. I need to be smarter, and not keep waiting for someone to save me.

Mama nods thoughtfully. "I see that. Your hand is swollen and the line indent matches the line in the floor. But hey, nothing says fine like the smell of puke."

As though her words are breaking a seal in my nose, the overwhelming smell assaults me out of nowhere. I look next to Alana where she's placed the trash can... which is weird. I don't remember her taking it from me.

"Don't worry," I say flippantly, scrunching my nose up in distaste at the smell. "I can still work."

Mama tilts her head to the side, studying me like I'm an exotic animal at the zoo. I snort at the thought. Exotic implies special, coveted—in short, it isn't me.

"I need to speak to Zoe alone," Mama says in her typical no-nonsense tone. "Go make sure Sasha knows she has to cover Zoe's shift for the entire night, please."

As Alana makes to leave, Mama catches her arm and pulls her close so she can whisper something in her ear.

When they're done whispering, probably about me, Alana leaves without looking back.

Without asking me or allowing me a say, Mama pulls me up so I'm standing. With her hand on my lower back, she guides me out of the storage room and up to Grayson's room. I haven't been back up here since that night. Instead, I've hidden everywhere possible. The storage room, the bathroom, even behind the small fridge under the bar. You name a nook, and I've hidden there.

As we walk by Grayson, I feel his eyes bore into me, causing my breath to falter again.

"Ignore him," Mama croons.

Reaching his room, she doesn't hesitate before unlocking the door. The room looks the same as it did when I left, minus some dirty socks on the floor. I don't know why that's the thing that sends me over the edge. All I know is that those fucking socks are the proverbial straw to break the camel's back.

I pick them up and throw them into the basket with a huff. Then I pick up an ashtray and hurl it at the window. Next is one of the chairs that I send sailing through the air, towards the wall. I'm panting with the effort, but I don't stop. I systematically work my way through the small apartment, throwing everything possible.

As I reach the kitchenette, I throw the drawers and cupboards open. I laugh with glee at the prospect of finally shattering something that isn't me. My laughter takes on a dark tinge as I shatter the first plate, then a glass. On and on I go, unable to stop until everything breakable is in so many pieces it can never be put back together.

I sniffle as a lone tear runs down my cheek. That's how I feel—exactly how I feel. I'm too broken. All that's left are jagged shards that hurt me or anyone coming into contact with me. The realization of how truly broken I am causes a sob to rise in my throat, and before I can swallow it down, it slips past my lips and into the room.

The broken sound fans the flames of my fury higher. I look around with tunnel vision as I search for something I can do to hurt Grayson back. But there's nothing in this room he'll even care about. If I thought he cared about me, I wouldn't be above hurting myself. That would be wasted, though. Because we all know he doesn't care about anyone but himself.

"Don't let me stop you," Mama grins when I come to a complete standstill. "I dare say there are more things you could ruin if you want to."

I huff, not in the mood for her mockery. "Whatever," I grumble.

Mama nods like I'm saying what she expected. "If you're done, I think you and I need to talk about your future here."

My breath hitches and my eyebrows shoot up in surprise. "O-okay," I stammer.

She gestures to the empty spot next to her on the couch. I frown as I realize nothing of what I've thrown has landed here. Or maybe she's cleared the area. I don't know, and I can't say I was paying attention to anything but my righteous tantrum.

"I need you to answer my question honestly," Mama says imploringly. When I nod, she goes on. "Why didn't you tell Grayson about Sasha and the other Cunts who dragged you up on stage at the club?"

My brows pull together as I frown. I'm not sure I know the answer to that question. Except... maybe I do. "He wouldn't let me say anything," I answer.

Mama shakes her head. "That's the explanation and not the reason. Try again."

I try to blow some of my hair off of my forehead, but it's sticky with sweat, so much to my annoyance, it isn't going anywhere.

"H-he was so angry," I stutter, licking my dry lips. "He was so angry, Mama. I've never seen him like that and... honestly, I'm not sure throwing someone else under the bus would have saved me. So why risk him taking his anger out on more people?"

My voice becomes even more hoarse towards the end, making it hard to speak above a whisper.

Mama studies me for so long I begin to fidget. Then she finally smiles softly. "That's both admirable and honest."

A soft knock on the door makes me whimper until I realize it's not Grayson. He would never knock on his own door, and if he did, it would probably be a lot louder. Like a bang. The thought is enough for me to realize how badly my hand hurts.

I look down at it, and Mama was right. It's swollen and looks really bad. At least my exterior is starting to match my insides, maybe that isn't a bad thing.

Mama walks over to the door and quickly opens it. I'm shocked to see Alana walk in with a rucksack in her hand. When she hands it to me, I immediately shake my head. Whatever it is, I don't want it.

"Take it," the Cruz Cunt urges. "It's for your... ahh..." She trails off and looks at Mama, clearly expecting her to say something.

After closing the door, the Cruz King matriarch sits back down next to me and takes my good hand into hers. "As I said, we need to talk about your future here. You don't have one."

Despite knowing I was doomed to die here, the words hit me harder than I thought they would. I sob into the quiet apartment.

"C-Can I... Leslie's riding coach left something for me," I say as the thought hits me out of nowhere. "Can I pick it up first? I want to see what my sister left me."

Mama and Alana stare at me with confusion.

"What are you talking about?" Mama questions.

"Oh!" Alana gasps, slapping her hand over her mouth as her eyes widen. "We're not going to kill you, Zoe," she croons.

Now it's Mama's turn to gasp, which sounds odd. The sound is so out of place for someone that's as cool and collected as her.

"You misunderstand me," she clarifies. "What I meant is that you need to get out of here."

Hope flutters in my chest, but before it can take root I smother it down and shake my head.

"You don't want to leave?" Alana sounds as though she doesn't believe me.

My breath comes out in heavy pants. "It's a trick. You're just trying to trick me," I whisper.

The two women exchange a look I can't decipher.

"No, it's not," Mama says sternly. "I've seen women like you before, Zoe. It never ends well, and I swore never to let another woman be treated the way Grayson has treated you. Don't get me wrong, I love him dearly, but that means nothing right now. The Cruz Kings were never meant to be a place to own or force women to do anything they didn't want."

I almost want to laugh at her words because since I've met him, Grayson has either forced or coerced me to do exactly what he wanted.

"There's something about you that has him acting like a fucking caveman," Mama sniffs. "I'm not making excuses for him. After what he did, there's nothing I can say. That's why I'm going to help you."

Narrowing my eyes, I look at her. I'm not sure I can trust her, which is kind of a given. The really messed up part is that I don't know if I can afford not to try. There's only so long I can hide from the monster in my nightmares, and once I'm running out of places... well, I don't want to stick around to figure out what comes next.

22

Grayson

My knuckles still sting from the brick wall I took my frustrations out on a few hours ago. The sting to my skin and ache to my hand doesn't feel near enough though. After what I did to Zoe, I deserve the single bullet in my gun sitting on the table before me.

I've barely eaten since it happened, when my entire being was possessed by a beast I'd never fully met before, until the moment I saw Zoe on stage.

It's fucking weird to have the reaction I did. The only reason I'm meant to be claiming Zoe is for her protection, but who the fuck is going to protect her from me?

"Gray." Mama C's voice is harsh as her presence looms in my peripheral.

"What?" I snap, not in the mood to talk to anyone, especially at four in the morning.

Nothing good ever happens at 4am.

"Get up." She snaps back, and I dart a glare in her direction, seeing her dressed in all leather, her arms crossed over her chest as she shoots an unimpressed glare right back at me.

"What the fuck for?"

Her dark brows lift, like I'm a fucking idiot. "You know what for. Get your ass down to the basement."

Shit.

I don't know why I'm so surprised to see her. Perhaps because I expected her to come for me days ago. Nevertheless, she's fucking here now.

"Now's not a good time," I snap, dragging my gaze back to the empty bottle of Jack and my gun that lies waiting for me to pick it up and play another round of Russian Roulette.

"We can do it here if you prefer. But I thought I'd give you the courtesy of avoiding public humiliation since I can clearly see how much you are already punishing yourself for your actions."

I gulp.

Humiliation.

I deserve it, but I'm a fucking coward. I've probably lost the respect of some of the men already, but for them to hear and potentially see Mama C doling out her punishment on me in our main bar isn't something I can fucking bear.

"So this is my punishment for what I did to Zoe at Dirty Diamonds?" I confirm, and she nods. "If anyone else had done that, they would be dead, or at least severely injured by now. Why haven't you come for me until now?"

"I've been busy cleaning up your mess," Mama C snaps, and my shoulders drop.

I eye my gun again.

Just fucking pick it up you coward. Press it to your fucking head and pull the trigger.

Slowly, I nod, pushing my chair back with a scrape as I stand.

Will this punishment be enough? Will it cancel out what I did?

I fucking doubt it, but as much as I don't want to go down to Mama C's torture chamber, I know I need to.

Within an hour of publicly claiming Zoe, I received another video, this time it was clearly recorded on a cell phone, showing me exactly how brutal I was on that stage. Not only do I see what I did to Zoe, and how we both looked on that stage, but I could see the expressions of the Cruz Cunts, as they bore witness to a side of me they've never seen.

I've wondered constantly if Zoe would have got the same message had she had access to her phone. I could probably check, but since it's locked in the club safe in Rocco's office, I know it doesn't really matter at this point.

What does matter is that someone has been able to gain access to not just the Millers' surveillance, and the coatroom from the funeral, but also used their phone to record us at the Dirty Diamonds Strip Club.

I should probably mention it to Cain.

As Mama C turns to lead the way, I follow, feeling unsteady on my feet as the room spins from the Jack burning in my gut right now.

I don't bother to check if Zoe has turned up in my room. She hasn't been sleeping there since the night it happened. Since the night I forced her at gunpoint to blow me on stage.

FUCK!

With my destination inevitable, I purposefully don't look around while I walk in case I spot where Zoe is hiding tonight. If I see her, I don't know what the fuck I will do.

She's lost more weight, and when I witnessed the scene in the storage room earlier and saw the dark circles around her eyes and how fucking scared she was, I was about ready to introduce my brains to that fucking bullet in my piece right there and then.

I don't know how to make this right, or if there's even a way to do that. Some things can't be forgiven or forgotten, and I'm pretty sure my actions fall under both of those categories.

Following Mama into the basement, she closes the door and doesn't look at me as she crosses the room to her tool cabinet.

The leather pants she's wearing, and the cropped leather vest to match, with long black boots scream power. Dominance.

It's fucking scary.

Just what I need.

"Usually, I like to have an audience, because humiliation plays a big factor in the punishments I deliver," she explains, even though I already know how she operates. "But I'm quite sure you feel the humiliation of your actions each time one of the Cruz Cunts looks at you, or any time your eyes land on Zoe."

I nod, my heart racing with anticipation of what's coming as I shuck off my cut and tug my t-shirt off, laying them neatly on the back of the chair by the door.

Mama eyes me, her expression unreadable, before pointing to the thick chain dangling from the rafter.

"I can secure you to it, or you can hang on to it."

"I'll hang on." I offer, and when she nods and turns back to her tools, I stand under the chain and reach up, clasping my hand around the cold metal.

Turning back to me with a sharp blade, Mama asks, "Do you think I should measure your punishment in a certain amount of cuts or lashes, or perhaps whatever I can inflict in a certain amount of time?"

My brows hitch. "If I were someone else, you wouldn't ask. You would just deliver what was deserved. So what would that be?"

Her eyes darken. "I would slice your sack open and make you watch your nuts tumble to the floor once I've severed them, then dice them up before your eyes so you know they aren't salvageable." A smirk tugs at her lips. "Then your dick would be next. The weapon you used. I'd turn you into a eunuch with one slice of this blade." She tilts the shiny blade from side to side. "Then I'd make you choke on your dick. And after that, if you weren't already dead from the pain or blood loss, I'd gut you until your heart slaps this fucking floor."

"Do it!"

I choke out loudly, suddenly desperate to feel her wrath, and her eyes darken as she shakes her head.

"You know, Grayson. Sometimes living with your suffering is punishment enough."

"It's not." I shake my head, clutching the chain tighter as I fight back emotions I'm not used to feeling. "I deserve the full punishment."

"You see, that's where you are wrong." She approaches, running the sharp tip of the knife over my peck and down my abdomen. "If you were here showing no remorse, then yes, Grayson, you would deserve the full punishment, because that would mean you are a true monster unworthy of breathing. But I can see how remorseful you are. So I will punish you, but not like that."

"Just do... something." I rasp, and she nods before she angles the knife and slices the blade across my abs.

I hiss as the sting engulfs me, burning like hot coals are embedded in the thin slash.

"More!" I yell, gritting my teeth as she gives me what I want.

I've never been punished by Mama before. I've never stooped as low as I did on that stage at Dirty Diamonds, but with each slash, each wound she inflicts, I know I've done the right thing by accepting what she is dishing out.

My hands hurt from gripping the chains above my head so tight. Not once do I consider letting them go and asking her to stop. Not even when she puts her blade away and produces her whip.

With each lashing across my back, I beg the monster inside me to feel it. To know that it's too fucking afraid to come out again.

"What the fuck?"

Gunner's voice has my lids flying open, and I slam back to reality to see my club brother looking fucking confused as he takes in what's happening.

"You should know better than to come in here without knocking first." Mama scolds and Gunner nods, his worried gaze darting from where Mama is standing behind me, to where I stand on shaky legs, covered in blood.

"Sorry... I uh... was looking for Grayson."

"It's five in the morning, Gunner. What on earth do you need to see him about at this hour?" Mama scolds again, but Gunner doesn't shy away. He steps further into the room.

"It's Zoe." He offers, looking concerned. "She's gone."

Instantly, I release my grip on the chains, and wobble on my legs as they take my full weight.

"What do you mean, she's gone?"

"She's gone." Gunner shakes his head like I'm an idiot. "She's run off. She's nowhere in the clubhouse, and I've just reviewed our video surveillance, and it shows her sneaking out the back of the property through the fence that only club members know about."

Rushing to the chair, I grab my t-shirt and tug it on.

"When did she leave?" I snap, before I feel a gentle hand on my shoulder.

"Did I say your punishment was over?" Mama snaps, drawing my attention again.

"I will return for more. But first, I need to find Zoe."

Sighing, Mama concedes. "Fine. But this isn't over." She points her talon-like nail at me. "You need to get cleaned up before you go looking for her."

I know she's right. I've got blood seeping from too many cuts to count.

"She left hours ago," Gunner adds. "While you were with Prez and Mama in the back room."

My brows hitch. "That was like, eight fucking hours ago. How come no one noticed her missing sooner?"

"She wasn't well. Sasha covered her shift, and Alana and I left her in your room after we cleaned her up," Mama offers and I narrow my eyes.

"Was that before or after she fucking trashed my apartment?"

Mama shrugs. "It was a good show. I'm not even sorry I let her."

"Seriously?" I deadpan and she shrugs.

Clearly she thinks it was deserving.

And it was.

Fuck!

I was angry when I came across my trashed apartment, but I figured I deserved it, so I left it alone and cleaned up what I could before starting on the bottle of Jack instead of eating dinner.

Eight fucking hours. I'd assumed she'd found yet another nook to hide in, when in fact, she escaped.

"This is my fault," I rasp, my cut in hand as I decide not to put it on. I can feel my t-shirt sticking to my wounds, becoming soggy with blood. "I went too far."

Gunner doesn't disagree, but adds. "What do you want to do? Go after her? Leave her?"

I shake my head. "She's mine. I can't leave her. Besides, she's in danger out there on her own. If the Reapers catch sight of her, she's fucking dead."

"She's yours?" Gunner asks, and I frown. Is that really what he took away from what I said?

Gunner doesn't know about the shady deal Rocco made with Brian. No one knows but me, Rocco and Mama C. Oh, and Brian, who is still in the fucking wind. Everyone assumes we have taken her to trade with Brian, or to lure him out.

"Was that not fucking clear at Dirty Diamonds?" I snap at Gunner, and he flinches.

"Uh. Yeah, I guess it was. But you two haven't been near each other since, and she hates you, man. So, I thought it was an act or something."

I glare at my best friend. "You think what I did up on that stage was an act?"

He shrugs. "Kinda. It was so out of character."

He's fucking right about that.

"I publicly claimed her. She's mine," I declare, even though I don't feel very fucking worthy of tying her to me like that.

But fuck.

Three years she needs to be safe in our care to get the money Rocco needs, so whether either of us like it or not, it's the way it has to be.

Gunner nods, and I turn back to Mama to see a slight grin tug at her lips.

"I'll be back for more once I find our escapee."

"A word of advice," Mama offers, but continues without waiting to see if I want it or not. "Instead of dismissing the beast inside you, Gray, perhaps you should listen to what he's trying to tell you. Maybe then, he won't explode out of you with such malice."

Her words make me stumble back, as if she's been able to read my thoughts or look into my soul this entire time.

"What the fuck is he trying to tell me? That I'm a predator? A rapist?"

She shakes her head and gives my arm a squeeze. "You're too focused on the act he did, instead of considering why he did it. Why *you* did it."

I shake my head. "You're talking to me in riddles, woman."

She smiles and nods. "Maybe. But perhaps it's something you need to think about and figure out. And hopefully before you find Zoe. She deserves to meet the real you."

"The hell is she talking about?" I ask Gunner and he shrugs.

"Beats me."

I leave the stuffy basement then, happy to be free of the metallic scent of my own blood.

"I'm going to clean up," I bark at Gunner as we walk back up to the main level. "Can you reach out to Tido? Get him to see if Zoe has turned up on any traffic light cameras, or security cameras in the area."

Tido is one of the cops on our payroll that works behind a desk and has access to certain surveillance that other cops don't.

Gunner nods at my order. "Will do. Should I wake Prez?"

"Nah. Mama will fill him in, and since Zoe is my responsibility, I need to take the lead on this."

When we reach the main floor, Gunner goes left towards the main clubroom, and I go right, towards the apartments.

I don't blame Zoe for running. The fact that she did, tells me I haven't completely broken her, and that's a good thing. Because in order for Zoe to stay alive, especially out on the streets of Santa Cruz until I can get her to safety again, she's going to need that bratty spark.

Especially when I get my hands on her.

After scouring the streets for twenty-four hours, and coming up empty on traffic camera surveillance, I order the guys to return to the club, and continue the hunt for Zoe on my own.

Having too many of our guys on the streets while the Reapers are out for blood is something we need to avoid.

For a whole fucking week I visit the local hotels, pay hookers to tell me if they've seen Zoe, only for them to tell me they haven't. Tido keeps his eyes on the Metro center to see if Zoe tries to catch a bus out of town, or the train to see if she tries to escape up to Roaring Camp. He even keeps an eye on the harbor, but still he turns up nothing.

The beast I've been trying to keep at bay comes out around day five, and then just fucking stays.

No longer am I a sane man asking, but a crazed man demanding as my fear that the Reapers have already found Zoe increases.

They have already taken too fucking much from my club. Too much blood has been spilled with little fucking reward, and I'll be fucked if I let them take Zoe too.

She never asked for this, yet here she is paying for her dad's actions.

"Loretta, I'm not fucking paying you again. You've been putting your hand out for payment and giving me fucking nothing, but I know you know where she is. So here's how it's going to go. You're going to tell me what I want to know, or you'll be choking on the barrel of my gun before I pull the trigger."

"Jesus. You're a grumpy prick these days, Gray." Loretta rolls her eyes as she puffs on her cancer stick. "But fine. I have no idea what you want with a girl like that, but she stands out a mile hiding away at the Sleep-Eazy."

"She's at the Sleep-Eazy Motel on the edge of town?"

She nods, blowing a puff of smoke up into the air.

"Lots of fast food deliveries going to room twenty-three. Gertie said the girl never comes out, so the only glimpse they get is when she opens the door to accept the food delivery. They aren't used to a motel room seeing so little action."

Fucking Gertie. I was out at the Sleep-Eazy two fucking days ago, and the bitch assured me she hadn't seen anything.

I knew if the local hookers knew anything about Zoe's whereabouts, Loretta would know.

She oversees most of the prostitution for their pimp now that he's in the lockup on drug charges.

"Give me one good reason why I shouldn't just shoot you for fucking lying to me when I came to you before?"

Loretta shrugs, not looking the least bit scared, which pisses me off.

Have I lost my fucking touch?

"You won't shoot me, because if you do, I won't be able to tell you about the Reaper information I fucked out of Senator Tipping last night."

My brows shoot up, and she grins past the cigarette hanging from her lips.

"The intel better be good!" I snap, and she nods.

"The Reapers have come into some money, it seems, and they are buying up property in the west."

Fucking hell. The assholes are using King money to buy housing for their fucking men.

On my fucking turf.

I don't say anything else to Loretta, I just chuck her a fifty and storm to my bike before shooting Rocco a text about that intel.

Then, I start my bike up with a rumble before heading towards the Sleep-Eazy.

Room twenty-three, here I fucking come!

23

Zoe

It's been a week since Mama C and Alana managed to sneak me undetected out of the clubhouse, and I've spent every minute of every day being scared of my own shadow. Every time I hear a bike, I'm sure he's found me. If he ever finds me, I know I'm done for. Even if he doesn't kill me, he'll find a way to clip my wings, making sure I can never fly away again.

After Mama C left me and Alana with clear instructions, she said she was going downstairs to talk to the Prez and VP. She made sure to emphasize she expected the meeting to take at least an hour.

My mind was so sluggish Alana had to explain the plan to me twice before it sank in. I tried to argue it wouldn't work, but now that I've had a week on my own, I wish I could send them an old-fashioned letter or postcard to let them know how genius they are.

After walking for a mile without bumping into anyone, I finally came across a taxi. Thanks to the driver who clearly didn't believe the rules of the road extended to him—I was safe at the rundown motel I've been hiding in since.

Thankfully, this is one of those places where all the rooms are outside with separate doors, giving me more privacy than I know what to do with.

And thanks to the phone I bought from the clerk with money from Mama—for about five times its value—I've been able to distort my voice to sound like an elderly man. Which has proven handy when I've ordered deliveries. Thank you ridiculous apps I never thought there'd be a need for.

Vending machine food and deliveries, my two major food groups now. It's funny how I once would never be caught dead in a place like this, now I'll most likely be dead if I'm caught here. Life is fucking hilarious, ain't it.

The phone also proved handy when it revealed I'm close to my start date at Harvard. While I would have loved to go straight there, I was afraid Grayson would track me down. I'm not stupid enough to think he won't be coming for me, and going there would be too predictable. As much as I hate it, I don't think I can ever go there.

No, I'd be better off finding a way to get more money, and then maybe move to Europe or something. Completely disappearing from the continent should put enough distance between us for me to be free. Right?

A week is a long time when the TV in your room is broken, so I've spent most of my time thinking. It's something I hoped to avoid, yet, here I am, doing little else. No matter how I replay things in my head, I can't comprehend the events. It all feels like I'm outside looking in, seeing it happen to someone who isn't me. But it is me, and I need a better plan. I already know I can't stay here forever, I'm lucky I've had a week.

Scrolling on the phone, I add some hair dye and fake tattoos to my online shopping. I don't know if it'll be enough to trick anyone, but I have to try. Hell, if I'm honest, I can't even be sure the order will turn up. Since I don't have a payment card, I'm using a small shop that took forever to find, and it's the only one accepting cash on delivery. So here I am, once again putting all my hopes on someone else.

Moving across the room I double-check that I've packed everything. Since I don't know if I'll have to leave at a moment's notice, I keep my bag ready at all times. I still don't own a lot of things. The bag Alana handed me had a few different outfits, and some cash. That was it. Yesterday I ran out of clean underwear for the second time, so I had to wash it in the disgusting water in the bathroom.

As I walk into the disgusting bathroom, there's a loud thud against the door.

"Open the fuck up, Princess. I know you're in there." There's no mistaking Grayson's angry growl.

The hairs on my arms and neck stand at attention as a shiver runs down my spine.

Shit.

I don't even have time to come up with an answer before he kicks the door down, and I come face-to-face with a very, very pissed Grayson Black.

His hair is in disarray, making his curls look wild rather than tight. There are prominent black circles under his

eyes like he hasn't slept in days, which causes his choco-
late brown eyes to look like two empty abysses.

"What game are you fucking playing?" he snarls while
closing the distance between us.

"I-I..." Words don't come to me, I'm rooted to the spot
as I watch him stalk closer and closer. "Get away from
me," I scream.

I try to run, but there's nowhere to go. I can't get
around him and... my thoughts are cut off as his hand
closes around my throat, and he forcefully shoves me back
against the wall.

"You fucking ran from me," he spits, squeezing harder.
"From. Me." He says the words with a deceptive level of
coolness, like he isn't fucking holding me by the throat.

At his words, my fear morphs into anger. "What did you
fucking expect?" I spit.

Gray's hold on my throat tightens, making it impossible
to breathe. If it wasn't for the calculated look in his eyes,
I'd think he's lost it. But I know he hasn't, and he proves it
further when he pinches my nose closed with two fingers
all while smiling like a glorified psycho.

I close my eyes, refusing to look at him and don't react
when he squeezes tighter, or when he licks up the length
of my neck.

"Open your eyes, Princess," he growls, but I don't. "I
said, open your fucking eyes."

He's so close I can feel his breath on my lips.

I still don't answer him, not that I think I can. Maybe
this is it... maybe he's here to finish me off for daring
to leave him. The thought is oddly enough not scary.
Everyone has to die one day, right? And at least I'll be
dying on my feet rather than on my knees.

As I run out of oxygen, my body tries its best to breathe, but it's impossible. Grayson's hold on me is calculatingly cruel, proving just how much of a madman he is. Despite not wanting to, my eyes open and the first thing I see is the black orbs in his face.

"When I tell you to do something, you fucking do it." With those words, he lets go of my nose and throat as he takes a step back.

Now that he's no longer holding me up, I fall to my knees while gasping for air. "Y-y-you..." I'm heaving, greedily taking in as much air as I can. "F-fucking b-bastard."

Gray's lips turn up at the corners, it's a mockery of a smile. "Actually I'm not," he says. "My mom was married to my dad."

I shake my head at his smart ass reply. Like I fucking care. But if that's how he wants to play it, we can. Game on, fucker.

"I don't feel too good," I croak. For good measure, I wrap my arms tightly around my middle.

It's not hard to fake being pathetic and weak, that's exactly what I am. My legs feel unsteady, my throat hurts, and tears stream from my eyes. But if I'm to stand a chance at escaping Grayson twice, I can't come at him head on. I need to play this smart.

Making a show out of it, I try to get to my feet. I fall twice, and I hate admitting that only one of those times was on purpose. Predictably, he rushes towards me the second time, immediately steadying me before helping me to my feet.

Not wanting to give him a clue of what I'm planning, I keep my facial expression passive while I patiently let him pull me over to the bed. As soon as I'm seated, Grayson stands in front of me, his hips almost perfectly aligned with my face which couldn't have been more perfect if I'd masterfully orchestrated it—which I suppose is exactly what I've done.

"Are you done now?" I quirk a brow in a challenge. "Or do you want to punch me a bit? Maybe kick me for good measure?"

At my words, Gray looks stricken, guilt swimming in his eyes. "Why the fuck would you even say that?"

I force a joyless laugh that hurts my throat. "I wonder why," I croak while making a show out of rubbing my sore throat.

It's with glee I watch as each of my venomous words hit him enough that he doesn't manage to school his expression.

"Zoe... I..." Closing his eyes, he slowly runs a hand down his face.

This is the opportunity I've been waiting for.

As quickly as possible, I reach for the gun holstered at his hips, pulling it free while I remove the safety and point it straight at him.

Even though I hate my dad, I mentally thank him for teaching me and Leslie how to use a gun when I was thirteen.

I don't know if it's the movement or the click that draws his attention. It's not like it matters. All that matters is that when his eyes fly open, they're as wide as saucers.

"Princess...?"

I get the urge to laugh at the dumbfounded expression on his face, but I don't. Instead, I say, "I'm not your princess, Grayson. I'm the woman you've scorned over and over. Since you're not as dumb as you look right now, I'm assuming you're aware that hell hath no fury like a woman scorned." My tone doesn't waver, and neither does my aim. "You have thirty seconds to leave. I never want to see you again."

Being the stubborn bastard that he is, Gray refuses to budge. We're standing so close our bodies touch with each inhale and exhale we each draw.

"So that's it?" he asks, not sounding even the least bit bothered. "You're going to shoot me, and then what? I hope you have a plan, Princess. Because the Cruz Kings will have questions, so I suggest you have the answers."

It's clearly an oversight on my part that I didn't expect this to be the outcome. I should have known that Gray would never cower.

"I'll claim it was self-defense," I coolly say. "Which it is. You came barging in here, you even tried to strangle me."

Throwing his head back, Gray lets out a booming laugh. "Trust me, Princess. If I wanted to strangle you, you wouldn't be alive to mouth off to me while pointing my own gun at me."

Shaking my head, I try to hatch a plan. I'm obviously not going to shoot him, but I don't know what else to do.

With shaky legs, I walk backwards around the bed and towards the door. Gray mirrors my every step, making sure not to allow any more space between us.

Everything goes smoothly until I reach the door and trip over the fucking threshold of all things. As soon as I lose my focus, Gray roars and lunges for me. Without thinking, I pull the trigger, watching through wide eyes as the bullet leaves the chamber.

My heartbeat echoes in my ears, making more sound than the gunshot that was barely more than a pop. Yet the aftermath is... there's so much blood. I sink to my knees, my eyes wide open. I'm unable to blink, to swallow, to... I shot him.

I fucking shot him.

My lips part as I look on in horror.

I. Fucking. Shot. Grayson Black.

TRIGGER
WARNING

Please note this is book 1 of 3 in a dark MC contemporary romance series. The book ends on a cliffhanger, and contains a swoon-worthy, alphahole MMC.

Somnophilia - enjoying having sex with sleeping or unconscious partner, often fuelled by not having their consent, or getting caught if they wake up.

Dormaphilia - getting aroused and/or enjoying being the sleeping/unconscious recipient of a somnophilic experience.

Blackmail

Non-con

Dub-con

Morally gray MMC

Bets

9 780645 649253